The Blood of Doves

MELISSA MCSHERRY

First edition

Editing: Renee Polks , Dana LeeAnn, T.M. Mayfield, Heather Creeden

Formatting: Dana LeeAnn

Cover Designer: Manuela Williams @Beholdenbookcovers

Character Art: @Paperwitches

Trigger Warnings

This book contains some dark and graphic content that could trigger some people. Your mental health matters, so please take the time to read over the list of warnings, and if any stand out to you, please set the book down.

Death

Graphic Violence

Graphic Sex Scenes

Blood/Gore

Murder

Abuse

Sexual Assault

Prostitution

Child Harm (Off-Page)

Thoughts/Mentions of Rape

Graphic Language

Feather Play

Blood Play

Biting

Whipping

Playlist

The playlist can also be found on Spotify.

PSYCHO - AViVA

Scars - Boy Epic

Up Down - Boy Epic

Not Your Baby - Cadmium, Jex

Battle Cry - Claire Guerreso

Sleepless - Dutch Melrose

Never Surrender - Liv Ash

Never Say Die - Neoni

Throne - Rival, Neoni

Empires - Ruelle

Monsters - Ruelle

War Of Hearts - Ruelle

Far From Home - Sam Tinnesz

Who Are You - SVRCINA

Fallout - UNSECRET, Neoni

Sand - Dove Cameron

Pronunciation Guide

Lethe - Le-the

Calanthe - Calan-the

Xerxes - Zurk-seez

Kasia - Ka-see-ya

Orion - Oh-ry-an

Senna - Senn-a

Viserra - Vis-cer-a

Niko - Ni-ko

Nymeria - Ny-mere-ia

Nefeli - Nef-eli

Erebus - Air-e-bus

Kenji - Ken-g

For the girls who dream of being saved by a winged High Lord, who will crawl on his knees and devour you before fucking you into oblivion beneath the stars.

Chapter One

KASIA

S tealing is a virtue of its own.

At least, that's what I've been telling myself for the last few days after I was caught killing and stealing from a few of Lethe's arrogant noblemen. A task that ended up getting me thrown in this frore hellhole. A cell of thick stone walls and iron bars that reek of piss and death in the dead of the never-ending winter—a curse placed on Lethe for the last twenty years. I'd give anything to have a mug of sweet, steaming thalla mint tea right now. To feel its warmth slide down my frozen throat, warming me from the inside out.

Each frigid breath I take feels like I'm inhaling tiny shards of glass into my lungs, but it's all worth it, even if my capture means I've been compelled to suffer for days in this icy cell of isolation. The silver coins I stole from those rich bastards and gave to the orphanage where I spent my childhood will be enough to heat the small building and fill their bellies for at least a few weeks. Plenty long enough for me to escape.

The rattling of keys and agonizing screams of the tortured inmates fill the air, echoing off the thick stone walls around me as I lay on the only piece of furniture in my tiny, windowless cell. A small wooden frame laid on the cold stone floor with no more than a thin and ratted linen blanket to keep warm; it's stained with Gods know what and smells foul, but it's better than nothing.

Curling myself into a ball on the thin wooden frame, I pull the hood of my fur-lined cloak up higher over my head to keep in the heat around my pointed Fae ears, which are painful to touch thanks to the freezing temperature. I wrap a disgusting blanket tightly around my shivering body as I watch each exhaled breath form a frosty cloud before dissipating into nothing. I twirl the small chicken bone I saved and sharpened from last night's dinner between my fingers, replaying my escape plan repeatedly in my head.

Visions of Sage's sorrow-filled eyes as she informed me of another child who did not return home to the orphanage after dark filled my thoughts with worry and concern. It has been happening more frequently, at least once a week, and we have searched for each of them. We spent days out in the brutal weather, searching and hoping, but we never found any of them, not even a trace. It's like they simply vanished, leaving nothing behind. The memory of their smiling faces and laughter has left a hollow space in my heart with their absence. What has become of them? Part of me wants to know, *needs* to know, but the other part already knows they'll never be found.

A cold draft blows through my cell, causing the stray strands of my white hair to tickle my skin. I brush them from my face and lift my eyes to the thick iron gate of my cell, knowing the draft means the door at the end of the corridor has opened: a new arrival. I pull my cloak tighter around my shivering body, trying to focus on the echo of footsteps through the corridor, but it proves impossible with the sound of my chattering teeth filling my head.

Surviving the cold is nothing new for me nor any of the other low-borns in the realm of Lethe. After twenty years of being forced to endure a never-ending winter, we've adapted well, and those who didn't die early on. The curse was placed over the realm with the royal family's assassination. I was too young to remember it, but it's a well-known tale taught to every civilian in Lethe, right down to the vivid details, per his request. It's an event he refuses to let the people of Lethe forget. His High Lord Draven Delephen, usurper and the one responsible for the brutal murder that changed the realm and the lives of everyone in it.

For twenty years, the low-born have struggled to survive, leaving them forced to steal, kill, and sell whatever they can including their children and bodies, just to afford the means to survive. Meanwhile the high-born or noble live lavish lifestyles in their well-heated townhomes, eating feasts of wild game and delicious sweets, never offering as much as a second thought to those who are barely surviving in destitute outside their doors.

It's why I never feel guilty for taking their lives, by drawing their attention with the hypnotic sway of my hips and flirty approach, like I'm nothing more than a common whore. Searching for the means to pay for my next meal. Watching their expressions change from desire to panic when my true intentions are revealed brings me more pleasure than I can express. I revel in the moment when my cold steel blade meets their warm flesh, and then they realize the low-born they thought was nothing more than a cheap fuck is ultimately the petty poison that infected them with a shake of her ass and brought them to a death they never saw coming.

They deserve it. The high-born rich scum who choose to turn and look away as the poor are left to starve and freeze to death. However, a select few of the high-born are not so cruel. Some still have kind hearts and spend their leftover silver trying to help those in need, not wanting to see their people suffer regardless of the faction they're born into. But the number of good-hearted Lethe civilians dwindles daily as resources become harder and harder to come by in this barren wasteland of ice.

Lethe wasn't always a frozen hell, full of death and poverty. It was once lush and green in the summer months, the soil rich in nutrients for growing an abundance of healthy crops and botanicals for the realm's people. No one starved to death or went without food. There was no high-born or low-born. They say that regardless of race or status, everyone lived peacefully together, Fae and dwarf alike but that was before, that pathetic excuse for a High Lord, Draven, took the throne.

His reign over the realm has brought us to this point, his sword that shed the blood of the former royal family, placing this curse on the realm. The day will come when he pays the price for the pain and suffering he has caused the people of Lethe, if not by the Gods themselves, then by my blade. I will avenge the people of Lethe, the ones who have been left to suffer while others have been thriving. I will be their voice, their vengeance, their warrior, whatever they need me to be. Regardless of what that is, it will always end with Draven's blood painting my blade and his discarded head rolling at my feet.

The echoing sound of approaching boots on the frozen stones meets my ears, pulling me from my murderous fantasies. Lifting myself from the wooden frame, I tightly grip the small, sharpened bone in my fist. I bring my attention to the iron cell door as three guards wearing the blue and gold emblems of the new Lethe High Lord reach it. One unlocks it while the other two stand behind a new prisoner, an older dwarf man with shoulder-length, greasy black hair that hangs around his filthy face. His sizeable hairy stomach hangs out the bottom of his stained shirt as the guards shove him roughly into my cell, throwing him to the stone floor.

"Ow! Why you doin' dis?! I'm innocent!" he pleads with slurring words, pushing himself to his feet and approaching me. As he gets closer, it's evident from the thick stench of ale that he's been drinking. "I didn't do nothin'! I was just trying to get through the veil like everyone else! I don't belong in hurr."

The guards ignore his pleading cries, their keys rattling as they lock the door before heading back down the corridor.

"No, no, no! You can't just leave meh in here! I'm innocent! I didn't take part in the riot! I swear I didn't!" he shouts after them, their laughter echoing back down the corridor in response.

I watch as he turns away from the gate, all hope of getting out of this frigid cell leaving his face as his eyes meet mine. I slowly tuck my sharpened bone into my pocket before bringing my cold hands to my mouth, cupping them over my lips as I exhale heated breaths to warm them.

Clearing my throat, "What riot do you speak of? What's happened at the veil?" I ask him with a shaky breath.

The veil is the portal between realms, the only doorway between Lethe, Amazath, and Calanthe. It's how people are able to travel between the realms...

"Lethe soldiers barricaded it off ay. There were guards everywhere, stopping people from crossing over or leaving," he explains as he sits across from me with his back pressed tightly against the stone wall. "The people were rioting, attacking the guards with whatever they had. It was madness."

"Why the hell would they block off the veil? What could they possibly gain by not allowing people through into Lethe?" I chuckle. "I think you drank so much your vision is clouded, friend."

His expression turns to anger. "I know what I saw! And I didn't have no part in the riot!" he shouts. "You'll see, you'll all see. High Lord Draven is up to no good, I tell ya!"

Rolling my eyes at the utter bullshit this drunken fool is speaking, I retort, "Whatever you say, now shut up. Some of us want to get some sleep." Only a few more hours till the guards switch shifts, and that's when the first part of my escape plan begins.

THE SOUND of my new cellmates coughing wakes me a few hours later. Cracking open my eyes, I find him standing in the corner by the cell gate, with his back to me as he pisses against the wall. I don't think I will ever get used to the stench of this place. I can tell by the dimness around me that it's nearly night. My dinner tray sits cold and untouched a few feet from the cell gate; the food here is equally as pleasant as the smell. The guards must have switched posts by now, which is all I needed. One of the night shift guards fancies me, and he does nothing to hide it. He's been trying to make a move on me for days, hinting that I should let him in my cell to warm me up with his big, manly hands. Well, tonight, I might just do that.

Lifting my stiff, cold body from the makeshift wooden bed, I head over to the cell door, carefully combing my fingers through my matted hair as my new cellmate finishes his business and returns to his spot against the wall. The iron bars are so cold they hurt as I wrap my hands around them, peering down the corridor in search of my target. It won't be long now. The voices of the guards chatting away echo through the passages. Most of the prisoners are silent tonight, which is odd but not surprising as many don't survive long once they get here. The conditions are too brutal.

I push the pain from the cold iron to the back of my thoughts as I wait patiently for the guard to make his usual nightly visit to my cell. It isn't long before his familiar voice hits my ears, growing closer as he reaches my door. My teeth chatter, and I can no longer stop my body from shivering.

"Well, there's my favorite girl. Waiting for me tonight, are we?" he says as he approaches the gate with a cocky smirk painted on his face. He's not horrible to look at, and if he wasn't one of Draven's toy soldiers, I might have indulged myself in his continuous offers to get between my legs; I might even enjoy it for once. Sadly for him, obedient little bitches do nothing for me.

"Perhaps." The response is shaky as my teeth chatter from the cold. I welcome the effects the cold has on my body, knowing I can use it to my advantage in this situation. "I - I was wondering if your offer still stood. Tonight is awfully cold, and well, I can't stand it anymore," I explain as I bat my lashes, pulling my chapped lip into my mouth with my teeth.

I can quickly tell by the look on his face my plan is working; no surprise. Men have one goal only, and that's to sink their cocks into anything and everything they can, spending their entire existence chasing a release that takes less than five minutes. Leaving a trail of unsatisfied women in their wake. It's pathetic, but I'm thankful they are so Godsdamn easy in situations like this.

His eyes rake across my shivering body as he brings himself closer to the thick iron bars. Sliding his hand through them, he grabs my cloak, opening it up to get a peek at what's underneath, and by the grunt that escapes him, I know he likes what he sees. My waist is thin and toned, thanks to years of physical training. I keep myself in decent shape, knowing it could be the meaning of life or death in a battle. His eyes roam from me to my new cellmate as he offers him a warning look.

"You best know how to shut your mouth, dwarf scum, 'cause if you repeat what's about to happen, it will be your tight little asshole I take next time."

"I ain't gon say shit. There are bigger things to worry about ay, like the veil being blocked off! But what do I know? No one listens to me."

"Shut up!" the guard shouts with aggression.

He pulls a ring of keys from his pocket, unlocking the cell door as he turns his sights back to me, his hunger-filled eyes burning into mine. He quickly makes his way into the cell, locking it again behind him. I slowly back myself closer to the makeshift bed, lowering myself to the floor as I keep my eyes locked with his, watching his approach.

I continue my flirtatious charade and offer him a forced smile that makes my frigid skin sting. "Please, hurry. I'm so cold."

"Don't worry, girl, I'll have you nice and warm soon enough," he smirks, removing his sword from his side, leaning it against the wall.

His lips part slowly, his tongue darting out to run across them as he lowers himself over me, supporting himself with his hands. He uses his knee to part my legs, putting his weight on one hand while the other hikes up my skirt. Lowering his head to my neck, he peppers hungry kisses along my cold skin. His breath is warm, and it smells foul, causing me to turn away to avoid vomiting. Keeping himself supported with one arm, he brings the other between my thighs, rubbing and circling his fingers around my dry folds. It irritates and begins to burn, but I push through, knowing it's only temporary. Tucking my left hand in my pocket, I grip the bone knife tightly as my other arm wraps around his neck, keeping him close against me.

Turning my head to the side, I force fake sounds of pleasure into the frigid air as my eyes scan the room. I find my cellmate staring as though he's ready to get off on watching us, yet his eyes are full of disapproval and disgust. I don't blame him. I'm not feeling particularly proud of this moment. The guard's moans vibrate against my cold skin while his hand moves from my skirt to his trousers, unbuckling them enough to free his hardened cock. My grip tightens on the sharpened bone as I carefully remove my hand from my pocket. His assault continues, his heavy breathing in my ear as he spits on his hand and strokes his cock, spreading his steaming saliva across his length, readying it. When he's finished, and he bends down to line it up at my opening, I bring the sharpened bone up above his head and plunge it down hard and fast, piercing his neck.

The sharpened end of the small chicken bone punctures his flesh with the force of my strike. I pull the bone out and bring it down again, this time hitting him right in the pulsing artery of his neck. Bright, steaming crimson blood begins to spray out, coating my face and hands. As he quickly reaches for his throat, shock stricken across his face, I push him to the side and roll him off me. The familiar metallic taste of blood rolls around my tongue as his gargled screams fill the cell. He rolls around the ground frantically, his eyes bulging from their sockets as they meet mine in the midst of chaos, his hands scratching and clawing at his neck wounds in an attempt to slow the bleeding. It won't help; he'll bleed out in seconds.

"Fucking hell! Help! Guards! Help!" my cellmate shouts through the iron bars, his voice leaking with terror. "She's killed him! Ah fuck there's so much blood!"

I waste no time, rushing to my feet and grabbing the sword he leaned against the wall tightly with my blood-slicked hands. At first, the warm crimson liquid is welcoming on my frigid skin, but as the seconds pass, it loses its warmth, only making my skin colder. My vicious attack has my new cellmate in a panic, his screaming and shouting to alert the guards only growing louder as the seconds pass. Finally, I reach my hand into the guard's right pocket, pulling out the ring of keys before using my arm to wipe some of the splatter from my face.

"Help! She's gon get away ay!" he shouts with a desperate tone. I turn my attention to him, bringing the tip of the now-dead guard's blade to the man's spine. The sound of boots meeting stone begins to echo through the halls, alerting me that the guards have heard his cries for help.

"You will shut the fuck up now, or I will gut you where you stand," I seethe through panting breaths. "You do realize you could've escaped with me, fool!"

A low chuckle escapes him as his body freezes under the pressure of my blade. "I don't need to escape, bitch! I'm innocent; they can't keep me in here forever. Especially if I help them catch you," he spits as he slowly turns to face me. "We both know you're not making it out of this place alive, so just give up now."

I laugh menacingly. "Oh, I will make it out alive. Shame the same cannot be said about you," I reply, watching his face as the cocky expression changes to confusion. That's when I push my blade through his chest. Through flesh, bone, and right into his heart. Innocent or not, his warning shouts will get me caught, and I can't spend another night in this hell hole. Especially after I just killed a guard.

He's dead instantly, and I pull the blood-coated sword from his chest, letting his limp body fall to the cold stone floor. Not giving him another thought as the sounds of the approaching guards get closer, I rush to the gate, stepping through the pools of freshly spilled blood. Trying key after key to find the one that unlocks my gate with shaky and frozen fingers. Finally, after four iron keys fail me, I find the right one and slide the heavy gate open before quickly rushing out and down the opposite corridor, leaving a trail of bloody footprints behind me.

Chapter Two

KASIA

Free from the confinements of my cell, I creep down the freezing corridors, searching for the easiest way out. Though not many of the passages will lead outside the thick stone walls of this prison, there are at least a few that will. This isn't my first time escaping from here. I quiet my steps, listening to the sounds of my pursuers echoing off the walls in their frantic search for me. I turn left, then right, carefully making my way to the passage I escaped through last time. When I turn the corner, I'm stunned to find it guarded by two large men.

"Ah, there she is. So, you thought you'd sneak out through the north passages again, did ya? Well, thanks to your new cellmate, we had time to make sure you had no way out," the first guard says, looking at me with satisfaction. I laugh, confident I can take them. It's only two against one, and I've faced worse odds and come out alive. They slowly step toward me, drawing their swords in a battle stance. "Drop the sword, pretty thing. I'd hate to have to cut up that pretty little face of yours."

"Speak for yourself. I wouldn't mind having to cut her up a bit," the other one chimes in as he eyes me up and down. "This one's wild. Just look at her, covered in her victim's blood. She even broke my nose just a few months back, eh!" I hold the sword strong and firm, keeping the blade pointed toward them as I slowly step back. Both guards may be tall and broad, but that doesn't mean they can move quickly. At least I have that advantage over them.

"Ah, that was you?! Well, looks like it didn't improve your looks. Still stuck with that ugly mug of yours, shame. I'd hoped I did you a favor. I apologize, I'll try the jaw this time. I heard women love a man with a good strong jaw," I reply with a smirk. He isn't happy about my new threat, the fury and rage clearly visible on his face.

"Bitch!" he seethes through his teeth before spitting on the ground to the right of him. I return his hate-filled glare with a smile. I love toying with them, getting them all pissed off. It always makes the kill so much better.

They continue to step toward me slowly, but without a good angle, I'm forced to back up, inching further down the narrow passages.

"I said drop the blade, bitch! You're not getting out of here. You're outnumbered, and all the exits are guarded. We've learned your tricks. Surrender now!"

"Surrender? Where is the fun in that?" I hiss before launching my attack. I charge at the enraged one first, but he's ready for me.

Our blades meet, blow for blow. He blocks my assault while the other comes at me from behind, wrapping his arms around my neck as he pulls me backward, away from the other guard. I bring my mouth down on the arm wrapped around me, sinking my teeth into his flesh, causing him to release his hold on me while he staggers back. Turning to face him, I run my blade deep into his stomach, catching him off guard. Holding the blade firm, I watch his face as his brain processes what's happened. Blood begins to leak from his lips, but enjoying the kill costs me. My attention is so focused on the man bleeding out on my blade that I forget the one behind me, and it allows him to make a move. His pommel smashes against the back of my head, knocking me to the ground.

The passageway spins as my head throbs, and I can feel warm blood leaking from a wound on the back of my head as I crawl around the cold stone floor, trying to escape his grasp. It's useless. I'm dazed from the blow, and the wound impairs my vision. He gets thick iron cuffs around my wrists easily and drags me to my feet. My legs shake under my own weight as he drags me through the passages and away from the carnage.

"I've got you now, you feral bitch. You should've surrendered when you could. Warden will see to it you're lashed for the lives you took tonight, *whore*," I hear him whisper before everything goes black.

———

THE COLD WIND brushing against my skin wakes me from unconsciousness. I struggle to open my eyes, my lashes coated in tiny icicles. My skin is numb from the cold, and my head throbs with intense pain. I quickly realize it's still nighttime, and for some reason, I'm outside. When I attempt to move, I find that I'm on my knees, and my arms are stiff and shackled, only now there is no guard holding them. Thick iron chains secure me to a pole in the middle of the frozen prison yard. Looking down at my pained knees, I can see I am completely naked. They must've stripped me when I was passed out; the thought alone turns my stomach, and whatever bit of food fills it threatens to make an appearance. The sound of someone clearing their throat pulls my attention, and I fight the pain of sore, frozen muscles as I turn to look behind me. I find the prison warden and a lineup of guards, including the one who caught me and put an abrupt end to my escape plan.

"Name?" the warden spits as his eyes scan the paper he's holding. I ignore him, my throat is dry and scratchy, and my body is so cold everything hurts. "I asked you for your name, girl!" I turn away from him, pulling my legs into my body as tightly as I can as I try to protect myself from the snow I'm resting in and the brutal winter air. "Fine, it's no matter. You will receive ten lashings for your crimes tonight. Three for each life you took, and one for failing to answer my question. Let's hope you've learned your lesson this time."

My heart begins to beat rapidly in anticipation of the punishment that's to come. I knew trying to break out was a risk, and the prison has been harder and harder to escape each time I'm captured. The guards have learned my tricks and routes. This time, they were ready for me.

Well, *most* of them.

I've been lashed before, so I already know what to expect. Searing pain, welts that last for months, and blood loss that will leave me dizzy, especially with my added head wound. But that isn't the biggest concern. Infection is what I really need to worry about in a place like this. An infected wound could take me out within days.

The sound of the whip cracking behind me brings my thoughts back to reality as fear and panic set in. I won't show it, though. I will not give these men the satisfaction of thinking they hurt me. Pain is nothing new to me; I've faced it many times and come out stronger, and this will be no different.

Heavy footsteps approach me from behind. My body shakes, and I can't tell if it's the cold or the fear causing it. The sound of the whip cracks through the icy night air again, and I hold my breath, readying myself for the pain I know is coming. I try to place my thoughts on happier things and times, doing anything I can to disconnect myself from this moment like my previous experiences have taught me, but it's no use. The second the whip slices through my frigid skin, I'm brought back from any possible escape I could've found.

One. A single tear slides down my cheek, freezing upon its descent. *Two.* The whip cracks again, another tear along my back, sending searing pain through my body. *Three.* I bite my lip, containing my sobs of anguish, refusing to show these vile men any weakness. *Four. Five.* My body tenses as warm blood begins to spill from the fresh gashes on my back. I can hear the guards whispering and laughing, but I keep my eyes on the pole in front of my face. My body is limp. Between the pain and the cold, I can no longer support my own weight. The warden continues his assault. *Six. Seven.*

I bite down harder on my lip, breaking the skin, but I don't make a sound. Not a single weep escapes me, and I can tell from the whispered voices that the men watching are shocked by my silence. *Eight. Nine. Only one left, Kasia. You can do this.* I tell myself over and over in my head. *These men are worthless. You are strong, and you will get through this. Do not weep, do not show them your pain.* I inhale a deep breath. Everything hurts; my back feels like it's on fire, and the slightest movement sends intense waves of pain through my entire frozen body. At this moment, I'm thankful for the cold weather and the effect it has on my naked skin. Its numbing chill offers little, but some relief. *Ten.* The final lashing of my sentence, and the most brutal, takes the last of my strength with it as I collapse to the snowy ground. The once pristine white snow is now painted with the crimson splatter of my blood.

"Take her back to her cell. Let her think about what she has done tonight and what it has cost her," the warden commands. Before I can even catch my breath or process what is happening around me, a guard unlocks my shackled arms from the pole and pulls me to my feet by the thick iron chains.

"Let's go, *pretty*," he chuckles, as though seeing me naked and bleeding like this is enjoyable for him. My head is spinning, and what parts of my body I can actually feel hurt like hell. I do the best I can to shield my nakedness from the eyes of every guard we pass on the way back to my cell. "Don't bother hiding," the guard smirks. "We all got a good view of your goods while you were passed out."

I push his confession to the back of my thoughts, choosing to welcome the pain from the lashes instead. The walk back to my cell feels excruciatingly long, each step harder than the last, and causing more pain as I'm dragged along beside him with his hand tightly gripping my bicep. The prisoners shout and make obscene gestures at their gates as I'm dragged by in my completely vulnerable and exposed state.

"Look at that ass!"

"Mm, bring her here. Let me get my hands on her!"

"Free show boys! Free show!"

"Quiet! All of you!" the guard shouts at them. "No one is touching her! Warden's orders!" Though I didn't expect them to allow other prisoners access to me, his announcement provides me with some comfort that I won't be raped, or *worse*. I'm in no condition to protect myself.

Finally reaching my cell, he quickly unlocks the heavy gate and shoves me roughly against the doorframe to my cell. The gesture causes me to cry out in pain as my back is slammed against the cold, rough stones. He brings his face to my neck, inhaling my scent deeply as a whisper of a moan escapes him. I turn my head away from him as he exhales, his warm breath in my ear making my skin crawl.

"Even after all this time in here and coated in blood, you still smell delicious," he whispers. "Warden said we can't touch you, but -" he pauses as he opens my tightly clenched thighs with his knee before bringing his hand to my center. All the tears and crying I had tucked in, hidden behind a dam of determination, are set free. The dam I worked so hard to build and maintain. My efforts were for nothing. With his touch between my thighs, in the most private places of my body, all my efforts come crashing down. His fingers swirl around my opening as he moans against my skin, causing my stomach to churn. He finally removes his hand, pushing me through the doorway and down to the cold stone floor.

The air smells like a smithy, raw iron and earth. The pools of blood from my victims are just beginning to freeze. I struggle to lift my body from the ground; the pain is unbearable, and my muscles are too weak, causing me to collapse. My eyes roam the dark cell in search of my clothing, but instead, I find the corpse of my second kill, still slumped against the wall, pale and lifeless, where I left him. My first kill still lies dead on the other side of me in a pool of his own blood. No clothes.

I turn my attention back to where the guard is locking the gate, clearly shocked they didn't return my clothing, even blood-soaked; it was better than being naked in this frozen hell hole. Surely they can't expect me to survive without some protection from the brutal chill.

"My clothing..." I manage to sputter, my voice cracked and quiet. The guard only laughs, a deep and dark laugh as though I'm foolish for even inquiring about my clothing.

"Don't worry, you won't be needing those clothes." He grunts as he rolls his shoulders before he starts undoing his belt. My eyes follow the movement as he slides his hand down slowly and into his pants, where he grips his hardened cock. He begins to pump himself while he watches me from the other side of the gate, his eyes raking over my exposed, beaten, and bloodied body. He brings his other hand up to his nose, sniffing my scent off his fingers as he works himself. "Fuck, you smell good. Better than the other whores we get in here."

Every part of me wants to turn away from him, wants to hide and disappear. But I don't; instead, I turn my head to look at him directly, taking in his face, every aspect of it becoming a permanent memory in my head. This will not be the last time I see him, and the next time I see his face again, I'm going to kill him.

"You like watching me, do you? Like knowing I'm pumping my cock for you, yeah? Nasty little whore you are. Look at the mess you made, coated in the blood of your victims." His comment causes me to look down on my body, and I realize he's right. My skin is painted with the cold blood of the men I killed earlier, but I don't feel guilty about it. His moans grow louder, and his hand begins to stroke faster, and he presses his body up against the gate.

He slowly pulls his pants down, exposing his fat little cock to me, its tip pointed right between the bars as jets of cum shoot out, hitting my feet and the stone floor as his body convulses and twitches with its release.

"Ahh, fuck yeah. Godsdammit," he moans.

I vomit. Unable to even process the fact that my feet are coated with his cum, I heave over and over, bringing up acidic stomach bile with each one. When I have nothing left to puke, I lay my head down on the cold floor. Every part of my body hurts. I'm weak and completely defeated. For the first time in my life, I feel like giving up. My will to survive no longer exists.

The sound of the guard putting himself away is the last thing I hear before his heavy footsteps head down the corridor and away from my cell. I let my eyes close, welcoming the darkness I've spent all night fighting, no longer caring if I wake in the morning or not. So long as it's over.

I'M AWAKENED by the sound of my cell door opening, but I don't hear any keys rattling. Footsteps approach me, but the closer they get, I realize they don't sound like the guard's boots. Someone kneels down beside me; I can feel them brush the hair from my face, and I try to turn away, not wanting to be touched. I force my eyes open, allowing them time to adjust to the new, bright golden light that's shining around my cell.

Once adjusted, I find the room is still spinning, my vision still unable to make out things too far away. I rub my eyes before opening them again, and when I do, I'm shocked to find a man crouched beside me. He's godly, the most handsome man I have ever seen, and definitely not a guard of Lethe. He's wearing dark green and black fighting leathers, with heavy black boots. His chocolate hair is pulled back out of his face, and his haunting whiskey-colored eyes are scanning every inch of my body with a possessive and angry expression I can't understand. Why does this stranger look at me the way he does? His body language and tone do little to hide the rage he feels. When his eyes meet mine, there's a glimmer of pain, of guilt, and for the life of me, I can't understand why a stranger would feel such things for me.

I try to speak but find myself without my voice; he notices and pulls a leather canteen from his belt, opening it and bringing it to my chapped lips before he pours some of the cold liquid into my mouth. It soothes my dry throat, but the cool liquid stings as it drips down my lips. Returning the canteen to his belt, he removes his chest plate before lifting his thick wool shirt over his head. Slowly, he lays it across my trembling body, the fabric instantly providing me some comfort.

"Tell me, little dove. Who did this to you? Which one of these fuckers touched you?" he seethes with a low and dark tone. I try to speak again, try to ask him who he is and why it matters, but find myself still unable to make out even a single word. Seeing my struggle, his expression changes as he brings his fingers softly to my lips before brushing his knuckles against my cheek. His touch is warm against my frozen skin, and I find myself desperate for more of it, more of the warmth surrounding him. "Hush now. Don't waste your strength. It's no matter who did it. They're all going to die regardless," he confesses before he rises and makes to exit the cell.

"Please..." I beg. It's barely a whisper, and my voice is shaky as I turn my head in his direction. "Please don't leave me here."

He freezes in place and slowly spins around, bringing his eyes to meet mine. "I will never leave you, Kasia. Now, save your strength. I will be right back." My name on his tongue is the most beautiful sound, and for a brief moment, I find solace in it, until the realization hits me that he knows my name. *Who is this man, and how does he know who I am?*

My head drops to the cold floor as I no longer have the strength to hold it up. The last thing to meet my ears before the pain once again becomes unbearable and the darkness claims me, is the echoing sound of shouting and screaming as the men who hurt me, the men who touched me, beg for their lives.

Chapter Three

XERXES

She doesn't remember me; the confusion in her eyes confirms that. I'm not completely surprised. It's been so long since we last saw each other, but I had hoped she'd feel the bond, feel something, some comfort by my presence. Even beaten, bloodied, and lying in filth, she is easily the most beautiful woman I've ever seen. Being near her for the first time in so long has my end of our bond aching to be near her.

"Please..." Her weakened voice calls out to me, begging me not to leave her. My heart sinks in my chest. Kasia was always a feisty girl; even as children I remember how tough and independent she was. She never took anyone's shit, let alone mine, but today that spark, that bravery, is nowhere to be seen. When I look at her, her minty green eyes fill with silent cries for help. *As if leaving her was even an option.*

Now, after twenty-three years of searching for her and finally finding her, I will never willingly leave her side again, not ever. I wish I could explain that. Make her see that she doesn't need to beg me to stay, not when I have no intentions of going anywhere.

Rage vibrates through my body, and my pulse quickens with thoughts of the condition I have found her in. No wonder she was silently wishing for death, to take her. These men have abused her, hurt her, brought her to the brink of death and left her to rot. They have broken her spirit as well as her body, and they will pay for every bit of it. Their blood will paint the blade of my sword, for that is the cost of touching what does not belong to them. Crouched down next to her, I can smell the putrid release of one of them on her. I clench my sword until my knuckles are white. His pathetic attempt to mark her in his own sick way, as though a woman like her could ever belong to a piece of scum like him. Marking her when she was broken and unable to defend herself.

My *little dove* put up quite the fight, though. The cold, lifeless bodies laying around her tell me that much. It brings a smile to my face. She fought hard, like the Kasia I remember as a child. Strong, tough, and never allowing anyone to push her around. I can't help but feel a swell of pride at how well she did before they actually took her out, especially without being able to use her powers in the hell-hole remains of this once great realm.

With my wool shirt covering her and hopefully giving her reassurance that I have no intentions of leaving her here, I turn on my heel and head out to find the guards who did this to her. I storm through the narrow passages of the prison. Passing cells of screaming prisoners in my search of the guard's quarters, craving vengeance and the spilt blood of those who touched what belongs to me. The cold air stinks, like rotting flesh with a hint of smoke, making me eager to get this over with so I can once again breathe in the fresh air of my home, my realm, Calanthe.

A realm of thick, dense trees and lakes, black as the night that fills the sky. Calanthe is in a constant state of night-fall; the native Fae depend on the moon's energy to access their well of power. Each moon phase determines how much they're able to pull from the source, making the full moon the time when we are at our most powerful. However, with the curse of Lethe, even my people are unable to access their power once here. I, being the High Lord, have ways around it, granting me the ability to store and use power outside of my well, but even that has its limits.

I slowly raise my arm at my side, pulling from my well of magic and conjure a thin, glowing white tether of moon-light, and weave it between my fingers so I can see as I continue through the corridors. It flickers in the cool winter draft that bellows through the passage ahead of me, tickling my skin as the sounds of shouts and laughter hit my ears. I follow their noise until the passage opens to a larger room filled with lit braziers and tables of steaming hot food. Lethe guards pile around small tables, pushing and shoving each other as they eagerly grab at the trays of food and begin filling their plates.

Tuning into their thoughts, most are fixated on the piles of food, but a few others who are off at a separate table have more sinister thoughts. They plan to share Kasia after their bellies are full, and finding it amusing, they snicker amongst each other, enjoying the plans they have for her when they think no one will be around to stop it. They're so caught up in the feast that they haven't noticed my presence.

With a flick of my wrist, the small tether of moonlight dissipates, and I open my palms to the ceiling as I raise them. The tables of food rise with the motion, knocking guards off their feet and onto their asses. Many panic, confused and unsure of what's happening. Most have never experienced any sort of magic, having been born after the curse was placed. Only when the hot food is pressed tightly against the ceiling do I release the tables, quickly motioning my hands down to the ground, causing them to slam down on the stone floor and shatter.

Drawing my sword, I prepare myself for the bloodshed. I don't know which one of these pieces of shit touched her, but none of them did anything to stop it, and most had plans to pay her a visit tonight. So, they'll all pay for it. I swing my arm, slicing the head off one of them, a dwarf. His limp body falls to the floor atop the corpse of a man who was crushed by the falling tables. The shocked expression is still etched into his pathetic, lifeless face. My first kill signals the others of my arrival, and of course, none wants to stand and fight. None of them are brave enough to fight. They run frantically about the room, cowering like insects, searching for some dark corner to escape into. But no dark corners will protect them from my wrath, not tonight.

My shoulders shake with a silent laugh, finding humor in watching them as they crawl and scatter. Knowing it's useless, I will find them all...every last one.

"Ah, so we're all big and strong when it comes to helpless women, but when a real contender faces you, you'd rather run and hide like rats. Well, you can run all you want, little rodents, but I will find you," I roar loudly, ensuring my voice echoes off the passage walls ahead of me.

I strike them down, one by one, my blade piercing through their thin armor and into their flesh with little effort as the metallic scent of blood fills the air around the room. Taking their lives means little to me, not with my thoughts flooded with visions of Kasia and what's been done to her. These men lashed her and left her untended, too. Allowing them to fester as she lay in frozen pools of crimson blood on the cold stone floor.

Thoughts belonging to one of the men pull me from my own as his fear grows with each of his comrades who falls to their deaths at my blade. His head fills with visions of Kasia, naked and beaten and pressed against the door frame as he touches her. The fear in her eyes at that moment replays in my head like a dream as he relives it repeatedly in his own, amongst the apprehension that I will find him. Of course, he has no idea I can reach him in his thoughts; no place is safe. Not for these men.

I storm across the room, my jaw clicking as I toss anything in my way to the side, my attention solely on the bastard who carries the scent of my little dove on his dirty fingers. He trembles in a corner, his back pressed tightly against it as I reach him, and the moment his eyes meet mine, the front of his trousers darkens.

"Bloody hell! Did he really just piss himself? Just from one look at your ugly mug?" Orion shouts from behind me.

"Took you long enough," I say cooly, keeping my gaze locked on the pathetic man before me.

"Well, like I always say, perfection can't be rushed. However, in this instance, friend, we don't have time. The Lethe guards almost completely control the veil again; we must go. *Now*."

"Pity. I was really hoping to enjoy this kill more." I growl as the scent of his urine hits my nose.

"Well, enjoy it quickly. I'll take out the rest," Orion calls as he moves with haste. Turning my head to the side, I nod in his direction before returning my attention to my victim.

"You touched what you should not have. Men like you are the worst kind of predators. The ones who feed only on the weak simply because you know you're no match for one at full strength. Pathetic."

The man moves to speak, but before he can mutter a single word, I thrust my hand out, using my power to pin him against the stone wall with my mind. Cocking my head to the side, I examine him and the way his body reacts to his terror and confusion. The sound of screaming men and the clashing of metal-on-metal echo around us as Orion takes out the last of the men.

"What- are- you?" he chokes out. His voice leaks of fear and confusion as to how I have him pinned on a wall while my hands remain firmly around the pommel of my sword.

I chuckle, finding amusement in his question. Raising one hand to his view, I summon my powers, and with a simple twist of my wrist, the fingers he touched her with are at his nose. His nostrils flare, and his eyes widen with shock.

"Go on, sniff, you sick bastard. Get one more whiff of her *delicious* scent in before you meet your end so that I can tell her you died with the scent of her still on your nose."

His body trembles under my magic's hold, and internally, my Fae ears can hear his heart beating so rapidly that I can only imagine how much pain it's causing him, but like the scum he is, he still finds it in him to inhale the scent off his fingers.

I push my hand towards the floor, roughly forcing him down on his knees before me.

"You know, it's complete bollocks that *you* can use your powers here while the rest of us are forced to actually wield a sword," Orion spits with sarcasm. I chuckle, briefly tearing my eyes off the man to inspect the moon-stone ring on my finger.

"Well, being a royal has to come with some perks; other-wise, where would the fun be?" I reply over my shoulder, returning my focus to the man before me. The thick silver ring is an heirloom passed down through the Aramis family for generations. The moonstone, intri-cately placed in the middle, has the ability to hold small amounts of the moon's lunar power, a second well of magic of sorts. Being the High Lord of Calanthe, it was given to me by my father when he stepped down and has come in handy with my trips to the cursed realm of Lethe, where magic is non-existent. Orion sighs with annoyance.

"At least you still have your wings. It is some advantage over these fools," I add through clenched teeth. Thank-fully, the wings the Fae of Calanthe possess do not stem from our magic, allowing us to summon them even in

Lethe. They're genetic, making them a trait all true-born Calanthians possess.

"Ha. I have plenty of advantages over these bloody wankers, even without my wings," Orion retorts.

With my power, I force his hands to his face again and use my power to constrict his throat as I lower myself to his eye level. His widened eyes meet mine, searching, silently pleading for mercy that will not come. There is no mercy for men like him. I clench my fist, and with the motion, his fingers snap one by one. The sound of bone cracking echoes around the frigid room. He screams in agony, and clouds of frozen, drool-filled sobs slip from his lips as he tries to fight against my magic and lower his hand.

Orion winces at the sound. "Seriously, Xerxes! You know, bone cracking is one sound I cannot handle!"

"Why do you think I did it?" I smirk. "Besides, I wanted to ensure that even in death, his fingers couldn't be used to touch a woman." I clench the man's throat with my power, silencing his wailing screams.

"Right, well, I highly doubt that will be a problem when he's dead. Now, let's get going; we don't have much time if we want to get back through the veil without having to fight Draven's men," Orion says, urging me to finish.

My fist grips tightly around the pommel of my blade as I lean in closer, bringing my lips mere inches from his ear.

"Now, I'm going to kill you, and with your last strangled breath, I want you to think about how good she smelt. Picture how beautiful she looked, even after you and your friends beat her and left her coated in the blood of the men she killed. I want you to die knowing that your pathetic attempt to mark her meant nothing and that I will be the one relishing in all of her while you rot in the frozen ground and insects feast on your decaying flesh."

His eyes flutter closed as the overwhelming amount of pain causes him to submit and accept his fate, and that moment is when I bring my blade up and through his chin. The pointed tip pierces through flesh and bone and protrudes through the top of his head, glinting in the brazier's glowing flames; rivers of blood leak from his slackened jaw as his lifeless body collapses. Pulling my blade from his skull, I wipe the brain matter and blood on his shirt before returning it to its sheath at my hip.

"Well, now that we're finished with the theatrics—"

"Let's go," I reply, cutting him off mid-sentence as I brush past him on my way down the passages toward where I left Kasia. When we reach her, Niko is at her side, his long black serpent tail spread around the room in a protective circle around her as he tends to her wounds. His thick onyx dreadlocks are pulled up and out of his face on the top of his head in a tight bun, revealing the inked ebony skin of his human half. He's just as concerned for her as I am, and if anyone can get her in good enough condition to make the trip back to Calanthe, it's him.

Being the High Lord of Amazath, his people, *the Naga*, are half human, half serpent. From the chest up, they appear human, but from the waist down, they have a thick-scaled serpent tail. The Naga are experts in poisons and tonics that they harvest from the plants and animals in their realm. Amazath is a tropical climate with scorching heat, thick rain forests filled with exotic creatures, and many insects and reptiles. Whether it be a poison or healing tonic, the Naga are the ones to seek for your remedy. I would trust no one other than Niko to take charge of Kasia's healing.

"Xerxes, the girl. She is in rough shape; we must get her out of here." Niko explains upon greeting me.

"Will she survive traveling through the veil?" I question as I kneel next to her, examining her wounds. She's unconscious, and the welts along her back are coated in a thick brown salve, no doubt some sort of healing remedy placed on her by Niko.

"She should, but Xerxes, without her Fae healing, I can't be certain."

Pausing, I briefly contemplate the risks before responding. "When we reach Calanthe, will her Fae healing return?"

"Again, that I am not certain of. It could take many days for the curse's effects to fade, or it could be instantaneous once she is out of Lethe."

"I always regain my power the moment we're in the veil," Orion adds.

"While this may be the way for you," Niko explains, "the girl has been here for many years; her body and power may not have the same reaction after being dormant for so long."

I know it's a risk, but I also know we can't stay here. She needs to get out of here. We all do. By now, Draven has heard of the attack on the prison, and I can't allow him or his men to find us here. Unbuckling my armor, I slide it off my chest and hand it to Orion. Taking care not to touch her wounds, I wrap her frail, naked body in the wool shirt I draped over her earlier before gently lifting her into my arms. Her long silver hair fans out over my arm; it's caked with a mix of blood and mud, but brings back so many memories of the tiny silver-haired girl from my childhood. She feels fragile and lighter than I expected, but something tells me she hasn't had the best life living in this shit hole.

"Xerxes—" Niko tries to warn me before I cut him off.

"Niko, I understand the risks, but we're in more danger if we stay. *She* is in more danger if we stay. Plus, she needs proper treatment."

"And a bath," Orion chimes in, and I glare at him as Niko smacks Orion upside the back of the head. "Bants, mate. I meant it all in good fun, so you didn't have to whack me," Orion smirks as he rubs the back of his head.

"Talkin' like dat, you're lucky all ya got was a whack from me. Coulda been Xerxes instead, and I doubt he'd have gone as lightly on ya as I did, wit ya talkin' bout his bonded like dat. Now, make yourself useful and carry your High Lord's armor," Niko chides.

No longer having the patience to deal with them and their bickering, I head into the passages toward the exit, and once we're free from the confinement of the thick stone walls of the prison, I summon some of my power to the surface. Large, thick, black, feathered wings sprout from my back and begin to beat through the frigid winter wind. Holding Kasia firmly against my chest, protecting her from the winter chill, I take off through the air toward the veil, eager to get her to safety.

When I reach the veil, I hold my position high above in the air and take in my surroundings. The veil's bluish glow reflects off the chaos around it, illuminating the surrounding area and giving me a clear view. Below me, I find utter chaos. The civilians of Lethe are rioting against Draven's men, clearly unhappy about the closing of the veil. Regardless, they're losing. Without magic and proper training, they don't stand a chance against Draven's men, and it won't take long for Draven's men to seize control again.

"If we're going through, we need to go now, mate," Orion shouts from behind me. His wings beat in the air as he hovers high above the veil.

"Where is Niko?"

Orion nods his head toward where Niko is on the ground; he's not far out from the veil and has a clear view of the battle below us. With just a couple of hand gestures exchanged between Orion and Niko, we're on the move. Unwilling to risk being stuck in Lethe, Orion and I descend into the chaos. Men are shouting and screaming, and children are crying over the bodies of their loved ones whom the Lethian guards have struck down. It's like an all-out war, and the civilians have nothing to defend themselves with.

"It's like a bloodbath," Orion says, with his face reflecting the tragedy.

"Of course it is. Draven doesn't care for the people of Lethe, and neither do his men." It takes everything in me not to help as we fly over them, but I know I can't. Kasia has to be my priority now because these people have no chance of survival without her. "Save as many as possible and get home in one piece."

"Hurry up and get her through the veil, ya? I'll do what I can while I wait on Niko," Orion shouts.

I nod my head in response. I look down at the woman in my arms, taking a deep breath before quickly heading through the veil.

Chapter Four

KASIA

"Why hasn't she woken yet? It's been too long. Are you sure she's okay?" a low male voice asks, his concerned tone meeting my ears as I wake.

Another male chuckles deeply before responding, "Xerxes, calm down, mate. She is fine. Niko told you the tonics he gave her for the pain will induce sleep. He also said *multiple* times that this is normal." A few moments of silence pass before he exhales loudly. "I don't think I've ever seen you so worked up over a woman."

"You and I both know she is not just some 'woman,'" Xerxes spits, keeping his eyes locked on my face.

"Ah, that we do. Come, let us get some dinner or a cuppa. It will still be hours before she wakes. You haven't left her side in days. You'll need your strength and energy when she wakes."

"I'll have Senna bring me something from the kitchen. It's not a bother. I want to watch over her until she wakes."

"I'm sure it is no bother. Senna will be just as happy as me to see you eating again. However, I don't know how she will tolerate your stench. Have you even bathed since we got back? You smell like proper shit, mate."

A loud growl fills the room. "I do not need you to oversee that I am tended to, Orion. Do not forget who the Lord of this palace is."

"Of course. Well, I will be off then. You may be willing to starve yourself and sit in your own filth, but I'd much rather fill my belly and soak in a hot bath before the night is over." He sighs again. "She will be okay, Xerxes. Because of you, she—"

"She never should have been there. If I had known where she was, I would've -" I hear him stop mid-sentence, and the room is filled with silence for a few moments. The longer it goes on, the harder it gets to pretend I'm still sleeping. "You can open your eyes, little dove. I know you're awake," the male closest to me whispers. I can feel his warm breath against my skin.

Slowly, I lift my arms, rubbing my eyes before forcing them open. I allow them to adjust to the room's light as I scan it, pushing myself to sit up. Shifting my weight, I feel something next to me in the bed, causing me to look down. The largest black wolf I've ever seen lies next to me, his body pressed snugly against my legs. Its golden eyes fixated on me, but it doesn't so much as lift its head. I find myself a bit afraid. I've heard of dire wolves but never seen one, let alone had one in my bed.

"*Relax*, Erebus will not harm you," the male closest to me appears and explains, putting my mind at ease. His thick hair is messy today and hangs around his handsome face, but through the locks, I can still make out his eyes. Their warm whiskey-brown color seem to see right through the walls I've built up and into my soul. He's gorgeous, easily the most handsome man I have ever seen. His black shirt hangs across his chest, unbuttoned from the top to the middle of his well-defined chest, exposing his tanned skin.

"Like what you see?" he chuckles, causing me to snap my eyes back to his.

"I've seen better, and your friend was right. You do smell like shit. Like a wet dog that rolled around in his own shit," I counter. Shockingly, where most men would be offended by my insults and tell me that it's improper for a lady to speak in such a way, this male does not. Instead, he counters with a cocky smirk of amusement that has my stomach fluttering.

"Bloody hell, mate. You may have met your match. This little bird has balls." The other male adds, and I turn my attention to him. He's tall, tanned, and toned like the other one. However, his hair is short and shaved close to his head. His expression is one of amusement as he pulls a chair across the room and sits down. I turn my attention back to the male closest to me, *Xerxes*.

"Thought you were leaving, Orion?" Xerxes asks, his eyes never leaving me.

"Well, I was, but I don't want to miss this. It isn't often someone besides Niko or myself has the balls to tell you off, let alone a woman," he replies, and for some reason, his referral to me being a woman rubs me the wrong way.

"What does being a woman have to do with anything? I don't need a cock to speak my mind nor hold a sword."

Xerxes grins as he sits forward to rest his elbows on his knees. "Is that so? Well, we shall see how well you can spar when you're healed. Now, tell me, how did you end up in that prison? Were you hiding before that, or have you been there since the assassination?"

"What are you talking about? What assassination?"

"The assassination of the royal family. The Satori family. Your family," he adds. I burst out laughing, unable to contain my reaction to his ridiculous assumption. "Is something funny?"

"Yeah, you thinking I'm royalty is hilarious," I spit as I sit up and lean back against the wooden headboard. "I'm not royalty, and I've spent many nights in that Gods-forsaken prison, but I always escape, and I would've again if you hadn't—"

"If I hadn't come in when I did, they would have beaten you again and then raped you," he says with an angered tone that catches me off guard. "They had plans for you. Their thoughts were filled with all the vile things they wanted to do to you. If I hadn't come for you, you never would've escaped. Not this time." His fists are clenched tightly as he turns his eyes away from me and to the floor before lifting himself from the chair and pacing around the room. The other male, Orion, clears his throat and adjusts his seat.

"Why did you come? You don't even know me, and I'm—"

He sighs loudly, cutting me off and then softening his tone. "I *do* know you," he pauses, lifting his eye to mine. "I felt you. I felt your pain, your wish for death. You wanted it to be over. I've been waiting, searching for some sign of your survival since your family was killed. Twenty-three years I spent searching, and at that moment, the moment you wished for death to free you from the pain and the suffering, I felt you, and I knew I had to come for you."

"You felt me?" I mock with a laugh.

"Yes." His voice is firm as he glares at me. "Though, I don't know why you're laughing. Is everything amusing to you? You almost died, Kasia!" My head snaps in his direction with the use of my name.

"How— how do you know my name?"

He stops pacing, his fists still clenched tightly at his sides. "Like I said, I have known you my whole life." He releases a deep breath. "When we were children, our parents had us bonded by the last and strongest Elder Oracle, Teun. Our parents were very close, and they wished for the two of us to rule over both realms together. The bond was meant to bring us and our families closer together," he explains. "When your family was killed, everyone thought you were killed too, but I knew you weren't. Even when no one believed me, I *knew* you were out there, somewhere. So, I never gave up searching. *You* are the lost heir of Lethe. The rightful High Lady and the last Satori."

"I think you're confused. Orion was definitely right. You need to rest. You're mad. Who spends their entire life searching for a stranger? I'm certainly no *High Lady*. I am an orphan. I grew up on the streets of Lethe. I grew up suffering through poverty, starving, living in filth, and stealing just to survive. No child should have to see the things I grew up seeing, let alone a child of royalty."

He sighs, his head dropping as he rests his hands on his waist. "Do you truly not remember me? From our childhood? How could you not remember your mother? Your father?"

Erebus lifts his head and cocks it to the side as he whines next to me, making it seem as though he understands the conversation.

"If I may," Orion cuts in. "It's possible her mother had her memory wiped, mate. They had to know they wouldn't survive the night, and it was possible they asked Niko to aid them in removing her memories. The Satori would've done everything to keep her from Draven. Dropping her off at an orphanage would only protect her if she herself didn't know who she truly was. It would explain why she doesn't know what you're talking about or remember you."

"No," I shake my head. "Niko wouldn't have done that and not mentioned it. Especially after all the years he spent helping me search for her."

"I hope you're right. I'd like to think Niko wouldn't, but let's be honest, Xerxes, if wiping her memories was the only way to protect the Satori line, there's a chance he helped them."

I sit in silence; my head throbs and my ears ring as I try to make sense of everything they're saying.

"Did the curse affect your powers too? I wasn't sure how it would effect those of the Satori bloodline. You must know how to control them by now. Have you had any training?"

"What powers? I have no powers," I scoff, trying to contain another laugh. "Satori bloodline? You both sound crazy. Is there a doctor here we can summon for you both? I think you should both get checked over," I interrupt, returning my attention to Xerxes. He meets my gaze with a cocky smirk on his face as he paces toward me, lowering himself to hover just above me. His eyes search my face, moving from my lips to my eyes, and I suddenly feel vulnerable, but in a good way. Like his darkened eyes roaming my body is everything I need at this moment, and suddenly, all the pain that was flooding my body just a moment ago is completely forgotten, replaced by a heat pooling between my legs, forcing me to clench them tightly together. This new male and his piercing gaze has an effect on me that most men don't, and I'm not sure I like it.

"The curse over Lethe could have affected her side of the bond; without magic and growing up as she said she did, she may not have even been able to feel the bond between you two with the curse over her realm, and if she did, I doubt she felt you as strongly as you felt her," Orion explains.

"Well, Calanthe has no such curse. Tell me, little dove, do you feel any different now that you are here?"

"If you mean do I feel more annoyed and murderous than normal, then yes, I definitely feel different. Thank you *so* much for asking," I retort with a venomous tongue.

Orion breaks out in laughter. "Oi, mate, you will have your hands full with this little bird. I fucking love it! Wait till I tell Niko!"

"It's a wonder how you managed to keep your tongue while inside that prison, assuming it was just as sharp during your confinement. Though, I'll admit, I'm pleased to find they didn't cut it from your seductive little mouth. I rather enjoy its verbal abuse. It's refreshing," he says with a low guttural tone before focusing on Orion.

"Orion, see yourself out. I'll meet with you shortly in my study," Xerxes commands over his shoulder. Orion lifts himself from the chair, offering me a smirk and nod before seeing himself out.

"You still haven't told me why you brought me here, or where I am, for that matter. Who are you?"

"So many questions," he smirks. "I brought you here because your realm is no longer safe for you. Draven has the veil completely under his control in Lethe. His guards have set up camp surrounding it, and they're no longer allowing anyone to enter or leave the realm. This tells me he may not have known where in Lethe you were, but he knew you were there and wanted to make sure you couldn't leave."

"What could High Lord Draven possibly want with me? I have already told you I am nobody."

He sighs loudly. "You are the furthest thing from nobody, Kasia. You are the only living Satori. The rightful heir to the throne Draven stole, the only one who can threaten his rule and break the curse over your realm."

"Let's say I believe all this to be true. Why do you care about Lethe? About what happens to me?"

"I care because I, like many others, want Draven removed from the throne and see to it that you sitting upon it where you belong."

"You mean to say you want me to rule so that you can rule beside me since we're supposed to marry and all that... That's what you said, right?"

"Yes," he laughs. "We were meant to marry and rule both realms together, but I also care because, with the veil under Draven's control, things will only get worse for Lethe as well as the other realms," he confesses, and for the first time, I find myself utterly speechless. Silence fills the room again. The tension between us fills the air so thicky a blade could slice though it.

This overflow of information seems completely unbelievable to me. Me? A royal? There is no way that's possible. Not with the life I have been left to live, and not with the number of frigid nights I cried myself to sleep with hunger pains. The squander I was forced to survive in, with dirty, torn clothes and the abuse I was left to suffer. No royal, highborn Fae would be raised like that, especially not the Satori Heir. I'd heard of her, though everyone assumed she was killed along with her mother and father that day.

"I slaughtered them all," he adds, breaking the silence.

"Who?"

"The men in that prison. Every single one of them. I killed them all, and the one who... Let's just say he suffered the most."

"Oh. But why? If Draven found out you were in his realm killing his soldiers, he could see it as an act of war. Why would you risk that for me?"

"I'm no stranger to sneaking into Lethe under Draven's nose, and it was worth the risk if it meant getting you out. The condition I found you in, Kasia..." He lowers his gaze as his body tenses again. "If I'd been just a few moments longer, it would have been too late. What they did to you, they deserved worse than death, and though I still hate that they touched you at all, I can promise it will never happen again. No one will *ever* harm you again. I will not allow it." His proclamation of protection fills me with an odd feeling. I've never had anyone to protect me before; no one ever cared.

"Right, well. I don't need you or anyone else to protect me. I can do that myself," I add, doing my best to hide the effect of his words on me. "I'll just be going now. I have people relying on me." I explain as I try to push myself from the bed. The small movement hurts as burning pains radiate across my back.

"No, stop," he shouts as he rushes to my side. "You cannot leave; you're in no condition to travel anywhere, and as I explained, the veil is closed. You can't get back through, even if you wanted to."

"What do you mean I can't get back through? You got me here, didn't you? Take me back. I will fight my way through if I need to," I seethe through clenched teeth. The pain becomes unbearable as Xerxes helps me lay back down.

"We snuck through when Lethe civilians were rioting over its closure. We will not get that chance again so soon. They've had days to set up their defenses and fortify their stations, and you are in no condition to fight anyone, let alone dozens of trained men."

"Clearly, you've never seen me wield a sword," I counter as the realization hits me. "Wait, did you say days? You mean I have been here... asleep for days?"

"Yes, three, to be exact. Niko has been tending to your wounds daily, but they're still healing slower than I'd like, especially for a Fae. The lashes across your back were very deep, and they will leave scars even with the Amazathian healing remedies. You need to stay in bed and let your body rest."

"This is your fault!" I shout. "Why did you bring me here knowing I'd be stuck here? Of course, you had to go and be all savior-like and try to save me. I'd still be in Lethe if it weren't for you! I would have been fine!" I scoff. Rage consumes me as I kick and shout, pounding my fists into his chest, ignoring the pain that courses through my body.

"Kasia, you would be dead if I hadn't come when I did! They would've done unspeakable things to you and left you for dead! You should be thanking me!"

"Thanking you? You, a stranger who kidnapped me and brought me to a foreign place against my will, and are now telling me I can't return home, and you want me to thank you? You cannot keep me here against my will!"

"I can, and I will!" he shouts.

I laugh menacingly as I scoot away from him. "Well, what's next, hmm? Are you going to try and force yourself on me too? After all, you said so yourself, we're meant to be husband and wife, right?"

"Oh, Kasia, I don't need to force myself on you. Do you think I can't feel what I do to you? I may be a stranger, but I have felt you my entire life, and I know my very *presence* affects you. I saw the hunger in your eyes when you first saw me," he adds, bringing himself closer to me. He runs his fingers up and down the exposed flesh of my arm, causing tiny goosebumps to prickle along my skin. A large silver ring with a glowing white stone on his finger draws my attention briefly. Growing up with nothing, the fine, shiny things often catch my attention, their beauty so enthralling. "I can scent your arousal this very minute, your body's natural reaction to me." I blush with embarrassment at his confession, turning my face away from him. "Don't be shy, little dove. You being so close has the same effect on me, especially when you show me how much you love to abuse me with that sharp tongue of yours. I don't mind spending every day with a hard cock if it means you're safe and here, where I can protect you, even if it is against your will. You can hate me, and I fully expect you to fight me when you're up for it, but trust me when I say I will do everything in my power to make sure you never leave here again, not if this is the safest place for you to be."

I pull my arm from his touch, shifting myself further back on the bed to get away from him. "Do not touch me again, unless you want to meet the end of my blade. The only thing you make me feel is nausea. You and your *presence* do nothing but repulse me, and I'd sooner let one of those guards have their way with me than ever let you touch me," I snap. "All you did was free me from one prison to place me in another, and I promise you I will escape from this one just as easily as I have escaped that one in the past."

He chuckles. "This is far from a prison, little dove, but see it that way if you must. You can lie to yourself all you want, but we both know the truth," he replies, running his hand through his thick dark locks as he backs away and strides across the room to the door.

"Xerxes," I add, causing him to pause. He turns, lifting his eyes back to mine. "A cage made of silver is still a cage." Erebus quickly rises, jumping down from the bed to rush to Xerxes's side.

He breaks his gaze with mine as he lets out a quiet sigh. "I'll have someone bring you up some food. You should rest," he replies before he leaves, with Erebus following behind him.

Alone, finally, I allow myself a moment to take in my surroundings and carefully lift myself from the comforts of the bed. The room is large and lavish—dark green walls with gold fixtures and beautiful tapestries hanging throughout the space. Massive cathedral windows make up the wall to the left of me, and as I peer outside, I notice it overlooks the dense forest landscape of Calanthe. There's a large reading bench in front of the window, stocked with piles of soft pillows and fur blankets that must've cost a fortune. *I can't remember the last time I felt such softness.* I run my hand through the thick fur blanket draped across the bench.

Far off in the distance, the thick forest gives way to a lake so dark it looks black. The large glowing crescent moon casts a glow over its mirrored surface, and as I lift my eyes to the night sky, I find it filled with millions of sparkling stars, bright and glowing like lanterns in the darkness. It's beautiful, even if I'd rather be anywhere but here. The pain radiating from the wounds across my back worsens with each tiny movement as I turn from the window and head back to the comfort of the bed. I don't want to be here, but I'm in no condition to fight my way out or escape. I have no choice but to rest and allow my body the time it needs to heal, and even though I don't want to admit it, mentally, I need time to take in everything I've been told.

I don't believe I am who they think I am. How could I believe that after the life I've been forced to live? The things I've seen and done in my life prove there is no possible way I was born a royal. No High Lord and Lady would ever leave their precious child, their heir, to the slums of Lethe, right? Thoughts of my childhood bring me back to the little faces I know are desperately waiting for me to return with silver coins and food. Without me to provide for them, the children won't last long, and knowing they're suffering will only cause me more pain than the wounds etched into the flesh of my back. A single tear glides down my cheek, my heart feeling heavy with sorrow at the little faces under Miss Sage's care that will surely fade without me. I quickly wipe it away with the back of my hand, not allowing myself to feel sad. Sadness and tears will get me nowhere. It's a lesson I learned early on in my life.

I don't care who Xerxes thinks me to be or that he thinks he can keep me in this cage of gold trimmings and silk. Once I'm strong enough, I will be leaving, and I will shed the blood of anyone who tries to stop me.

Chapter Five

XERXES

I curse myself as I make my way through the large stone halls of Eventide Palace. The sounds of Lake Arachai's waves crashing against the high palace walls echo through the nearly empty halls. Servants, clearly sensing my mood, quickly move to the side to avoid my approach, lowering their heads as I pass. I never should've touched her, but the pull to be near her is so strong and so much harder to ignore than I initially thought it would be.

My side of the bond calls to her, craves her closeness, and even though she fights it, I know she feels something. Her body's natural reaction to me was similar to mine, and though she tried to hide it, I could feel it. She's attracted to me, and she hates that I have an effect on her. Her thoughts can't be kept hidden from me, though. I know exactly how I make her feel, and it would take more than the bond between us to have her heart racing the way it was.

My chest physically hurts from how angry she is with me, and though I understand why, there's nothing I can do to change it. If Draven were to get his hands on her, he'd kill her, and if hating me keeps her safe, then I will have to learn to live with it.

"Xerxes!" someone shouts from the other end of the hall, pulling me from my thoughts. Lifting my eyes, they land on Niko as he slithers towards me from the direction of Kasia's room with a satchel of herbs. Panic sets in with the fear that something could possibly be wrong with Kasia.

"Niko, what is it? Is she alright?"

"Relax, friend," he replies, calming as he directs me to walk next to him down the hall. "Your bonded is fine. She is healing well, and since she seems to have woken despite the tonics I gave her, I imagine her Fae powers are slowly returning, too."

"That's good news then, isn't it?"

"Ah, yes, but also concerning," he states before clearing his throat. "Da girl has never used her powers. I doubt she even knows what her magic feels like. She'll have no control over it, and well, that could prove to be problematic, especially with her temper."

Raising my brow, I reply, "I see Orion wasted no time filling you in." Niko laughs as he pats his hand on my back.

"Now, why would you expect any less? Dat boy loves getting you going, always has. Not very often does anyone other than he or Senna give you a piece of their mind, High Lord. I imagine to him it is quite the show."

"Yes, well, she's certainly strong-willed, as were her parents, so I'm told."

"The Satoris were good people. They did not deserve the death they received, and many, including myself, wish we could've done something to prevent it," he adds before pausing, "Orion mentioned she has no memory of them or anything else."

"It's true. She has no memory of who she is and refuses to believe me when I tell her, but I swear to you, Niko, it really is her."

"Xerxes, I do not doubt the strength of your bond. Besides, I believe your suspicions are correct. Days before their murder, the Satoris paid me a visit," he explains, looking solemn. "They asked me if I'd be willing to give them some of my scales for a potion."

"Salome potion? They wanted to wipe her memories?"

"Indeed. However, I understood why, and I denied giving any to them. Friend, you have my word. I did not have anything to do with that girl's memories being taken from her."

"I believe you. Thank you for explaining. I think it's safe to say we know why she doesn't remember, but without your help, how could they have done it?"

"There are others in Amazath who know the sacred way of making Salome. I will see what I can find out when I return," he adds gently. "Do not fear for her. That girl is her mother through and through. I knew who she was the moment I laid eyes on her in that cell, and in time, she will, too. We will find a way."

"I won't stop until she knows the truth of everything," I admit. "What of the newest Lethe child? The one Orion brought back from the riot at the veil. Did you find proper arrangements for him?"

"I did. A family in town took him. He seemed to be in good spirits when I last left, and he was filling his belly with a warm supper along with their other children," he explains as he nods his head. "It's a good thing you're doing for those children. That last one surely wouldn't have survived much longer with how thin he was."

"I'm just doing what I can. None of them deserve to live like that. Kasia didn't deserve to grow up like that."

"Ay, she didn't, but something tells me it's made her the woman she has become."

I sigh. "It definitely made her strong, that's for sure. And you said she's healing well? Do you truly think her Fae power has returned?"

"I do, but we will know for sure tomorrow. If I'm correct, most of her wounds should be completely healed between my tonics and her Fae healing. I will check over her in the morning to be certain. For tonight, you should try and rest. Perhaps allow yourself to indulge in a hot bath," he adds jokingly.

"Thank you, Niko," I reply, giving him a side-eye glance. "I'll check in with you tomorrow." Bidding him goodnight, he continues down the hall as I slide open the door and head into one of the palace's finer guest rooms.

The large room is cold and empty. Nothing like my chambers, but instinctively, when we arrived from Lethe, I put her in my bed like she belonged there. Because she's the only woman who ever has. Though I've had my share of women over the years, none have touched the bed in my own chambers. Other than the maids who change the sheets of course. Being in this room is an odd feeling. However, I'm no stranger to it. Over the years its become the room I bring women. The moonlight pours in through the large open windows, casting a bluish glow across the tapestry-covered walls and the dusty shelves of books that never get read. I should have Agatha in here to clean at some point now that I'll be staying here.

I slide out of my filthy clothes, dropping them to the ground as I make my way straight to the bathing chamber and turn on the faucet, filling the large porcelain tub with steamy hot water. The small room is bare, save for the large tub and small table of supplies, but still luxurious for a guest room. The wall furthest from the door holds a huge window that overlooks Arachai Lake with piles of pillows scattered around the floor beneath it so one might sit and enjoy the cool night breeze.

A small brass table sits next to the bath with vials of scented oils, a box of matches, and bars of oatmeal soap. There's also a large crystal decanter filled with golden liquor and a singular glass. Grabbing two tiny vials, I pop the corks, dropping a few drops of lavender and lemon oil into the water before stirring it around the steaming waters with my arm.

As the bath fills and the scented oils fill the air around the room, I quickly light the pillar candles placed around the sides of the bath, one by one, until their flickering flames resemble stars in the night sky. My body aches from days of sitting in a small chair next to her bed, and though I'd do it all over again, I crave the comfort the heated waters will impose on my muscles.

With the bath filled, I turn off the faucet, slowly stepping into the tub. Lowering myself to sit down, I welcome the sting of the scalding water as I rest my head on the back of the tub, allowing my eyes flutter shut.

"You haven't been to visit me since you returned with her," a hushed voice whispers over my shoulder.

"Nymeria."

"Lord," Nymeria answers as she reaches the side of the tub. Lifting my eyes, her long black braids hang down her petite body, barely covering her bare nipples. The blue shine of her scattered scales painted across her ebony skin glint off the array of pillar candles placed around the tub. She lowers herself to my level as her crystal blue eyes feast on my naked body submerged in the bath water. "Why have you not come to see me? I have missed you."

"I've had more pressing matters to attend to."

"You mean, *her*. She is not worthy of your affection. She is nothing more than a peasant," she hisses. Her aggression toward Kasia quickly angers me.

"You will watch your tongue when you speak of her."

She scoffs. "My, you seem easily agitated. Let me help you relax," she whispers against the shell of my ear as she trails her fingers across my chest.

I quickly remove her hand, finding her touch nauseating. "Your touch is not wanted."

"You never minded my touch before. In fact, I quite remember you enjoying it," she growls. "Many nights we spent in this room together, touching each other. Have you forgotten?"

"No, I have not forgotten how easy of a fuck you were when I needed one. Now, see yourself out. I wish to enjoy my bath."

"She's not worthy of your company. She's used-up goods."

"Rich, coming from you, *siren*. Tell me, is that the scent of three or four human men I smell on you? How many of them did you lead to their death after you fucked them?" I spit. "Now leave, I said."

"She's barely been here a week, and you have already changed, Xerxes."

"Nymeria," I add as I pour myself a small glass of liquor from the decanter on the table. "What we had is no more. You will stop these visits, for you are no longer wanted here. And, if you so much as whisper any ill will toward Kasia, you will live to regret it."

"Threats are beneath you, *Lord*."

I bring the glass of liquor to my lips, taking a sip, and swallow it down. "It is not a threat. It is my word." With that, I bring my power to the surface, wrapping it around Nymeria's body. Sensing it, she pauses, looking down on herself with a shocked expression.

"What are you doing?" she says with a hiss. She quickly tries to get her bearings. Knowing what's to come, she frantically tries to grab onto anything she can in order to fight my magic.

With a wave of my hand, she's forcefully dragged out of the bathing chamber with the door slamming and locking shut behind her. Releasing a sigh, I smirk—

content with the solace of being left alone with nothing more than my thoughts of Kasia. I allow myself to relax again in the heat the bath provides as I stare out the window. The moon is nearly at its fullest tonight. I can feel its energy across my exposed skin, giving me strength and refilling my well of power after my trip to Lethe.

My lungs release a breath I didn't know I was holding as my thoughts trail back to Kasia and how her very presence affect my side of the bond. Even after so many years, when I look at her, the memories of our childhood and the reckless little girl I once knew become so overpowering that it feels like just yesterday I was chasing her through the forest; her silver hair swaying in the wind behind her in the pursuit. Orion was always fond of finding new ways to annoy her; he found it amusing, much like I do now. Her venomous tongue makes me feel things I didn't know were possible. Sure, I'd been with women before, but none that sent chills through my body or had my heart beating so rapidly, not until her.

One of our favorite pastimes as children was to soar high above the forest around the palace together, even though it was against our parent's orders. Sometimes, we'd travel as far as Culzean just to watch the Centaurs from the safety of the trees as they went about their day. I'll never forget how closely she watched them like she was studying them. It was odd back then, but now I've come to know the little girl with the white wings, whom Orion and I thought was just a silly girl, was actually much smarter than she led on. I think she knew even then that the fear we had been raised to have of the Centaurs was misguided, and not entirely truthful, though I don't know how, yet.

With my aches and pains finally subsiding after soaking in the heated waters, I decide it's time to head back out into the room I'll be calling my own for the time being and start preparing for a sleep that most likely won't come. Carrying the decanter and small glass in my hands, I stride across the stone-cold floor with nothing more than a thin linen towel wrapped firmly around my waist. When I reach the bed, I place the glass and decanter on the night table beside it and stretch my arms above my head. The sore muscles along my back are finally feeling some relief thanks to the long hours spent in the heated waters of the bath. I should've listened to Orion about bathing sooner.

Even when freshly washed, I can scent her on me, feel her on my skin like she's right here, touching me. It's an odd feeling, though it's one I hope I'll come to get used to as I imagine it will only grow in intensity with how frequently she will be near me. I don't plan to ever let her wild heart stray very far. I won't lose her, not again. If Niko is right, Kasia will start to feel the bond between us sooner rather than later now that she is free of Lethe's curse, and I can't help but feel curious as to how my little dove will react when it does. Will she continue to try to fight it, or will she give in to the constant pull that stems from the deepest parts inside her?

Laying down on the fresh sheets, I cross my arms behind my head and stare up at the ceiling in a blanket of moonlight, picturing the way her nose crinkles when she tries to lie to cover her true feelings and the sound of her beating heart makes when she's cursing me with her mouth, yet yearning for me to kiss her in her thoughts.

"Such a predicament you find yourself in, little dove. Whatever will you do?" I whisper to myself with a smirk before letting my eyes flutter closed, and I welcome the sleep I didn't think I would get.

Chapter Six

KASIA

I wake the next morning expecting a golden sunrise, but as I peer outside, I find myself confused. My eyes are met with the same dark star-filled sky that I fell asleep to lastnight.

"It's always night in Calanthe," a feminine voice breaks the silence. Startled by the unexpected visitor, I sit up, gripping the covers tightly against my chest. I scan the room until my eyes land on a woman with a tall, lean face. The pale, pointed tips of her ears peek through her long auburn hair as she flips the page of a book she's reading at a small table across the room. An ornate silver tray sits near the empty seat with a steaming silver teapot and matching tea cups. A vase filled with the most beautiful red roses, all at various stages of blooming, sits in the middle of the table with bowls of mixed fruit and baked goods.

"Oh? I did not know Calanthe was cursed like Lethe," I mutter. Though it's not the morning I expected, it's a welcome sight from the grey skies of Lethe.

"It isn't," she replies, her eyes never leaving the pages of the thick book she holds. "In Calanthe, it is always night because without the moon's presence, our people wouldn't have access to their power for long. We draw our power from the moon."

"Interesting. Wait-" I pause, not quite understanding. "But how did he manage to bring me here from Lethe? Without magic?"

"Ah, you mean Xerxes? Being of royal blood and our High Lord, he does not need to have the moon as a constant in order to draw power from it. It's a rather long and boring explanation," she says as she slams the book closed. "Come eat. You must be hungry, and he's going to have my head if we don't get some food in you." Her eyes finally meet mine, and she gestures to the chair across from her.

I slowly lessen my grip on the thick blanket, feeling silly for being so startled. I don't usually scare easily, but being in such a new place, full of new people and things, is an odd feeling, which fills me with a weird sense of vulnerability that I'm not familiar with. Carefully, I turn in the bed, placing my shaky feet on the floor before pushing myself from the bed. My legs feel weak under my weight; having not used them the last few days, I'm not surprised, but I push through it, ignoring my body's weakness, and step by step, make my way to the table.

The closer I get, the stronger the rich aroma of fried meats and sweet treats gets; notes of cinnamon and apple tickle my nose as I pull out the wooden chair across from the red-haired woman and delicately sit down. I scan her with my eyes, a common habit I've picked up living the way I have, never knowing who can be trusted. She's beautiful, with bright green eyes that shine like emeralds in the fire's golden glow, and a pale complexion with specks of freckles dusting her cheeks. Long, bright red hair hangs perfectly straight around her face with the front two sections braided tightly and clipped to the back of her head, leaving a clear view of her pointed Fae ears. Though her features look friendly enough, with large doe eyes, pouty lips, and a perfect nose, I can't shake the feeling that she isn't happy to be stuck sitting here with me. I can't say I'm happy to be here either. *I don't trust her. I don't like her.*

"I guess growing up in poverty means you were never taught proper manners, hmm?" she snaps. "Staring is rude, and I don't appreciate you raking your unappreciative eyes all over me."

Maybe it's her tone, or the fact that I'm starving that has my blood boiling as a response to her arrogant comment, though it doesn't matter. I've never been one to take shit from someone, and I'm not about to start now. "Do not speak as though you know me or how I was raised because I can promise you, your assumptions are wrong," I snap. "I'll have you know, one of my favorite things to do is prove entitled bitches who think they not only know everything, but also think they're so high and mighty above everyone else, wrong."

Her expression changes before me, a coy smirk replacing her blank stare. "Interesting. Orion was right, for once. This is going to be so much fun!" she explains with a smirk.

"What is? And who are you?"

"Oh right, I'm Senna, precious and favorite little sister to our great High Lord —"

"More like pain in my ass little sister, I'd say," Xerxes cuts in. I avert my eyes to the door where I find him leaning against the frame with a cocky grin on his ridiculously handsome face, but his stare is fixated on me. *No one should be able to look like him.* The pressure and weight of his piercing gaze makes me feel all kinds of things, but I refuse to show it. It doesn't matter how fucking sexy he is or how much my heart races when he's around me; he's still my captor, still someone I can't trust.

"Well, still. Favorite sister, nonetheless. Besides, you would be quite bored without me around," Senna adds, bringing the small cup to her lips.

Xerxes chuckles as he turns his eyes on Senna with a raised brow. "Favorite sister is a title easy to come by when you are in fact my *only* sister, Senna. Besides, I have a feeling with our new guest, my days of being bored are not over, even if you were not here to drive me mad with your ridiculous torment of telling me random facts you read in your dusty old books."

"Yes, well, I agree with that. Quite the mouth on her. I, however, can't wait for her to chew you up and spit you out! It will be so entertaining, Brother."

"Are you two done? I prefer to eat in silence, not listening to sibling chit-chat," I add. Using my fork, I grab a thin strip of fried meat and sniff it before bringing it to my mouth. It's salty and smokey taste is new and delicious as it swirls around my mouth. It's flavour is unlike anything I've ever tasted before, and involuntarily, a small moan slips from my lips.

Noticing the silence around me I bring my eyes to Senna, finding her wide-eyed and staring at me. I pause my chewing, "What?" I ask.

"Um, well, nothing. It's just that I've never seen someone be so excited over a piece of bacon," she stutters. As I lift the bacon to my mouth again, it flies from my hand to Xerxes's. Snapping my eyes to his, my jaw drops with surprise.

"How did you do that?" I ask with a curious yet sharp tongue. A cocky grin forms on his face that has me feeling both weak in the knees, and wanting to slap it off his face.

Xerxes clears his throat from the doorway. "Senna, head down to the seamstress. Let her know I'll need her to pay a visit to our guest later. She will be in need of new clothing, and I want her to have whatever she wants."

"Oh, yes! You will love Glinda! She makes the most beautiful gowns, you just wait! I swear that woman can turn the ugliest of silks into the most glorious wardrobes. She's in *high* demand with the nobles of the court, always wanting her to create new and fancy gowns for them." She brings her hand to cup around her lips as she lowers her tone to a whisper, "They're always hoping a new dress and more cleavage will catch my brother's eyes," she giggles. Somehow, in the few minutes that have passed, I've grown to like this strange girl, and I find I may have judged her too early. The fact that she enjoys egging her brother on doesn't hurt either. I feel like we could have some fun together, since I am trapped here. For now.

"Senna, as a Fae, you should know even when you're whispering, I can hear you as though you're right beside me," Xerxes explains as he approaches us.

"I know, Brother. But it's more fun when I pretend you can't," she smirks, rising from the small table and collects her items. She offers me a kind smile and nods before patting her brother on the shoulder and exiting the room. Turning my sights back on Xerxes, I leave him no chance to change the subject from his little bacon trick.

"How did you do that? With the bacon?" I ask, crossing my arms over my chest. Xerxes chuckles, as he quickly takes Senna's place at the table. His frame is large for the small chair, but he makes it work.

"Just one of my many talents, I assure you," he replies as his eyes darken briefly. "I apologize for her, little dove. I had meetings to attend, and I did not want to leave you without someone watching over you. She can be a lot, but you can trust her."

"So, your plan is to treat me like a child who is in constant need of being watched, as well as a prisoner then?" I question, bringing another strip of the salty meat to my mouth. I find myself wondering what other hidden shows of power this man has that I have yet to see. Keeping my eyes locked with Xerxes's, I slide my tongue across the crispy meat from one end to the other. Its salty flavor assaults my tongue, and I can't control the orgasmic taste it fills my mouth with as another soft moan leaves me.

"Is this what every meal with you is like?" he asks, adjusting himself in the tiny chair. His shoulder-length hair hangs over his face today in messy waves. He's wearing the same style of tunic today. Again in black and unbuttoned halfway down giving me a perfect view of his tanned and toned chest like he knew I'd enjoy it. I find myself watering at the mouth, not because of the bacon. *No. No, Kasia. He is not gorgeous. He is not the most perfect male you've ever seen. He is your captor. You do not like him; you do not want to be bedded by him.* A smirk forms on his face as his eyes rake across my body.

"Uh, no. I just— I just haven't eaten in days, and I really like food," I retort, doing my best to push the thoughts of his perfect face and well-defined chest from my thoughts. My response only makes his smirk grow as he arches his brow.

"That's not the only thing you like, it seems," he replies with a guttural tone. "Though, I'll admit, if those are the sounds you make with every meal, I shall never skip another supper."

I swallow the bacon down like a lump in my throat. Flirty comments from men aren't anything new for me, though they usually don't affect me. I'm pretty enough, and I've never been one who is afraid to use my body to get me what I need. Even if that means pretending to show interest in return. But with Xerxes, his flirtatious behavior is different. It affects me in ways I'm new to, and I'm not sure I like it. I am angry with him, even if what he said is true and he saved my life. It is his fault I can't return home, and it is his fault the children at the orphanage will suffer and starve without me. I hate him. I hate everything about him. Even his sexy, toned body and fuck-me eyes. I hate his husky voice and the way he makes me wet just by being near me.

"I don't know what you mean. Besides, who is to say I want your company at every meal? I think I'd much rather dine with Senna thank you," I spit, doing my best to hide my reaction.

"Little dove, you can tell whatever lies you wish with those luscious lips, but you can't hide the truth from me," he adds before grabbing an apple from the silver tray on the table. "You see, my gifts, one of them allows me to read one's thoughts, so just now, when you were thinking of my, well, how did you put it 'tanned and toned chest'? Right? Yes, well I heard all of that."

The bacon drops from my grasp as his words hit me, and my cheeks flush with a mix of anger and embarrassment. "Stay out of my head!" I seethe through tightly clenched teeth.

"No need to be angry, Kasia," he chuckles, amused. "Back to your thoughts of me bedding you, I'd happily oblige to that little fantasy whenever you'd like. I find your aggression to be quite the turn on, especially when it's directed at me."

"We shall see if you feel the same when my blade is directed at you!"

"Oof," he mocks, bringing his hand to his chest as though my words have hurt him. "Every time you use that venomous mouth of yours against me, my cock twitches for you, little dove. So much so, that I find myself wondering what else you can do with it." Fully understanding the hidden message in his bold statement. I snap back with annoyance.

"Idiot. Just because I won't kiss your ass like the women you're used to doesn't mean I don't know what to do with my mouth. Though," I pause, bringing my eyes to his crotch. "I doubt a pint-sized penis is even big enough for a woman to suck."

A loud laugh erupts through him as he leans forward, placing his elbows on the small wooden table. "Ah, and do you often find yourself thinking about the size of my cock? I can assure you it's not, well, how did you put it? 'Pint-sized'? I'd even be willing to show you if you'd like." His voice is confident and cocky as he speaks.

I mimic his movement, leaning forward and placing my elbows on the table the same way he did before leaning in close. Our faces are mere inches apart as I pull my bottom lip in with my teeth. His eyes catch the small movement and his gaze fixates on my lips. "Hmm, no thank you. To answer your question, I don't think about it. Usually, my thoughts of you involve me ending your life, but now I'm wondering which hole in your corpse to shove your tiny cock in when I'm finished with you. Your ear perhaps? Or maybe your ass? So many choices, High Lord," I mock, ensuring I'm sporting my best flirtatious smile.

My breath catches in my throat as he leans closer, bringing his lips to ghost over mine, sending a chill down my spine. Tonight, having washed since the last time he was so close, he smells different, like a midnight rainstorm, damp and earthy. It's enthralling. "Little dove, you know just how to get me going." Before I can react, his Fae fangs softly nip at my bottom lip, pulling on it before he releases it with a pop. "Such a sexy little mouth of venom, and yet I'd happily let you bite me." With that, he rises from the table. His hardened cock clearly visible through his leather trousers as he strides toward the door. My heart races and I find myself breathless when he offers me one last glance over his shoulder. "Finish eating. I'll have the maids draw you a bath before Glinda arrives. I have business to attend to. I'll be back later tonight," he adds before closing the door quietly behind him.

Alone at last, I allow myself a few moments to process all these new and confusing feelings. I *hate* him. I blame him for everything that has happened in the last few days, and yet he consumes my thoughts, my very being. I want him close; I want his touch, to drown myself in his intoxicating rainstorm scent, but I won't allow myself to, not after what he's done.

I exhale slowly, forcing myself to calm my quickening pulse as I slowly grab another piece of bacon from the tray and bring it to my mouth. Biting into the crunchy meat, my thoughts replay the last few days over and over again. In my head, I'm trying to make sense of all that I've learned from these strangers. Looking around the room, knowing now that Xerxes is High Lord of Calanthe, I'm not surprised to find it decorated with the finest of things. Plenty of silk pillows and fur blankets to keep one comfortable and warm. Trays full of delicious and warm food brought in by maids, the same maids who tend to their every need. It's sickening. One would expect me to enjoy this, to take full advantage of the luxury I'm being treated to, but all I can think about is the people back home and the way they must be suffering without my daily food and silver coin deliveries.

Clearly, the people of Calanthe and Amazath sleep fine, resting their heads on silk pillows while the low-born in Lethe starve and freeze to death. Anger flows through my body as I toss the piece of overly salted meat back on the plate. *How am I supposed to eat these fine foods knowing what's happening in Lethe.?* My skin tingles, like tiny vibrations coursing through my body that continue to grow until it's overpowering, like every inch of my body is on fire. It's a feeling I've never felt before, and it startles me. Shoving the wooden chair back, I rise to my feet, bringing my hands to cover my face in an attempt to calm myself. I try slowing my breathing, but it doesn't work. The burning tingle only grows.

Suddenly, the large window across the room opens as a strong wind bellows in, and I remove my hands from my face just in time to see it knocking a vase of red roses from the table. The vase crashes to the stone floor, shattering. I panic, unsure of what's happening and terrified of this feeling coursing through my body. It's completely consuming me. Thunder booms outside as the wind grows stronger, knocking things over in a circular assault around the room. Confused and scared, I stumble backward, grabbing the back of the chair to keep my balance as the burning sensation wreaks havoc on my body.

Just as it seems the floor is calling my name and my body can no longer withstand the pressure or the burn, the door to the room bursts open, and I feel the presence of someone at my side, catching me before I meet the cold stone.

"Ma 'lady! Come here; you need to calm down. Just breathe. You're going to be okay."

"What's happening? Who are you?"

"I'm sorry. We did not mean to frighten you!" and older woman apologizes. I glance toward her voice, finding her waist-length salt and pepper hair pulled into thick braids on the sides of her head, her face aged with wrinkles and kind blue eyes. She's short, thin, and has a grandmotherly aura about her. Her aged expression leaks of concern, and kindness as she reaches me. The burning feeling slowly begins to fade, along with my anger and thoughts of those I left back home, in Lethe.

"Let us get that cleaned up for you," another woman adds with a softly. Lifting her hand, she snaps her fingers and all the shards of broken glass disappear. Suddenly, the roses are back on the table in a new vase. She appears to be much younger than the other maid. With shoulder-length black hair and narrow brown eyes, she's petite and her olive skin glows.

"How did you—?" I stammer, finding myself utterly lost for words.

"Magic, ma 'lady, of course," she replies, giving me a puzzled look. "Have you never seen one use their magic?" *Magic? Was that what happened with the roses?*

"No, I— Well, I came from Lethe, and well—"

"Lethe! Oh! You, poor dear! That would explain why you have no control over your powers."

"My powers?"

"But of course. That little storm there, that was you, dear. My guess is you were having some not-so-happy thoughts or emotions," she chuckles.

"My thoughts did that?"

"That they did, but that's a topic for a different day. In time, you will, in time, learn to control them. Thank goodness you are here now, and allow me to apologize on behalf of myself and Ingrid; we were not made aware of your situation. The High Lord only said you were to be looked after and that anything you wished for was to be brought to you immediately. This is Ingrid, and I am Agatha. It is our job to see to it you have everything you need."

"Ah, yes, I am sure he did." I roll my eyes. "I bet he demands that for all the women he kidnaps and holds prisoner."

"Kidnaps?" she pauses. "Ma'lady, I mean no offense, but you should be happy to be here. High Lord Xerxes is a kind man, who cares deeply for all Fae people, including those in Lethe. He does what he can to help them, without catching the wrath of High Lord Draven, of course."

"He does?" I ask curiously. "He never mentioned helping them."

"Oh, but he did admit to kidnapping women like it's one of his favorite pastimes. Did he also say he held them hostage in his own chambers? While he moved to a lesser room? Our High Lord, sleeping in a guest room so you could have his," Ingrid responds abruptly, turning her back to me whilst tending to the room. "You know little of our realm or our High Lord, so perhaps before you speak so lowly of him, you should spend some time getting to know him."

"Ingrid!" the older one snaps. "Go and run the bath!" Obeying her elder's demands, she turns back to me and curtseys before heading off toward the bathing chamber.

"No, it's okay. She's right. I know nothing of this realm or your High Lord," I apologize, suddenly feeling guilty for offending them. "Is this truly his room I've been staying in?" I ask with a pained expression, guilt consuming me as I glance around the large open space.

"It is, and I assure you. I have been a maid in this palace since before the High Lord was born, and he has never once brought a woman to *his* rooms, nor given them up for one. You are the first. Now, let us get you cleaned up. Glinda will be here in a short while, and we can't have you smelling like that when she arrives," she adds, gesturing with her arm for me to stand before a tall silver mirror. I follow her guidance, my reflection shocking me as my cheeks flush. I can't believe I've been walking around looking like this. Her hands grasp the fabric of my robe as she begins to untie it.

"Wait," I shout, grabbing her frail hands in mine. Bringing my eyes to hers, I offer her a genuine smile. "My name, it's Kasia."

"Well, Lady Kasia. It is nice to meet you," she replies, before continuing to undress me. I turn my attention to the full-length mirror before me. This is his room, his bed I slept in. He gave up his personal place, his sanctuary, to me, a stranger. Why do I feel a sense of relief knowing no other woman has laid on his silk sheets? I force the thoughts from my head as Agatha begins to help me undress. *It doesn't matter, and I don't care.* At least that's what I tell myself.

Chapter Seven

XERXES

Fuck. Her plump little lip felt too good pinched between my teeth. The breath she released brushed against my lips, sending chills down my spine, right to the very core of my side of the bond, and it wanted her. The pull to kiss her, mark her, to even just touch her has never been stronger than it was in those brief seconds where her moss-colored eyes locked with mine. Her heart beat erratically and the world around us seemed to freeze. She wanted me to kiss her; she practically begged me in her thoughts of all the places she wanted me and my touch. Her thoughts were so vivid I could practically feel myself touching her. But I know she isn't ready. I know she's still angry with me. That sharp tongue of hers proves it, but I can't lie, I'm fascinated by it, and thoroughly enjoying her verbal abuse especially while her thoughts are the complete opposite. She's brave, despite what she's been through, and for that, I'm glad.

She'll need that bravery for what's to come. Her birthday is fast approaching and with it she'll gain access to the entire well of her power. However, her magic has already begun to return in small forms. I can't help but wonder if she even notices? After so many years of being powerless, and not having that burning spark of magic flowing through her veins, how will she react when things start happening around her without her control? She will need to start training as soon as she's strong enough. By the looks of her tonight, she isn't far off from being completely healed. Being in Calanthe and away from the Lethe curse, her Fae healing has finally kicked in.

Pacing down the halls, I'm eager to get to my meetings and discuss with my men how things should move forward. It won't take long for Draven to suspect she's in one of the other realms, and with him knowing about our bond, he'll surely search for her here before Amazath. We need to be ready for it. Kasia needs to be ready for it.

"Xerxes!" Orion shouts from behind me. I spin around and find him jogging towards me, his expression sporting his usual comical grin. "I don't think I've ever seen you late to a council meeting," he adds as he reaches my side. We continue on our way, walking side by side through the large halls filled with members and staff of the court.

"Yeah, well it couldn't be helped today."

"Ah," he chimes, jabbing his elbow into my side. "She's got you all worked up, doesn't she! I knew this was going to be great," he adds playfully.

"My late arrival has nothing to do with Kasia, *Orion*. You're overthinking it, as usual." I smirk, knowing full well he's going to see right through my words. Orion and I have known each other for years; he used to play with Kasia and I as children. We've been best friends for as long as I can remember, and because of this, he knows how to read me like a fucking book.

"I don't think I am, mate. But whatever you need to tell yourself to feel better about the fact that you are completely and utterly swooned by her very existence," he spits jokingly as he places a hand over his heart mockingly. "On another note, you might want to prepare yourself for this meeting."

I freeze in place, confused by his statement. "Prepare for what exactly?"

"Well, let's just say not everyone is happy about our little trip to Lethe, and some are even more upset about the part where we brought home the long-lost heir to the Lethian throne."

"Well, unfortunately, I'm their High Lord, and they have no choice but to accept my decision to bring her here. Don't they see-"

"Mate, nobody understands more than I, why you did what you did. But your men? They're scared. For themselves and for their families. Draven's wrath is no secret, and they fear for what will become of them and their loved ones when he discovers that not only is she here, but that they have been helping guard her." His honest words anger me. I understand their fear, but do they have so little faith in me as their High Lord that I won't protect them and their families if it were to come to that?

"I know what I am asking of them, Orion, and I know the risks, but if we didn't get her out of there, if we hadn't brought her here when we did, she would already be dead. Lethe would never be free from Draven or the curse he caused. None of the realms, or their people would ever be free of Draven. They must know that once Lethe collapses under his rule, which it will, and there is no one left for him to rule over, he will simply move on to another realm until there is nothing left."

"As I said, I understand *why* you did it. If I didn't, I wouldn't have fought by your side to ensure she was brought back here safely. But I also understand their fear." Taking in his words, I nod. We continue walking down the halls until we reach the large arched doorway that leads to the courtyard. Heading outside I fill my lungs with the humid night air, a sure sign that a storm is headed our way tonight. Lifting my eyes to the night sky that always looms above, I find its stars seem to twinkle a little brighter, giving me hope that my choice to bring her here was the right one.

In every part of my being, I know it was, and I know there was no way I was leaving her to die. Erebus reaches my side, followed by Kenji, their tails wagging excitedly behind them as they greet me.

"Erebus, Kenji. What trouble have you been getting into?" I ask, cocking my brow. Erebus ducks his head, a sure sign he was up to no good, but Kenji continues his excited little dance around Orion and I as we reach the group of men awaiting me in the middle of the court-yard. My most trusted men, and privy council stand together, talking amongst themselves, but their voices quickly lower with our approach.

"Men," I start with a tone of authority. "I know what you're thinking, and I understand your concerns. I wish I could tell you that Draven won't come through the veil looking for her, but I can't. Once he realizes she isn't in Lethe, he will begin to search the other realms, and that will eventually bring him to our door. But," I pause briefly, taking a moment to look into their eyes, giving them the chance to read my words, and know that my words are honest. "When he does come for her, we will be ready, and we will face him and his army head on if that is what it takes to protect our families. If fighting a war with Draven means protecting Kasia and Calanthe, have no doubt we will charge into battle without a second thought, and we will win."

"But what of the costs?" one of the men shouts from the back.

"I don't care what it costs!" I snap back.

"Of course, you don't!" a man argues as he pushes through the group of men to bring himself forward. I instantly recognize him as Marcus, one of the men who served under my father. He was an older gentleman, well known around the court for his loyalty to my father, which is why his opinion is a shocking one to hear. "You don't care because you can afford to lose things, luxuries, while a war means men like us risk losing *everything* we have worked so hard to build, to earn."

"You won't lose anything." Orion counters, as he brings himself to stand next to me. "Have you seen me in battle, Marcus?" the question rolls off his tongue cockily. "I'm practically untouchable, and I know for a fact most of the men before me are too. I trained them myself. Now you lot of oldies, from before my time, I can't speak for when it comes to the training you've had, but I'm willing to give you some lessons, if you think you can keep up," he adds. "With my training, Draven won't stand a chance against us, not in Calanthe, and not without magic."

"Pft, everyone knows the curse doesn't extend past the veil. Draven would regain his power as soon as he crossed over, and then what?" another man counters.

"Actually, that isn't entirely true," I interrupt. "When we brough Kasia back through the veil, she didn't have access to her powers for some time, and even now she hasn't dipped into the full potential of her well of power."

"But how do we know the same will be said for Draven?"

"Well, we can't be sure, but I would assume, seeing as before the curse his power was nowhere near to the level of Kasia's, that he would take even longer to see any signs of regaining it. It would take weeks, possibly even months for it to return fully, and he'd never last that long here without it."

"But how will we know when he crosses over?" a shorter man shouts from the back as he does his best to peer over the other men.

"We will set up camp at the veil, on our side. Four hundred of my best trained men will head out tomorrow and begin to scout and prepare the area for the camp to be built, and then we won't miss him. We will know the minute he or anyone else crosses through, and we will be ready for them."

"And we will be there to aid in your defense," a deep female voice emanates from behind me. I turn around in time to see Nefeli, Queen of the Centaurs, who lives in the Somnia Forest. She approaches me with her entourage of guards. Her long red hair cascading down her shoulders and blowing through the night's wind around the tall antlers that resemble branches, protruding through her thick locks. Her rosy nose is coated in a thick dusting of freckles as she bows her head to me in a show of respect. I also return the same courtesy to her, bowing my head upon her approach. Though the top half of her body is that of a human woman, the lower part is that of a large horse. She stands on four muscle-filled legs coated in a thin reddish-orange coat of hair that leads down to strong pointed hooves. Her hooves are covered by a layer of longer and thicker bristle, which helps quiet the sound of her steps on the stone paths around the courtyard.

"Nefeli, to what do we owe the pleasure?" I ask playfully. Nefeli and I have grown closer since I took over as High Lord, and even though our parents had their differences in their ruling, we chose to make peace and put the past behind us. The Centaurs are peaceful, and mostly keep to themselves, but it wasn't always thought to be that way. *The little girl with the white wings from my childhood was right all along.*

"Well, you had to know word of the Lethe heir being in Calanthe would reach Culzean at some point. Though I would've expected you to be the one to tell me yourself of her arrival, assuming you had something to do with it, friend." I dismiss the men and give Orion the signal to follow them out and make the arrangements I set in place. As they head out, their expressions soften. The thoughts in their head have calmed, and they know this is a good plan. They still have concerns for the safety of their loved ones, but they have faith in me. They have hope that this plan we have built will work.

Satisfied, I withdraw my power from reading their thoughts and focus back on Nefeli, "Your assumption would be right, and I had meant to tell you." Not a lie; I did mean to tell her and ask for her support in the battle that is sure to come. "Things have just been over-whelming with her return, and until I knew of my plans, I didn't want to include you or your people. What right do I have to ask you to help me defend my realm without a set plan in place-"

"No right is needed for such a request, Xerxes. Calanthe is our home as much as it is yours. We do not wish to see it, nor its people fall, regardless of their race."

Just like Nefeli, her people stand tall and proud. Nefeli is a good and gracious queen to the Centaurs, and their love for her is well known across Calanthe. I've been lucky to call her my friend. But knowing that friendship has brought her here, where she openly offers me and my men aid, is something I didn't expect. The Centaurs have never offered their help before, not to me, nor to my parents during their rule.

"Why do you wish to help me? Even if Draven was to cross into the Calanthe, his battle would not be with Culzean or its people."

"It will matter little to Draven who his problem is with, especially if he manages to cross into Calanthe. This is a war that we must all fight, *together*. I know better than to think he will stop after he takes Eventide. The sooner we can put an end to him, the better."

"I agree. I've already arranged for a camp to be set up at the veil, my men will be the first to know if Draven or anyone else makes it through-."

"Tell me, Xerxes. How is she?"

I pause briefly. Contemplating my words before deciding how I want to answer the question. My fists clench at my side as the memories of how I found her, how her silent wishes for death to come, echoed around in my head, pulling me to her for the first time in twenty years. The pain and sorrow I felt in my bones from her through the bond still haunts me, and nothing has ever terrified me more than the thought I might not get to her in time.

"She's alive," I whisper, through tight lips.

"Well, that *is* a start. How is her spirit?"

"That of a Satori. She refuses to give up and has a mouth that could be mistaken for her mother's, from what I hear." Nefeli chuckles with my remark.

"Ah, well she will be good for you then."

"You're not the first to say that," I add grimly. "Am I to assume you have been talking to Orion then?"

"Not recently, but I am glad he sees what I see," she explains, a smirk on her face. "Orion knows you better than anyone, and anyone close to you knows how long you have searched for her, how persistent you were that she was alive. Having this life-long mission finally come to an end, might finally bring you some peace, friend."

I pause, "I may have found her, but I won't stop. Not until she's sitting on the Lethe throne where she belongs, and Draven is rotting in the earth, where he put her family after slaughtering them."

"Well, allow us to share such a burden. Let us fight this war, together, as one. Centaurs and Fae alike. For Calanthe. For Kasia."

"I'd be honored to have you at my side in battle, Nefeli."

"Good, it's settled then." She slides her fingers into her mouth, and whistles. Its high-pitched sound echoes around the courtyard, and her entourage of armed Centaurs slam the bottom of their thick, sharpened stone spears on the ground once, twice, then freeze. "These men will head to the veil with Orion. They are yours to command, and I shall send more with supplies in a few days. We will face Draven and his cruel offspring together."

My loud laugh fills the air. "Cruel offspring? Am I to believe you're not a fan of Draven's son, Drake?"

"What woman could be? Though I entertain him when I must, that man is intolerable. He believes every female, regardless of race, should just fall at his feet and please him in any way he commands." Drake's thirst for women is well known across all realms. He truly knows no bounds when it comes to the women he wishes to bed. Regardless of race, marital status or even social status, he has been known to seek out the ones he wants until they finally give in and then he tosses them aside, like a child's broken toy. The fact that he has tried with Nefeli doesn't sit right with me at all, though I can't say I'm surprised to hear of it.

"Ah, so you have met." I chuckle.

"A few times you could say, and I would very much like the chance to show him what I can do with my spear," she adds. Her tone reminds me much of Kasia, stirring something inside me and though I just left her a short while ago, *I miss her.*

"In that case, I will save him for you on the battlefield. Again, I thank you, Nefeli."

"No thanks needed, I'll return now to Culzean and make the necessary arrangements. Send word when the camp is prepared."

"Of course. Safe travels home," I add as I offer her a nod. I watch as she heads back out of the courtyard and into the Somnia Forest.

"My Lord." One of my guards approaches with Nefeli's absence. "I've been told to inform you that the lady Glinda is unable to attend to your guest this evening, but that she has had some clothing put together and arranged for them to be brought up to your chambers."

"Alright, thank you." I nod agreeably and wave off the guard.

As the guard leaves to return to his post, I head back inside to inform Kasia that Glinda won't be coming tonight. Not that she needs to know, I doubt she'll even care, but it gives me an excuse to stop by her chambers. *My chambers*. Any excuse to silence my bond's pull to her for a few moments more.

Chapter Eight

KASIA

F inally, alone and stripped of my clothing and wearing nothing more than a silk robe, I head toward the bathing chamber attached to the large room I've been staying in, as Ingrid directed. The large wooden door to the bathing chamber is carved with intricate designs of vines and trees that must've taken someone many hours to carve out. I run my fingers along the grooves, appreciating their beauty, before taking the handle in my hand and swinging the door open. Entering the room, I'm immediately hit with a cloud of steam that carries the scent of honey and lavender. The room is larger than I expected, with dark walls that match the bedroom and decorated with ornate fixtures. The bath, however, is more of a small private pool. It sat level with the marble floor in the center of the room, with steps leading down into its dark and heated waters.

Untying the gossamer black silk robe, I let it slide off my body to the cold marble floor, before stepping into the bath. Each step takes me deeper and deeper into it. It's heated water hugging my body. Reaching the middle, I crouch, submerging myself to my shoulders. I breathe in and deeply as though each breath in and out releases more stress and tension. The heat soothes my aching body as I make my way to one of the submerged seats in the corner of the bath and sit myself down. I slowly lean back against the marble side of the bath, the wounds on my back sting briefly with the contact. I let out a quiet hiss as I attempt to find a comfortable position.

I can't remember the last time I had a bath. Back in the orphanage in Lethe, all we had was a bucket that we filled with snow we melted over the fire, if we had the means to do so. Then it was shared amongst all of us, as was the stained rag we used to wash our bodies. We rarely even had soap and resorted to using whatever plants we could find growing through the snow that had any sort of scent to them to wash away the stench of sweat and dirt. This tub was nothing like I'd ever imagined, nor expected to be lucky enough to experience. My entire body could fit in it thrice, and there'd still be room to move around.

I run my hand across the dark marble, following the tiny veins of gold that trickle through it; as they glint in the glow of the lit candles around the sides of the tub. Knowing I plan to leave when my body allows it, I decided to enjoy this bath while it lasts. After all, this High Lord has made it his mission to ensure I have everything I want; perhaps, for once, I should indulge myself in the finer things.

Though my heart hurts for those I left behind, the ones left to suffer, I know that with the condition I am in, I am of no use to them. All I can do right now is focus on taking care of myself and letting my body and mind heal. I haven't forgotten what happened in that prison; even if I don't show it, its scars will stay with me long after my lash wounds have healed. They'll remain deep inside, where I have piled a lifetime of scars and traumas hidden away from the world so that I never appear weak or damaged. Those qualities would only bring on more danger in the world I was raised in.

A knock on the door pulls me from my dark thoughts. Keeping my back to the door, I tense up in the heated waters and take a breath before I cautiously respond.

"Yes?" I mumble quietly. The wooden door slides open behind me as its hinges creak quietly in an echo around the room. I could feel him before he even spoke. My skin prickled with his approach, like lightning across my skin. I hated it and silently cursed my body for reacting to his presence.

"Niko sent this up for your wounds," Xerxes said quietly as he slowly approached the side of the bath. "Stand up. The sooner we get this on those wounds, the better."

"Leave it; I can do it myself," I reply, keeping my back pressed firmly against the side of the bath. The contact hurts, but I ignore the pain.

"Please, Kasia, as much as I find your stubbornness refreshing, let me help. Besides, we both know you can't reach your own back." His voice is soft, as though my rejection to allow him to help bothers him. I sigh, knowing he is right. Had he listened and just left it, I wouldn't have bothered to put it on at all. But the sooner that I am healed, the sooner I can leave. Without another word, I slowly rise to my feet, keeping my waist down submerged in the water and only exposing my naked back to him. I can feel his eyes on me, scanning my flesh before a deep growling sound vibrates through him as he takes in the damage done to my skin.

He is the first to see the collection of scars on my skin. Though the fresh lashes will be the ones to stand out the most, it is impossible to hide the others. I have collected many scars over the years, and they're painted across my skin like stripes on a tiger.

"Who is Niko? You have mentioned him a few times now." I ask, but my question is ignored as the tension in the air grows thick.

"Who did this to you?" he seethes. His tone has me feeling uncomfortable in my own skin for the first time in my life.

"Many men over the years," I reply. "I have not had the best life, I told you that. I—I did what I had to in order to survive, but that doesn't mean I always made it out unharmed."

"I will kill every fucking person who has touched you and all who dare try to from this day forward," he growls. I can sense his fury as he brings his hand to my flesh. The salve is cool, and its contact with my heated skin causes me to gasp and jump. Xerxes pauses, pulling his hand from my skin. "I'm sorry, I didn't... I didn't mean to hurt you," he whispers. His tone is leaking of concern.

"No. You didn't. It's just... it's cold." I explain with a small smile, though he can't see it. "It's okay, you can continue."

He clears his throat before continuing, his touch softer this time as though he's afraid of causing me pain. His concern for my well-being is something new and confusing. No one has ever cared if I was in pain or not before. Sure, Sage and the children cared if I returned at night or not, but not because they cared for me; they cared for what I brought them. It was no secret; I knew all along they never cared for me as a person, and I never held it against them. It didn't stop me from caring for them, even if I lacked in showing that. Showing emotion has never brought me anything but pain. Over the years, I learned to hold everything inside and handle everything in silence and on my own. It's why I don't know how to feel about Xerxes and his openness about how he feels about me and my safety. My body instinctively stiffens under his touch with the thought of there being any sort of feeling for him other than distain or hatred. After all, he is holding me here against my will.

"You seem tense... I'd be happy to help you with that if you'd like; I know a few tricks I think you'd rather enjoy." He whispers against my ear with a lust-filled tone. It catches me off guard.

"You truly know no bounds, do you? It's like you're trying to make a hobby out of touching me. I'm honored, truly. Who would've thought, the High Lord of Calanthe, chasing common Lethe pussy." He smirks, as he pulls his hand back and pushes himself to his feet.

"*So,* fucking feisty. It's like you speak directly to my cock, little dove. Well then, I supposed that should be good enough for the night." He explains. "Oh, and Glinda is unable to make it tonight, but she did send up a few gowns she thinks will fit you."

I nod, swaying my arms through the fragrant bubbles floating across the surface of the bath. "Thank you. Is that all?"

"Yes, that's all. I guess I should leave then?"

I turn to face him, finding his eyes darkened and lustful. *Oh, this is going to be fun.* I think to myself. "Yes, you really should. I'm sure you have some sort of company lined up tonight, and I'd hate to keep them waiting." I reply, slowly moving myself into the water, careful not to wet my back.

"You almost sound jealous," he replies with a smirk that sets my blood on fire. Me? Jealous? "Alright, I give up, you win. Listen—" he changes his tone to a serious one, clearing his throat. "There is an oracle, a few days' ride out into the Somnia Forest, off the coast of Arachai Lake. She is known around the realm for having... certain powers. I think it might help you. She could be able to help return some of your memories. If you're willing to allow her to try."

"I see, and what if there are no memories for her to return to me? I still don't believe I am who you think I am."

"Well then, this trip to her can't hurt, right? If you're right, and there are no memories for her to return, then at least you got a chance to experience more of Calanthe. There is a whole realm outside of these walls, little dove."

"I suppose you're right," I add, silently considering his request. "Alright, I'll go."

"Really? So easily? Hmm. I had expected you to fight me on it."

"Why? The sooner it's proven I'm not this Satori heir you think me to be, the sooner I can figure out how to get back to Lethe. Now, if you don't mind, I'd like to get out of the bath before I turn into a prune." His expression changes to one of annoyance, clearly unhappy to hear that I still don't believe myself to be the lost heir he seeks.

"Right, I'll wake Senna and have her come help you—"

"No. You don't need to wake her or anyone else up; I can dress myself. Not everyone grew up with people at their disposal to tend to everything for them, you know." I snap, annoyed with his incessant need to wait on me as though I'm a child and unable to do things for myself. I rise from the water and slowly make my way toward the steps. I can feel his eyes on me, scanning every inch as each step reveals more of my naked body to him. A low vibration emanates from his chest as his eyes follow my every move as I stride across the room. I grab a towel from the folded piles that Ingrid and Agatha left for me on a small table by the door. "If you don't mind, I'd appreciate some privacy to dress, High Lord," I add over my shoulder with a soft low voice.

He chuckles as he lowers his eyes to the floor with a teasing grin. A light pink hue coats his cheeks, and I smile, knowing I've affected him like I'd hoped. I've always known I'm pretty enough and have never been ashamed to use my body to my advantage. However, even I can't deny that this time feels different. Usually, a man's eyes on my body repulse me, and I have to force myself to ignore it, but with Xerxes, knowing his eyes are on me and having this effect on him sends tingles across my skin, and my pulse speeds up.

"Oh?" he questions with a smirk. He clicks his tongue and runs it across his teeth as his eyes pierce mine through the steam from across the large room. "Well then, I suppose I should go," he replies as he lets himself out of the bathing chambers, clearly aroused. The wooden door's latch clicks behind him just as I tighten the towel around my slick body. He wasn't wrong. As amazing as soaking in a hot bath for the first time in, well, probably forever was, my body and mind are still tense.

There is too much confusion and too many questions on top of the never-ending concern that has been flooding my heart for days for the children I left behind that depend on me. Feeling so many emotions is new for me and uncomfortable. While I know Xerxes wants to help me, in more ways than one clearly, I don't know how to let him. I've always only had myself, never had anyone want to help me, not without gaining something in return. No one ever cared for me, and now that someone does, I don't really know how to act or feel about it. My instinct is to push him away so he can't hurt me. But there's this feeling, this speck of emotion deep inside me that speaks to him and begs for me to let him in, to trust him.

He's done nothing but show me how much he cares for me in the time since he brought me here, and I can't lie, part of me returns his feelings, even if I don't want to admit it. But does that mean he doesn't expect anything in return, he's made it clear he wants *something* but is that something all he wants from me? I've seen first-hand how hungry men are for the release women can give them. The lengths they will go to, to lie and take it even if the woman doesn't want it. Memories of the prison guard before me suddenly replay in my head. His grotesque face as he stroked himself to my naked and bloodied body—the warm feeling of his release coating my feet. I cringe at the thoughts, reminding myself how lucky I was that is all he did.

The worst part is that I want that something too, I can feel it. He affects my body in ways no man ever had, and it both excites and enrages me. He may have saved me, but he brought me to a place I can never leave, away from everything and everyone I know. He speaks as though he knows me, like these memories he claims to have of us as children, mean he knows the woman I have grown to be, but he doesn't. He has no idea about the life I have lived, or the blood I have shed to stay alive. Would he still view me as this innocent lost princess if he knew the truth? Or would he look at me with the same disgust the men I have killed did?

I slide my feet into the silk slippers Agatha left me, before grabbing the matching silk gown. I slide it over my body, peeling it from my damp skin as I adjust it. My long white hair is wet but smells clean again, finally. Running my fingers through its length, I untangle the knots before using the towel to suck up any leftover water and tossing it in the laundry basket. Finally washed and dried, I head back out to the bedroom, eager to get into the soft sheets and sleep away the confusion that has taken over my head.

As I enter the large room and head towards the bed, I freeze, and my breath catches in my throat as I find it's already occupied by the High Lord himself. He'd fallen asleep waiting for me to dress, and of course, it had to be in my bed. *His bed.* He's shirtless, his black tunic sitting on the small table by the bed. He has his arms crossed behind his head, thick dark hair is pulled up into a messy knot on the top, giving me a good view of his face as I approach the side of the bed. Thick dark lashes rest on high-tanned cheekbones, and specks of freckles are dusted across his nose and cheeks. His lips, so full and luscious, I can't help but wonder what they would feel like against mine.

I force the thoughts from my head. He is radiant, and there is no denying it. Easily the most handsome man I have ever seen, almost like he was sculpted by the Gods themselves. But that doesn't change who he is or what he's done. He may have saved me, and may be trying to help care for me while I'm here, but it is still *his* fault I am here. Had he left me in that cell, I would have made it out, and I would have still been in Lethe and not trapped in a foreign realm with strangers. All the thoughts about his beauty and how his lips would feel, are quickly replaced by an emotion I am more familiar with, fury. I tear my eyes from the sleeping High Lord, only to find his belt, with his sword and dagger resting on the floor beside the bedside table.

Without a second thought, I wrap my hand around the pommel of the dagger; its metal is cold against my heated palm as I unsheathe the small blade. Carefully, I climb onto the bed, straddling him in his sleep. His frame is larger than I expected under me, and his body is warm against my bare skin beneath the thin silk robe. Slowly, I bring the cool steel to his throat, pressing it against his flesh. *This is all his fault, and he is the one keeping me here, the one refusing to let me leave.* My hand trembles as I hold the blade to his throat, trying to find the courage to do something I've done hundreds of times, but for some reason, can't.

"I always knew you'd end up on top of me, little dove," he whispers, his voice hushed and raspy. "Well, go on then. I am not afraid of you nor death."

"Is that so? Then why is your heart beating so rapidly?" I ask confidently. Men always claim they're not afraid of me, but when I look into their eyes, it's always only fear that's looking back at me. But not Xerxes. When his whiskey eyes opened and locked with mine, they were filled with a dark and lustful hunger.

"Well, it has been some time since I had a beautiful woman in my bed. Can't blame me for being excited, Kasia. After all, I may be a High Lord, but I am still a man."

"From what I hear, you've never had a woman in your bed; perhaps you prefer the company of men."

"Ah, so you've inquired about me, have you? Well, in that case, I'd love to show you just how thankful I am that you are the first and convince you that while I hold no grudges on those who prefer men, I am not one of them." With his words, I feel him harden beneath me, and I remember that I'm completely naked under the silk robe. I drop the dagger on the bed and climb off him in a panic.

"You're disgusting! Repulsive!"

"Now, that is a shame; what fun we could've had together," he says cockily. "Truthfully, I suppose I missed the comforts of my own bed more than I originally thought. I didn't mean to doze off." He admits as he runs his hand through his hair.

"Then why didn't you just have me placed in another room? You could've had yours." I ask with confusion. No one has ever done anything nice for me. Not for free, anyway.

"This room is the most secure and the easiest to guard."

"Oh. Meaning the strongest cage to keep me—"

"No, Kasia. I mean, you are safest when you are here. I wouldn't have been able to sleep if I knew you were staying in any of the other rooms. So now," he adds, gesturing around the room with his arms, "this is *your* room."

"And what will your people think about you having a commoner from another realm staying in your room?"

He laughs, and a genuine smile forms on his handsome face. "My people will not care. They wish for the same thing as me: to keep you safe. Your social standing does not matter in Calanthe, nor does anyone else's. If you're important to me, you are important to them."

I allow myself a moment to awe over his words. It's odd to hear a High Lord speak of his people so kindly. Draven has always treated the people of Lethe like dirt on his boot, but Xerxes seems to genuinely care for them as a whole.

"Right, okay. Well, thank you then." I reply softly.

"What was that?" he jokes, cupping his hand around his pointed Fae ear. "Did the mighty Kasia just thank me?"

I shake my head in disbelief. *Is he ever serious*? "Don't let it go to your head."

"Oh, little dove, no, no," he adds, placing a hand over his heart. "I'm taking that one right to my stone-cold heart."

Catching myself smiling, I turn my eyes away, fidgeting with the silk sheets. "Truly, I don't mind staying in another room so you can have yours back. I'm fully capable of protecting myself should something happen."

His smile grows, "I have no doubt you are, but I would feel better knowing you are here. Besides, I don't imagine it will be that long before you and I are in my bed again, though the next time I'm sure you will view me as less repulsive," he replies with a smirk as he rises from the bed. He grabs his belt from the floor, strapping it firmly around his waist before retrieving the discarded dagger from the sheet and sheathing it. His eyes scour my body; the tight silk robe leaves nothing to the imagination, and I watch as he bites down on one of his luscious lips.

I climb into the bed, quickly wanting to shield my body from his eyes. "That will never happen," I growl. My blood boils beneath my skin, a fury like no other, as he laughs. Turning away from me he heads toward the door. Without thinking, I grab one of the small decorative pillows. Swinging my arm back I whip it at him, but just as it's about to hit him in the back of his head, two large black feathered wings sprout from his back. My jaw drops, as the pillow hits them and drops to the marble floor. Xerxes freezes and turns towards me with a playful grin on his face. He bends to pick the pillow up from the floor and he lightly tosses it back at me with a chuckle.

"Well, I guess we will have to see about that, won't we? Get some rest, little dove. We leave in the morning," he adds with a humorous tone as he heads out of the room. I grab the pillow tightly in my fists. Bringing it to my face, I scream into the pillow, releasing all the emotions I've been holding in. I scream until my lungs burn and my throat aches, using the pillow to muffle the sound, and when I'm finally done. I calmly place the pillow down at the head of the bed, lay myself down, and close my eyes. Forcing whatever thoughts I had into the back of my mind and welcoming sleep if it means the end of this night.

Chapter Nine

XERXES

The cool night air whips around me as I stride through the large arched passages of Eventide palace toward my temporary room, and I rub my hand along my chin. The moonlight shines through the arches, casting intricate floral shadows across the stone floor. I've been unable to contain the smile that's been etched into my face since I left her. *Kasia*. The fierce look of anger she gave me when I summoned my wings and blocked the pillow she threw at me will forever be a memory I think back on. Especially because, though her behavior was that of a rabid animal, her thoughts were filled with shock and confusion.

Her body felt so good on me, *so right*. The way she pressed the dagger to my throat as though she or the tiny blade were a threat to me had my blood pumping. In those few moments, through her internal battle of hatred and lust, I couldn't help but see her as the most beautiful thing to ever walk the realms. Regardless of how she feels for me, I know her side of the bond is slowly returning with her magic. I can feel it. Behind her self-made armor is the girl from my childhood; she is hiding, and nothing excites me more than putting a dent in that armor to watch her come out and play.

With the arrangements made for our journey tomorrow, I'm eager to get some rest. I know this journey will be a rough one, especially with a Fae of her power and so uncontrolled. Agatha informed me of the episode in her chambers, and how it startled Kasia. This is only the beginning of what is to come. When I reach my new room, I quickly enter, closing and locking the door behind me.

"Tell me you weren't harassing that poor girl again, *Brother*."

"Harassing is a strong word, *Little Sister*."

"Ah, well then, what would you call it?" Senna retorts with a debating tone.

Offering her my brightest smirk, I reply. "I was merely offering my services."

"Well, that's disgusting and not what I needed nor wanted to hear," she explains with a look of distaste.

"Not what I meant. Niko needed me to bring her some salve for her wounds." I chuckle as I reach the table Senna sits at. I can't help but see the resemblance to our mother, especially the way her long auburn curls hang loosely around her petite face as she sits with her legs crossed and her nose shoved in a book. She loves reading, something she and our mother used to do together before she and my father left court to live a quieter life on the other side of the Somnia Forest. Leaving me responsible for our people.

Senna is every bit the spitting image of our mother, right down to the gown she wore today. With its thigh-high slits for easier movement in a fight. Not that it would matter. When my darling sister isn't reading, she's training. Archery being her sport of choice and she is deadly with a bow and arrow. Any foe wouldn't stand a chance of getting close enough to her for those slits to even be put to use.

Grabbing the large crystal decanter, I fill a small glass with the amber liquid and toss it down my throat before placing it back on the table. I shrug my shoulders, "Though I did offer that as well."

"Seriously, Xerxes. You cannot push her."

"I'm not pushing her. I'm just having a bit of fun."

Lifting her eyes from her book, she glares at me. "To you maybe, but have you ever stopped to think about what your advances could mean to her? Especially after what you told me those disgusting guards did to her."

"Oh, trust me, she doesn't mind my advances as much as you think she does."

"Gods! Stay out of her head! You're only going to push her away more." She adds as she rises from the table. "I know what she means to you. We all do, and we all know how hard it is for you to be so close yet so far away, trust me." Her tone leaks of compassion as she places a hand on my shoulder. "She will get there, just be patient with her, please." I know Senna means well, and I know in many ways she truly does understand how hard it is for me to be so close to Kasia, yet so far away from truly having her.

"I don't intend to push her Senna, that I promise," and I mean it. I don't want to push her away, but part of me likes this little game we have between us, especially when I know that she doesn't truly feel the way she claims she does. Part of me wants to see how long she fights it, and how long it will take for her to give in to her side of the bond.

"Good, because if tonight's little windy episode was a sign of anything, it's that the smallest thing can set her off right now and that girl has no idea how to control the power flowing through her veins."

"Agatha told you as well, then I see," I add, cocking a brow. Looking down on me her expression changes to one of surprise.

"Of course, she did. She knew you'd need someone to help you figure this all out. Lord knows you can't rely on Orion to help you," she adds as she rolls her eyes.

"Why do you pretend to hate him when—"

"I swear to the Gods, if you finish that sentence, I will cut out your tongue and feed it to Kasia on a silver platter," she snaps, "and for the last time, stay out of my head. You have no right to read my thoughts!" I smirk, knowing full well she has a thing for my best friend. She's been sweet for Orion since she could walk, always following him around everywhere she could, but she's never mentioned it to him, or anyone else. In Fact, she usually goes out of her way to make it seem as though she hates him.

"Is everything ready for tomorrow then?"

"Of course, the stable hands will have the horses geared and ready to go, the kitchen staff have packed enough food for a few days, and the men are preparing everything else. Orion will wake Kasia in the morning as you asked, though I don't know why you wouldn't wake her yourself."

"I have meetings to attend to before we leave. Niko will stay behind to make sure things run smoothly with setting up the camp at the veil, and he'll guide Nefeli's men out when they arrive."

"Yes, I must admit. This plan for a camp at the veil is one I didn't expect you to make. Usually, you rush into battle without a second thought."

"Usually, yes, but this time I have more to lose. This time, things need to be done right. We have the best chance of defending if we know the moment he comes through the veil."

"Do you truly think he will come?" she asks with a hushed tone.

My hands grip the sides of my chair so tightly my knuckles turn white. "Draven will come."

"You know that isn't who I meant," she adds, her tone doing little to hide her concern. "Will *Drake* come?" Her fear both hurts me, but also angers me. It's barely been a year since the meeting of the High Lords. A yearly celebration and feast where we meet to discuss trade routes and goods between realms over a meal. Last year, however, Drake found Senna indisposed. She'd had more than her fair share of wine and instead of seeing her to her chambers, he took advantage of her. With potent amounts of alcohol pumping through her veins leaving her unable to stop him or defend herself, there was nothing she could do. He raped her, using her how he pleased, and left her to be found by the maids the next day.

"I wish I could say for certain," I explain, turning my eyes to hers. "I do not know what their plan will be, but I do know *he* will not touch you. *They* will not touch you or Kasia, not while I am standing. Never again."

"I— I know that. I just don't think I could stand to look at him againafter— after—"

Quickly, I rush to her side to comfort her. "Shh, it's okay. I understand your concern, and you're right to have it. I will always hate myself for not being able to protect you that night, for not stopping it."

"You can't blame yourself, Xerxes. It was no one's doing but his. I do not blame you."

"He will pay for it. I promise you that." She silently nods her head at my words, as she makes her way over to the window. She fiddles with the silver locket around her neck, a family heirloom passed on to her before my mother left. Passed on through the Aramis woman, it's of great sentimental value to our family and Senna never takes it off. Lifting the locket to her lips, I watch as she softly presses a kiss to its front before clearing her throat.

"I still have nightmares sometimes. When I wake, it's like it's happening over again. I can still feel the weight of his body over mine, his warm breath on my skin," she adds as a shiver rakes through her body. Hearing how it still haunts her has my blood boiling under my skin and my blade aching to pierce Drake's flesh, shedding his skin from his body as he screams and begs me to stop.

At first, I don't say anything in return. Unable to find any words to console her, that she hasn't already heard from me. I make my way over to the fire and crouch down, placing a new log on the fading embers as she continues to stare blankly out the large window over-looking the forest around the palace. With the flames catching, and the fire once again beginning to roar, I return to her side, staring out at the beauty of our realm in silence.

The night sky is clear tonight, and full of glittering stars that seem to dance around the moon's glow. Its energy seeps into my skin in tingling waves, refilling my well of power as we stand in this light. I have always relished in the moon's healing touch.

"Do you think taking her to Viserra will actually help?" She whispers, breaking the tension and silence.

"Truthfully, I have no idea, but I am hoping Viserra is able to do something for her."

"I don't understand, why does it matter if she remembers or not? She is still the last Satori, whether she remembers herself to be or if she doesn't."

I sigh at the ignorance of my sister's comment. Though I know that's not how she meant it to come off. "It matters because she's been through enough. She doesn't trust me, Senna. She doesn't trust anyone, and I can't blame her for that. Not after what she's been through. The easiest way to gain her trust is for her to have at least *some* of her memories."

"Xerxes." She exhales as though she's annoyed with my persistence. "Even if her memories return, her only memories of you will be as children, and from what I heard from Mother, you and Orion were nothing but little shits when it came to Kasia."

"I don't care what her memories are of me. I want her to remember them. Don't you see, Sister? If she remembers her mother and her father, then she'll remember how loved she was, she'll remember all the warnings her mother gave her, and everything that led up to her memories being taken."

"Yes, but have you considered that maybe her losing her memories has made the loss of her family easier to bear? What happens when she *does* remember them?" she adds as she turns to face me. "What happens when the most powerful Fae in Calanthe remembers her family and how brutally they were taken from her and is unable to control her emotions, or her power?"

"I will make sure she can control her power."

"How? You have no idea how to train someone with her magnitude of power, and you constantly poking at her is not going to help. You need to help her keep her emotions to a minimum, at least until she learns to control her power."

"Don't you think I know that? I'm trying!" I snap, finding myself frustrated with her attack. "I know I need to stop messing around, I know I have no idea what I'm doing when it comes to training her, but I will do it. I'll do whatever it takes."

"No, Brother, we will. Together, we will do whatever it takes," she adds as her expression changes to a soft smile. "I'll be coming with you to Viserra, so I should get some sleep. Promise you'll leave her alone for the night?"

"You have my word. I won't bother her for the rest of the evening. Besides, I should turn in, too. I imagine if we're to ride across the realm we're going to need our sleep."

"You, maybe, but I don't plan on sleeping. I'm way too excited to watch Kasia put you in your place for the next few days," she says with a smile, as she makes her way to the door. "Goodnight, Brother. Sleep well." With that she's gone.

With my sister gone, I strip out of my clothing, and make my way to the large bed. The sheets are cold on my heated skin as I climb in, but I welcome it. The conversation and memories of Drake has my blood pumping, and the coolness aids in simmering it down. There's nothing I can do about it... Yet. Part of me is hoping he'll come through that portal looking for Kasia, but the other part is praying he doesn't. While I'm willing to go to war to protect her, to protect Calanthe, I'd rather not have to if we could avoid it. Draven will want her dead, and I doubt he'll come himself. He'll send Drake through first, and that's when I will claim my revenge for what he did to Senna. That's when he will learn to wish he was dead, and I will show him what a gracious High Lord I can be, by granting his wish on the tip of my blade.

Brutal and cold. The same way his father killed the Satori family. Draven will get a taste of his own cruel punishment, and I can't wait to dish it out to him. I stretch my arms above my head, tucking my hands under my head as thoughts of Kasia fill my head. It's been nearly impossible to keep myself from thinking about her. When I'm with her, I want to be closer to her, touching her, and when I'm not with her, I need to be with her. It's maddening.

This trip to the oracle will be hard, but I know it needs to happen. If there is anyone who can help her remember, it's Viserra. I just hope that she's willing to help. As the last living oracle of the Seer Tribe, without her wisdom and sight on the matter, I fear we will never know how her memories were removed from her.

Chapter Ten

KASIA

When I wake the next morning, I'm parched. My throat is scratchy and raw as I sit myself up and reach for the glass of water on the bedside table. As I'm swallowing down the cool liquid, my eyes scan part of Xerxes's room, taking in his decorative choices. I find myself a bit taken back at how homely his room feels for a High Lord. Placing the cup down, I let myself fall back to the comfort of the silk pillows, which seem more attuned to a man of his rank.

"Well, good morning, Birdie."

I jump, the voice catching me off guard. I turn my head to the side, finding Orion sprawled out across the bed next to me. He's lying on his side, with his arm supporting his head, fully clothed in his black fighting leathers and boots, with a big ass grin on his face.

"Bloody hell, Orion! Why are you in my bed? Do you people wake all your guests this way?"

He chuckles, "Not all, just the special ones, I promise." he replies with a coy smile. "Anyways, I was sent to see to it that you were awake and prepared to leave, but considering I have found you still soundly asleep, I'll assume you're not ready to go."

"Let me guess. Xerxes sent you?"

"Ay, indeed he did," he nods.

"Did he also tell you to climb in bed next to me? I highly doubt he'll be thrilled to find out about that tiny detail."

"That he did not," he whispers, bringing himself closer to me. "This was just for me." His tone is soft and laced with seduction. But I'm not buying it.

I laugh, cocking my head in derision. "I think what you mean to say is that your plan was to piss him off, and you know being close to me is going to do just that."

"Exactly! I'm so glad we agree this is going to be hilarious," he replies with a large smirk before falling back into the pillows. "You do have to get up though, that part was true. We should be leaving very soon; the first camp is already going to take us nearly all day to ride to."

I take in his words, letting the thoughts of everything I have learned the last few days soak into my head, and for a minute I forget he's even in the room.

"Kasia. Did you hear me?"

"What? Oh, yes. I'll be ready soon," I mumble.

"You seem distracted. Are you alright? Should I fetch—"

"No, I'm fine. Really." I quickly replied. Not wanting to worry anyone. "It's just been a lot the last few days." His eyes meet mine with the confession, and his expression softens.

"That I can understand, and I know Xerxes can be... Well... a lot, but you can trust him, Kasia."

"That is easy for you to say. I have known him, what... three days? While it's clear to anyone around you two with the way you bicker, you've known each other for so long you're practically family." I pause. "Wait, are you family?" I ask, lifting a brow in his direction. My question causes him to chuckle.

"No, we're not. In blood anyway, but you are right. I have known him almost my entire life, and you know what? I knew you once before, too. When we were very small." His words hit me like a shock wave. Orion too? How is it possible I have none of these memories they seem to share? "And since the day we heard of your family's murder, he hasn't stopped looking for you, Kasia. The entire time I have known him, he has been holding on to *you*. Even if you don't feel the bond, he has felt it for the last twenty years. To him, it's like you have always been here, with him, even if he couldn't see or touch you.

I know it's all a lot to take in, just... give him a chance, ay? You might find yourself surprised."

I have no doubt there is much to Xerxes that I don't know; if anything, his little wing show last night proved that all too well. The problem is I don't care to get to know him. I don't feel the way he does. To me, he is a stranger, and I can count on one hand the amount of times letting a stranger in has been good for me. He can claim he wants to help me, wants to protect me, yet here I sit in a realm I don't belong in, with strangers I do not know, dictating where I can and can't go.

"If Xerxes is the type to keep those he claims to care for prisoner, then I don't want to get to know him. I don't care about what *he* feels. What about me? You all claim I'm this lost heir that I'm royalty, and yet you treat me like a child. You all seem to forget. While you may all remember me, I don't remember any of you or this place. I don't have these memories you all share. In my eyes, a bunch of strangers have brought me to a different realm against my will, and you all refuse to let me leave!" I snap, tossing the thick blankets from my legs before swinging them over the side of the bed. I exhale deeply. It feels like no one is listening to me. Like my feelings about being here don't matter.

"I do understand why you feel this way, Birdie. Listen, let's just get out to see Viserra. If anyone can help you restore any of the memories taken from you, it is her. You could feel differently after you remember."

"Fine," I reply with a sharp tone. I just want this all to be over so I can return home. For the first time I miss the cold wind on my skin, the pain in my fingers and toes from the snow. "I'll be down when I'm ready."

"Perfect. I'll wait so I can escort you down."

"Like hell you will."

"Well, how else am I to be sure you won't get lost on your way? You haven't been here long enough to know your way around the halls."

"I haven't even been allowed to leave my room, you mean? So how could I possibly find my way down to the stables?"

"Ah, well yes that too."

"Orion, you will leave me to get ready on my own, in private, or I will tell Xerxes I was forced to show you my entire naked body, and I highly doubt—"

"Say no more, I'm leaving. I'll have the men outside your door escort you," he explains, raising his hands in defeat.

"Right, thanks." I sigh with annoyance as he quickly jumps up off the bed and heads out of the room. Once he's gone, I rise from the comfort of the mattress and head toward the bathing chambers, stopping to pour myself a cup of tea from the kettle Agatha must've brought in earlier. Bringing it to my lips, I'm welcomed by the sweet scent of Thalla Mint and citrus, which instantly brings me back home to Lethe. One of the only things we could get to grow in the frigid temperatures was Thalla Mint and making it into tea was one of the easiest ways to keep ourselves warm.

Entering the large bathing chambers, I observe the reposeful room, admiring the patterns that adorn the tall cathedral glass windows. Stepping down slowly into the natural hot spring bath, I find myself comfortably resting my head back on the ledge, with a satisfied smirk on my face. If I'm expected to travel for the next few days, a bath before I leave is a must, besides, I said I'd meet them down at the stables, but I didn't say when.

A LOUD KNOCK on the door pulls my attention from my reflection in the mirror.

"Who is it—"

But before I can even ask, Xerxes is barreling in the room with Erebus behind him. He's dressed in his usual leathers. Half of his thick hair is pulled up in a knot on the top of his head, while the rest hangs down freely. Every time I see him, I find myself in awe with his beauty, and today is no different. Even with a look of annoyance etched into his face, heat builds within me.

I can't explain why but pissing him off excites me. I'm thoroughly enjoying this game between us. Even though I blame him for so much, there's a part of me that finds it amusing and almost exciting to test him, though I'll

THE BLOOD OF DOVES

never admit it. Erebus reaches my side and rubs his head against my legs as his thick black tail wags excitedly behind him. I give him a few pats on his head, ensuring he knows I'm just as happy to see him before he lays down at my feet. Turning my attention back to my reflection, I mess with my hair, trying to control the ice white strands while I wait silently for his reply, but it doesn't come.

Confused, I spin around in the chair, and find him standing behind me with darkened eyes as he takes me in, inch by inch. He devours me with his eyes, like a predator watching their prey, but instead of fear, a familiar heat begins to build in my core.

"What is it?" I choke out.

"You look... That dress is..."

I smirk, "My, my. The Great High Lord Xerxes, rendered speechless by a common whore in a pretty dress." Within seconds he's bent over at my side, gripping my chin as he tilts my head up and forces my eyes to his.

"If you ever, refer to yourself as a 'common whore' again, I will fuck those words right out of that pretty little mouth. I'm tired of hearing them. You are neither of those things, little dove," he growls. His eyes trail down my body, as he pulls his bottom lip into his mouth with his fangs.

"You wouldn't dare," I mutter, doing my best to hide the desire burning within me to have him do just that. *I need to feel his fangs against my skin, between my thighs. I want to taste him on my lips.* I swallow the lump in my throat and find myself clenching my thighs closed.

"Is that so? Why don't you utter one of those words again then, go on. I dare you," he adds as he lowers his lips to ghost over mine. His rainstorm scent fills my nostrils and I find my eyes fluttering shut on instinct, until his chuckle meets my ears, and he releases my chin from his grasp. "You forget, not only can I scent your arousal but I can also read your thoughts. I know you want me Kasia, no matter how much you pretend not to. Now let's go. Everyone else is waiting on us," he explains, his expression unmoving as he stands back up and heads for the door.

Feeling a mix of rage and embarrassment, I clench my thighs tighter. *He can smell me? What does that even mean?*

"It's your arousal I smell, little dove, and it smells fucking divine so don't try and hide it from me," he says coldly, turning his attention back on me. Sensing my confusion, he sighs and returns to my side. "Kasia, I know this is all new to you, and I understand that it has to be hard, but I promise it's natural. It comes with the bond. Your body craves mine just as much as mine craves yours. It would be less complicated if you stopped fighting it and let things flow as they're meant to," he explains, trailing his fingers down my arm. He softly takes my hand in his as he kneels before me.

I sit there mesmerized by this stunning man, as he lifts my hand to his perfectly full lips, placing soft kisses along my wrist. "I know I'd rather be indulging in every inch of your body. Touching every freckle, kissing every scar, until you smelt of no one, or nothing but me," he whispers. My heart races in my chest as the need between my thighs grows. He's not wrong. I do want him. Every fiber of my being is pulling me to him and why I fight it, I don't know. He affects me like no man ever has, and while he makes me feel things I've only ever dreamt about, I can't seem to bring myself to act on how I feel.

Just when I can feel myself beginning to give in, he retreats to where he was standing. Erebus lifts his head and lets out a small whine as he tilts his head to the side.

"I'll wait for you in the hall. Please do try and hurry up, little dove. As it is, we will be lucky to make it to the first camp before dark."

"Right," I stutter, finding it hard to speak. I watch as he lets himself out of the room, leaving Erebus with me. I rise from the chair and pat down the long, red, flowing gown I chose from the wardrobe for the journey. Since Glinda has yet to measure me for my custom clothing, I'm stuck wearing the gowns she sent up; though they're not my usual style and limit my movement, I have to admit, they're beautiful. This one is by far my favorite, with its deep red silk and tiny gems sewn on around the sleeves and bodice which cuts low down my chest.

I furrow my brows with confusion at the mix of feelings I find myself plagued with. It's like an internal war between the anger and hatred I feel towards him for holding me here against my will and the pull to have him as close as possible. Whether it's the bond he claims to feel or not, the more days I spend here, the more I see him, and the closer that side gets to conquering.

I make my way toward the bed, where the bag I packed for the trip sits on the freshly made sheets. Erebus follows close behind me; no doubt Xerxes ordered him not to leave my side. Not that I'm complaining, I've grown quite attached to him in my days here. The large wolf nudges me with his nose seeking affection, and I run my fingers through his thick black fur.

"Your master sure is one confusing pain in the ass," I mutter.

"Fae ears, Kasia. I can hear you," he shouts from the hall where he waits.

I roll my eyes, I turn to the door and poke my tongue out like he can see me, while Erebus nudges me again, softer this time as though he understands my frustrations. I take one last look around the room to ensure I haven't forgotten anything. Satisfied, I grab the bag and make my way to the hall as Erebus follows. As I reach the door, Xerxes opens it from the outside, using his arm to guide me out before he closes it behind me.

"This way then," he explains as he heads off down one of the long corridors. I follow, eager to get this awkward trip over with.

FINALLY FREE OF the thick stone walls of the palace, the night's air kisses my skin. I lift my eyes to the sky and find it to be the most beautiful night sky I've ever seen. Millions of sparkling stars glitter across the inky black sky, and the moon's glow casts down its radiant glow over the palace. The air smells damp and earthy, like melted snow as I inhale deeply, filling my lungs with the freshness of it. *I've missed being outside.*

When we reach the stables, I'm surprised to find Senna along with Orion and a few other men. Senna is tending to what must be the largest black mare I've ever seen. A floor-length evergreen gown with a delicate floral pattern cascades down her tall, thin frame, the perfect contrast to her deep auburn hair, which is hanging loosely down her back today.

"Raven," Xerxes explains as he reaches my side. "She is Orion's pride and joy. He rescued her as a colt. Her mother had been killed by wolves in the forest, and when Orion came across what was left, he found little Raven stranded by her mother's corpse. They've been insepa-rable since."

"Ay that we have. No girl will ever measure up to this one in my cold heart," Orion chimes with a smirk as he approaches Senna and Raven. I watch as the two interact; Senna's eyes light up with excitement as Orion helps her finish strapping the large leather saddle to Raven's back. She tries to hide it, but when they lock eyes, even for a brief moment, it's impossible to miss. I've seen that look before, and I know all too well what it means. *They're definitely fucking.*

"Hop on, little dove."

The use of my nickname pulls my attention, and I turn my head in the direction of Xerxes's voice, finding him seated on a large light grey horse with his hand outstretched to help me up.

"Like hell, I am riding with you!" I snap.

"Sorry, little dove. Only so many horses are available right now with the men needing them to set up the camp at the veil."

"Well, then I'd rather ride on Raven, with Orion," I spit, crossing my arms over my chest. Xerxes's low growl is clear as day, as he averts his eyes to his best friend. They exchange a look and Orion's lips pull into a smirk. The gesture has me giddy inside.

"Ay, Birdie." Orion starts out doing his best to contain his amusement. "While I'm flattered, riding with me would be, well, inappropriate. Especially with the whole court knowing of the whole bonded thingy you have going on with our dear High Lord."

"Oh? Well, was it not inappropriate for you to be in my bed this morning when I woke, then? I imagine that is much worse than sharing a damn horse!" I retort with a smile, knowing full well I'm stirring the pot. If I thought Xerxes growl was loud before, it was nothing compared to the sound he made with the mention of Orion in my bed. Orion's smirk quickly disappears as he raises his palm in defense.

"Mate, calm down. She's overplaying it to be something it wasn't, I assure you," Orion tries to explain before mounting Raven. I lock eyes with Senna briefly, catching the change in her expression. Hurt flashes in her eyes, and in the pit of my stomach, I instantly regret my insistent need to cause problems for my own amusement.

"Enough!" Xerxes shouts. His eyes fixate on Orion. "We will discuss this later, *mate*," he mocks. "Kasia, get the fuck on this horse."

"No," I reply, glaring at him.

He chuckles, deep and menacingly. "I am done asking nicely. Either get that perfect little ass on this fucking horse, or I will tie you, gag you and strap you to the back. I assure you, riding with me will be much more comfortable."

I stand in silence for a moment, pretending I'm actually weighing my options. When truthfully, I know I don't have any other choice but to ride with him. I've ridden tied up on the back of a horse once before, and I don't intend to ever again. My body was aching and bruised for weeks after. Accepting defeat, I huff, taking his hand and allowing him to help pull me on to the horse.

The beast is larger than any of the horses I've ridden before. However, we didn't have many in Lethe, and we had scarce food. Its long white mane flows down the side of its head in waves. Running my hand through them, I'm surprised by how silky it feels through my fingers until the moment when my eyes meet the ground below us, and I realize just how high up I really am. Suddenly, my stomach tightens with a flash of fear that I might fall off.

Xerxes wraps his arm around my middle, gently pulling me back snug into his chest, as he brings his mouth to my ear. His lips brush against my ears' pointed tip softly as he whispers soothingly.

"Don't worry. You've never been anywhere safer than where you are right now, little dove."

Goosebumps perk up along my skin, and my breath catches in my throat as he tightens his hold around my middle and directs the horse through the giant stone gate of the courtyard and out into the Somnia Forest, with Erebus and Senna's dire wolf, Kenji, on either side of us, and our company following behind us.

Chapter Eleven

KASIA

The Somnia Forest is unlike anything I've ever seen or even imagined would have existed. Sure, I'd heard tales of its beauty and the way it seemed to beckon you into its heart. But now that I'm here, I find myself wondering how anyone could resist exploring such a lush and beautiful place. Coils of thick vines climb the overgrown trees that seem to stretch up to the sky, and branches of velvet flowers in the most beautiful golden color drape down from the thick oak branches.

The air seems sweeter under the forest's canopy, and as we make our way further into it, I expect things to get darker without the moon's glow. However, I find instead that the forest has a glow of its own. Speckled along the trees like tiny decorations are thousands of glowing mushrooms, and the ground is littered with thick foliage with pops of different glowing plants and flowers.

"Breathtaking, isn't it?" Xerxes says softly behind me.

Awestruck, I whisper as my eyes scan across the mysterious and magical forest, "It's incredible. The most beautiful thing I've ever seen."

"Well, growing up where you did, I can't say I'm surprised," he chuckles. "Though I have to agree with you. I've seen every part of all three realms, and only one thing measures up to the beauty of this forest."

"Not every part," I add. "You've never seen the part of Lethe that I know. The place I call home."

Tightening his arm around my waist, it's clear the mention of Lethe has him on edge just from the way his body tensed. He doesn't like to discuss what I've been through or where I come from. It's as though my suffering hurts him as much as its memory hurts me.

"I've seen more of your *home* than you think, little dove," he explains with a click of his jaw. Before I can reply, Orion and Senna reach our side.

"We're going up ahead to make sure the camp is cleared out and to oversee the set-up," Orion says. Senna keeps her gaze away from me and stares off into the dense forest. Her cold shoulder hurts more than I expected, though only knowing her for a short time, she's the one I feel I can relate to the most. Having her ignore me isn't the best feeling, even though I understand why and know it's my own fault. Xerxes offers him a nod, and they take off ahead of us with two other riders behind them. The wolves move in closer to us for protection as the others ride up ahead.

"How much longer?" I sigh.

"Why? Is riding with me that terrible?" Xerxes counters.

Every part of me wants to tell him I was wrong, and how much I've truly enjoyed having him so close. The way his body's heat radiates into mine when he holds me close. I feel safe with his arms tightly wrapped around me. But I won't. I won't tell him any of the truth I feel.

"Much worse, actually, I've even considered willingly throwing myself off the horse's back just to be trampled to death rather than spend another moment on this damn horse with you," I say with a playful yet venomous tone.

"That would never happen," he chuckles. Glaring over my shoulder at him, I scoff. *How dare he doubt me.*

"Oh? You don't think I'd do it?"

"Oh no, I have no doubt you'd happily throw yourself off this horse if it meant keeping this little game we have going, but I'd never let you hit the ground, let alone get trampled by Oscar here."

"Oscar?" I ask with confusion.

"Yes, Oscar," he replies. "The horse's name is Oscar."

"Well, that's a stupid name for a horse." The horse huffs at my comment as though it understood me. Accepting defeat, I slouch back and let my back rest against his hard chest. This close, he's much larger than I thought. His broad shoulders and frame box me into this small space of safety in his lap, and I'm growing to like it. It's warm and smells like the night air after a rainstorm. *Like him.* "Fine. It's not terrible, but my legs are numb and I'm starving, so how much longer?" I ask, turning my head over my shoulder and lifting my eyes to his.

He smirks, his face beaming with victory as he pulls me in closer, and for once, I don't fight against him. Being in his arms on Oscar is a welcome break from the cool night air of the forest. It's comforting in ways I don't fully know how to understand after growing up in Lethe, but I know the more he touches me, the closer we get, the harder it gets to hate him and the more I wish he would touch me everywhere, forever.

"Not much further, little dove. You should rest." My eyes look out at the forest around us as I try to peer through the trees with curiosity. I find myself wondering what could be lurking just beyond the brush, watching us. Xerxes presses a gentle kiss to the top of my head, clearly sensing my concerns. "I promise you're safe. I have you." As though his words are a magic spell, my eyes flutter shut as I melt into the warmth his body gives off, and everything goes black. The strong arms of the man I thought to be my enemy have become my safest resting place.

THE BLOOD OF DOVES

THE FEELING of gentle fingers brushing stray hairs from my face tickles against my skin, pulling me from my dreamless sleep and causing me to stir. Snapping my eyes open, I find Xerxes looking down on me. His whiskey brown eyes hooded, and his expression soft.

"Wake up, we're here," he whispers. His tone is husky and deep, but he never takes his eyes off my face.

"Oh. Sorry, I didn't mean to doze off," I explain, quickly sitting myself upright on Oscar's back. I wipe the drool from my face, feeling embarrassed I slept for so long, but looking around, it's clear we're very deep into the forest. *I must've been asleep for hours.* As he helps me get down, something inside me feels different, like small vibrations pumping through my blood. Similar to the vibrations I felt that night with the wind.

"Don't apologize. It was nice, for me anyway."

"What do you mean by that?" I ask curiously as I lift my eyes to his. Knowing he can read my thoughts, I do my best to hide these new sensations coursing through my body.

It's probably nothing anyway.

"Nothing, Kasia. We're almost done setting up the camp. Can I trust you not to run off if I allow you to explore unattended while I help the men?"

"Hmm... Tell me what you meant, and I will promise to stay close by," I reply coyly.

He sighs, "I meant that having you be so close, knowing you were safe, with me. Spending the long ride with you in my arms while I filled my lungs with your sweet scent, and didn't have you fighting me for once, was nice. That's all." His confession strikes a tinge of guilt inside me, which is new. I never feel guilty, especially when it comes to men. But Xerxes's feelings towards me are genuine, that much I can tell even if I don't return those feelings.

Who am I kidding? Yes, I do.

"Oh, I-"

"No, you don't have to say anything. Just promise to stay close to the camp, please? The forest can be dangerous at times," he adds as he turns to head off toward where the setup is happening.

"I promise," I reply, and for once, I genuinely mean it. I may not like being stuck in Calanthe, but I'm no fool. I have no idea where I am or what monsters lurk in this glowing forest. He pauses, and quickly turns to bring himself to stand in front of me. Tucking a loose strand of my hair behind my pointed ear, a lump starts to form in my throat. I tilt my chin up, bringing my eyes to his, unsure of what he's thinking, but refusing to back down.

"Take Erebus and Kenji with you to be safe, please."

"Okay," I agree, giving him a smile. I kneel to greet the dire wolves as they reach my side. Erebus is quick to lick my face, while Kenji isn't as friendly with me yet and only allows me to pet him a few times on the top of his furry head before he backs off. His fur is thick like Erebus's, but where Erebus's fur is black as ink, Kenji's is a sable mix of grey and white.

Turning my eyes back on Xerxes, I find him smiling and his eyes sporting a faint sparkle before he clears his throat and heads off to where his men are setting up the tents. *Fuck, I'm getting soft for him.* If he truly can read my thoughts, he already knows how much he affects me, and having me fight it must be hard for him to endure. I don't even fully understand why I do it. Fear, I suppose. If I let him in, I'm just opening the door for him to hurt me, and I've had enough pain in my life. I don't need more.

I huff. "Who even am I? Since when do I care how other people feel?" I mutter to myself as I rise. I give one last look toward the men setting up the camp before turning to the forest, excited to finally have the chance to explore it. The deeper I venture into the thick glowing foliage, the more intense the vibrations under my skin get. It's an odd and new feeling, but I do my best to ignore it, assuming it's nothing. Just my body waking up from spending such a long journey on a horse.

Erebus stays close to me while Kenji wanders off a bit further but never allows me out of his sight. It's clear he's untrusting, and I can't say I blame him. I'm a stranger, and I'm in his home. I'd be cautious, too. Erebus, on the other hand, and I have been close since I woke to him at my feet on the day of my arrival, and I've been thankful for having his company during my days stuck in the palace.

As we reach a small clearing, my jaw drops at the sheer beauty around me. The trees are filled with glowing petals of thousands of flowers of all shapes, sizes, and colors. They give off the most fragrant scent I've ever smelt, like fresh lavender, but sweeter. Reaching the middle of the clearing, I turn my gaze up to the forest canopy and open my arms as I spin around in a circle, wallowing in the aurora the forest gives off as the vibrations within me grow.

Crunch.

Something crunching under my foot breaks my focus, and I stop. Lifting my foot, I find a tiny sapling I must've stepped on, squished under my boot. A feeling inside me that I can't explain snaps with its tiny stem, and the vibrations I've been feeling grow in intensity. Pausing, I crouch down beside it, inspecting its tiny glowing stem and the damage inflicted by my carelessness.

It's snapped in the middle, its stem now drooping as a sap-like glowing liquid drips down and seeps into the forest floor. Reaching out, I touch the tip of my fingers to the delicate leaves of the tiny sapling, but with the contact, the glowing light grows, and with it, the vibrations coursing through my body. A force of some kind stops me from pulling my hand away as the glow becomes so strong I'm forced to turn my face away from the blinding light. Erebus whines behind me with confusion; his ears perk up as though there's danger as he paces from side to side, unsure of what to do.

The vibrations grow so intense they're almost painful, my fingertips burning in the bright glow. Panic begins to set in, and my heart races in my chest. It takes everything in me not to cry out for help, for *him*. But just as I begin to find it unbearable, just when I'm ready to call for help, the bright light slowly dims, and with it the vibrations fade, allowing me to finally catch my breath. I quickly pull my fingers away from the sapling and hold them close against my chest tenderly as a hiss slips from my lips.

"Well, I guess it's safe to say your powers are finally returning," Xerxes says as he approaches. "Are you alright? How do you feel?" he asks as he crouches down beside me.

"Yes—I mean—I think so," I mutter. Sensing my discomfort, he takes my hands in his, and rubs them softly.

"You will get used to it, in time."

"Are you sure? It didn't hurt this much last time."

"Last time?" he asks, cocking his brow. Realizing my error, I know there's no way of avoiding the topic now. I can't hide what happened that night from him anymore.

"There was an incident in my room. The wind—" my voice catches in my throat as he brings my fingertips to his lips, pressing soft kisses along them, but it's when he takes them in his mouth, and his fang skims across the sensitive flesh that I come apart internally.

He smirks, "Go on..."

Clearing my throat, "I- I don't know how to explain it, but the wind, it's like it fed off my emotions."

"That's because it did," he replies. "Lethian magic is linked to emotions. The stronger your emotions, the stronger the magic. I'm guessing this little wind incident happened after one of your little hissy fits," he adds, brushing his thumb across my bottom lip. Something deep inside me is pulling me to him. No matter how small his touch may be, it always sends tingles through me that my body and mind crave. "You'll learn to control it. I will help you, Kasia."

"Okay," I whisper, finding myself in such awe that forming more words proves impossible.

"Just okay?" he asks, cocking a brow.

"Yes. Just okay," I explain as Kenji returns from his little wander and lays down next to Erebus. Still holding my hands tightly in his, Xerxes helps me to my feet before leading me out of the clearing and back towards the camp.

"Little dove, I need you to understand something for me. This, what happened both here and back at Eventide, with your powers... You can't tell anyone."

"But Agatha-"

"Agatha and Ingrid won't mutter a word of it, they are loyal to me. So are Senna and Orion, but no one else must know. It isn't safe, not yet."

"Why isn't it safe?"

"Because Draven is looking for you, and if word of your magic, of what it can do, gets out, he will know exactly where to find you."

"Do you really think Draven will come for me?"

He raises his brow at me, "Does this mean you finally believe you are who I say you are? Do you truly believe yourself to be the last Satori heir?"

"I don't know what I believe. I don't remember any of the things you or Orion tell me." With the mention of his best friend's name, he tenses, and a low growl slips through his lips. I suddenly find myself feeling like I need to set his mind at ease.

"Nothing happened. This morning, I mean. Between Orion and I."

He chuckles, "I know that."

"Then why do you act like you're so bothered by the mere mention of his name?" I ask with a confused tone.

"Because I know what game he is playing, and if ever there was a woman he should not play with, it's you."

"Truthfully, I don't think he even has any interest in me. I think it's Senna who has his true interest."

"I know he has no interest in you, that isn't why his little game bothers me. It's because when it comes to you, I can't control myself, which Orion well knows. This playful game has always been a thing between us. But when it comes to you, the bond is so strong that if it views him as a threat to what I'm meant to have with you, I don't know that I can stop it. Orion thinks it's funny to get me going, but you're correct in your assumptions of him and my sister. They've been seeing each other for months; they just haven't told me yet."

I stop and choke out a cough. "So, you know they're seeing each other? How? Wait, don't answer that. I already know the answer. This mind-reading power of yours sure does come in handy, for you."

He chuckles at my comment. "I suppose you could say that. It's difficult to keep things from me when I can enter your head."

"So why haven't you said anything to them then?" I ask as we continue walking through the forest.

"Because it's amusing to watch them. They think they're doing a great job keeping their little secret, but I knew before they even did how each of them felt about each other."

"That's both cruel and hilarious."

"I'll tell them one day. Right now, I like watching them squirm when they think I suspect something."

"And are you okay with there being something between them? After all Orion is your best friend, and Senna your little sister."

"I think there is no man I'd trust more with my sister's heart. He may come off as a joker, and he loves to play his games, but he has a good heart. He's a good man, and he'd die to protect her."

"Well then, I suppose he also isn't as horrible as I first thought."

"Ah, does this mean you don't hate me anymore? You've given up your plans to kill me while I sleep?" Xerxes whispers, with a coy smile.

"Hate is a strong word. I think it's safe to say I don't hate you, but I strongly dislike you, so I wouldn't say I've given up just yet."

"Lies, little dove. So many cruel and vicious lies that beautiful mouth of yours likes to tell." Standing before him, I lift myself to my tiptoes, keeping my eyes fixated on his as I ghost my lips over his. I softly bite down on his bottom lip and pull it into my mouth with my fangs. "Lies or not, it's all you'll ever get from these lips," I whisper, before I turn to leave him.

His strong hand grabs the back of my neck, pulling me back to him as his large onyx wings sprout from his back and wrap around us, shielding us from prying eyes. I only have time to draw a quick breath before his hand is fisted in my hair and his lips crash onto mine.

The kiss is heated and full of hunger. I deepen it eagerly, wrapping my hands around his neck and pulling him into me. At this moment everything is forgotten, all the hate, Lethe, nothing else matters except this need to have more of him, more of his luscious lips against mine. I need it more than I need air, and just as a small whimper slips from my chest, he breaks the kiss.

Resting his forehead on mine, we share panted breaths as I try to make sense of what just happened. My heart races in my chest, and my body pulses with so many new and confusing feelings.

"*Fuck*," he whispers against my mouth, as he cups my face in his hands. "I will give you my realm in its entirety, the stars, and the moon along with it. Anything you ask, it's yours. I am yours, little dove."

My lips form a small smile, "All that from just a kiss? Well, High Lord. Who would've guessed it would be that easy." I reply playfully. He lifts his head from mine with a handsome smirk on his face, and our eyes lock briefly before I turn to leave him, lifting his wing with my arm so I can duck underneath it before I head off toward the camp with a huge smile and Erebus close on my trail.

This High Lord and our bond is going to be the death of me.

When I reach the camp I see several pointed structures, and as I look around, I can see that all of Xerxes men have finished setting up their shelters for the night. Someone has even set up one for Xerxes, and there is no doubt in my mind that I will be sleeping in there too, although it doesn't seem to bother me as much as I expected.

A group of men are sitting around a small campfire talking to each other, while some others are sitting down by their shelters with a meal. As I walk through the camp, I get engulfed by a smell so good that even my soul cries out for whatever food is available: *spices, meat, and a hint of... honey, maybe.* I turn and head in the direction of the decadent smell until I come across a kitchen where I can see Senna and Orion hard at work.

I find Senna handing out bowls of steaming broth to a lineup of guards, while Orion tears off a piece of bread to hand them. My stomach growls at the thought of a hot meal, so I quickly get in line. When I'm next in line, Orion offers me a nod of his head, while Senna barely makes eye contact as she hands me my bowl of broth and a chunk of bread. Before I can even apologize, she's shooing me away and filling a bowl for the man behind me. It stings, but I understand her coldness. *I'll talk to her in the morning, I'll explain.* I tell myself. With my bowl of meat and broth in hand, I find a quiet place to sit and eat, away from the rowdy men.

The hot liquid is a welcoming feeling as I swallow its richness down my parched throat. The flavor is unlike anything I'd experienced in Lethe. Not that I should be surprised. The soft bread practically melts in my mouth after dipping it in the broth. A soft moan slips from my lips and my eyes close as I indulge in its moist fluffiness. The sounds of commotion cause my eyes to snap open, as a group of the men head off into the forest. Continuing to chew my food, I watch them curiously, wondering where they could possibly be going.

"They're going to the cove," someone says. Turning my head in their direction, I find one of the older guards, his long salt and pepper beard pulled into a thick braid that hangs off his aged face as he sits with his back against a large oak tree. "The cove is beautiful at night, ay."

"Oh, I didn't know there was a cove," I add, intrigued with his remark. "How does one get there?" I ask.

"You just follow that path, dear, straight on out about fifty meters. You'll hear the waves of the lake when you're close."

"Thank you," I reply, placing my bowl on the ground next to me. I rise to my feet, scanning the men for Xerxes, but I don't find him. "Come on, Erebus, let's go see what all the fuss is about."

Chapter Twelve

XERXES

Running my fingers across my lips, it's like I can still feel hers pressed up against mine. I dreamt of what it would feel like to finally kiss her, but those dreams were nothing compared to the real thing. My bond hums beneath my skin, content with the progress I'm making with her, even if it is slower than I'd like. Her thoughts are enough to tell me things are heading in the right direction, and the fact that she opened up to me about her powers making an appearance, means I'm earning her trust.

Pulling my long hair up, I tie it up on the top of my head before turning to head back to the camp. When I get there, I find Orion and Senna, still handing out bowls of meat filled broth and bread to the men. My stomach growls with hunger as I approach the small table they're set up at.

"Brother." She greets me with a nod. "Do you want some before it's gone? Frederick has already had at least six bowls, I don't know how he expects anyone else to eat at this rate."

"No, thank you. Save it for the men. Have you seen Kasia?"

Senna rolls her eyes at the mere mention of my bonded's name. "Okay, enough of this," I add as I bring myself to stand before both Orion and Senna. "I'm fully aware of whatever this is between you both, I have been aware of since before it started."

"What? I don't know what you're talking about?" Senna snaps, turning her eyes away from me as her cheeks glow red.

"Senna, you've been infatuated with Orion since you were nine, and you know full well I've suspected it, and Orion..." I add, snapping my eyes to his "well, you fell for her that day in the woods when you saw her take down that bear with an arrow between the eyes."

"Mate, how could you possibly... Never mind." Orion replies, pointing at me.

"So, if you have known this whole time, why haven't you said anything?" Senna questions with annoyance.

I shrug. "Well, mostly because I enjoyed watching you two squirm, but I have tried to mention it; your stubborn ass just wouldn't let me finish."

"Seriously?" she hisses.

"Yes, but the point is, because I know how Orion feels for you, I know nothing happened this morning with him and Kasia." Orion goes to speak but I raise my hand, stopping him. "Not that I thought it would've anyways, Orion is like my brother, he wouldn't have hurt either of us that way."

"As annoying as your brother is, especially right now, he's right, Senna. I was just taking the piss, ay. I like to get him goin', it's funny as fuck, but I didn't know Kasia would bring it up in front of you. I should've expected it, though, that woman is ruthless."

I chuckle, "That she is. Speaking of, have you seen her?" I ask, scanning the groups of men for her silver hair.

"Not since she got her dinner," Senna replies, placing her hands on her hips.

Without another word, I rush to check our tent after not finding her around the camp, leaving Senna and Orion behind. Panic begins to set in when I pull back the flap of our tent and don't find her safely inside. I notice Erebus is nowhere to be seen either, which should offer me some relief but for some reason, it doesn't.

"She went down to the cove, Lord," a male voice shouts, pulling my attention.

"Gage," I nod "To the cove?" Any relief I had is now completely gone. The cove is where Nymeria hunts and nothing would please her more than getting her siren claws into Kasia. Into what belongs to me. She didn't take me declining her advances lightly. I knew she wouldn't. Sirens are famous for their jealous and uncontrolled behavior. "How long?" I ask.

"Uh, about ten minutes or so, she followed a group of your men out there, Lord. I mentioned how beautiful it is with the stars and the moonlight. The lass seemed intrigued and with your men, headed down there as well, I didn't think there was any harm in it. I apologize." he stammers as though he's done something wrong.

"Not your fault, Gage. Thank you," I reply.

Kasia venturing down to the cove isn't his fault, he may have told her how to get here and what beauty it holds, but he did so innocently. No one suspects the danger that lurks beneath the water's surface, especially when the face of danger presents itself as a beautiful woman who knows how to use her body and song to lure you in.

It's no secret I'd been lured in by Nymeria many times. Though my heart and soul have always belonged to my bonded, to my little dove, I still needed to find release. I'm sure she did as well. I push the thoughts from my head as I make my way down the trail, through the thick foliage, eager to lay eyes on my little dove, to know she's safe.

The closer I get the louder the sound of the waves crashing on the beach gets, and with it the sound of laughing men.

"Why don't you join us then?"

"Yeah, the water is warm, and the stars are beautiful, but not as beautiful as you lass." another man shouts with a playful tone.

My blood boils in my veins.

"Common then, don't be a tease, give us a peek at what you have hiding under that pretty little dress then ay?"

I'm close enough to pick up their thoughts, and none of them please me. They're wondering who she is to me, who could be of such importance that I escort them on a trip to the Oracle. They're thinking of her tight little body under her gown, and how it flows down her curves. They want to see what's under it. Touch what's under it.

No longer able to contain my temper, I push off from the ground, beating my large wings as they carry me up above the forest. It takes mere seconds and I'm landing in the cove with my feet sinking in the damp black sandy shores of Arachai Lake's cove. The men grow silent. A loud growl rumbles in my chest as I bring myself to stand before Kasia. She lifts her eyes from the men in the water to mine briefly. Amused with my show of jealousy, she brings her fingers between her two plump lips and chews on it. My jaw clicks before I turn my back to her and focus my attention on my men.

"Tell me, men. When did it become common courtesy to try and convince our guests to strip down their clothing and go for a midnight swim?" I yell out at them. The tone of my voice does little to hide the aggression building inside me. Small tethers of glowing moonlight stem from my clenched fists. Flickering about like flashes of lightning in a storming sky.

"We didn't mean anything by it, Lord."

"Yeah, we were just messing around. She's not even my type," one mumbles. My eyes snap to him.

"Not your type?" I hiss through tightly clenched teeth. "Then why is your head filled with thoughts of touching her? Touching what does not belong to you? To any of you!"

"We're sorry, Lord," the other pleads, placing his hands up in surrender.

"Yeah, we weren't aware she belonged to you."

"Excuse me?" Kasia says, pushing herself past me. "I belong to no man."

"Kasia," I whisper with a stern tone, hoping she'll sense how close I am to losing my patience.

"No!" she snaps. "Who are you to claim that I belong to you? To tell me I can't do as I wish. Hmph." she huffs as she slides the gemmed sleeves of her red gown down her arms. My eyes trail it as it glides down her perfect petite body, revealing her soft, milky skin until it pools at her feet. For a brief moment, I'm rendered speechless, but it's when the men's thoughts of her little show grow louder that I'm pulled back to reality, finding Kasia bare and striding towards the inky waters of Arachai.

"Return to the camp, now!" My voice booms over the silence of the cove. Hearing the anger in my tone, the men waste no time making their way to shore, quickly grabbing their piles of discarded clothing. "And if I were any of you, I would not consider even glancing in her direction again for the remainder of this journey."

"Yes, Lord," some of them whisper as they scurry back down the trail through the forest. Turning my attention back to Kasia, I find her waist-deep in the water. Her bare chest exposed to me. The ends of her long white hair swaying in the water around her as she wades. Turning her gaze on me, her expression changes as the most gorgeous smile forms on her face. *I am done for. She is trouble and she knows just how to play me.* My jealousy got the better of me and she finds it entertaining.

"Find something amusing, little dove?" I question looking over my shoulder as I will my wings back inside of me.

"Jealousy doesn't look good on you, Lord. You really shouldn't make empty threats towards your men, not when you expect so much from them." Annoyed with her little game, I growl.

"Do not test me, little dove. Continue seeking the attention of other men, whether it be in thought or touch, just so you can continue your *little game*, and I will show you just how *easily* I'm willing to shed their blood."

"Must everything end in bloodshed with you?" she replies seductively as she trails her left hand across her bare chest. I watch as she runs it up and down the swell of her breast before circling her peaked nipple. All the while watching my reaction. "Your jealousy ruined my fun."

I laugh, "Fun? Well then, I suppose you have no other option other than to have fun with yourself now, seeing as none of my men will dare even look at you." I add, crossing my arms over my chest.

"You'd like that, wouldn't you? To watch me have fun all alone in this cove, playing with myself," she adds with hooded eyes. Pulling her bottom lip into her mouth with her fang, she eyes me.

"Kasia-" I hiss as her hand slowly trails below the water's surface. "We can have this conversation back at the camp, the cove isn't safe."

"It was safe enough for your men," she purrs as her submerged hand reaches her core and begins to move in circular motions. Her free hand moves to her breast where it pinches her peaked nipple as a soft moan slips from her lips. My cock begins to swell in my leather pants as I watch her touching herself, knowing full well I'm falling right into her trap.

"They aren't you."

"Oh? So, it's safe for them and not me? Well, in that case, you better come and fetch me, *Lord*," she replies playfully as she swims further out. *Fuck*. Quickly I strip off my clothing, welcoming the moon's energy on my exposed skin as I head to the cove's shore. Kasia stops and turns her sights back on me. The water is getting deeper now, reaching high enough to just barely cover her perky little breasts. The lake is colder than I'd like tonight, but I ignore it, knowing every second she's alone out there puts her life at risk. This is Nymeria's territory, and she could be lurking anywhere below the water's surface.

I slowly swim out to her until I'm a few feet from where she's wading. The water here only reaches to my waist, but I keep myself submerged to my shoulders as I watch her. My blood is pumping right to my cock with her little show, and she knows it. Even my side of the bond is affected. The cool night air carries the scent of her arousal right to me, and her thoughts tell me everything her mouth won't. She needs this. She needs to find release. Her body aches for it. I just wish she'd let me help her.

"What? Not going to drag me back to the shore by my hair?"

I laugh, "I don't need to. I'm close enough that no harm will come to you."

"Is that so? The big bad Lord of Calanthe is here to protect me. So sweet."

"I'll always protect you, Kasia," I reply.

As if sensing the seriousness in my reply, she stops her little show, and dives under the water. When she doesn't immediately rise, panic sets in, and I quickly stand. Peering into the blackened waters, I search for any sign of her but find nothing. Suddenly, she surfaces directly in front of me. She inhales a deep breath before wiping the water from her face. When she opens her eyes, she scans my chest. I look down on her, as her eyes devour each ridge of my toned chest in the moonlight. Softly, her hands trace the muscles. Standing before me, she barely reaches my shoulders, and she's forced to tilt her chin to look up at me. Her beautiful green eyes are full of lust and hunger as she brings herself closer.

Instinctively I reach out, wrapping my hand around her waist, and pulling her closer, when suddenly her lips crash on mine. With her bare breasts pressed tightly against mine, a low growl rumbles in my chest. *Mine.* She quickly pulls back, breaking the kiss and bringing her eyes to mine.

"This means nothing," she whispers from swollen lips.

"No, little dove. That's where you're wrong," I reply, tucking a loose curl behind her pointed ear. "This moment means everything. You just don't know it yet," and with that her lips are back on mine. She tastes of pure passion. Her lips dance with mine like they were born to waltz together, and they were. She wraps her arms around my neck and her legs around my waist as she deepens the kiss. Sliding my hands down to her ass, I hold her against me while my fingers grip into her flesh.

Her hips begin to grind against my hardened cock as I lower us back into the water. Seeking friction for the release she so desperately craves. Feeling her against me is almost enough to make me come undone. Every fiber of my being wants to claim her, here and now, but I know it has to be her choice. I want it to be her choice. Each run of her pussy along my shaft bringing me closer to the edge of my breaking point.

Reaching down, she grabs my shaft firmly in her hand, as a shocked expression forms on her face. I smirk through kisses, as her thoughts fill with remarks about the size of my cock. When she realizes I'm reading her thoughts, she stops and smacks my chest, bringing her smiling eyes to mine before her lips are back on mine. Her hand tightens around my girth as she begins to stroke it. A moan slips from my lips, and she breaks the kiss. Just when I think she's going to run, she surprises me. Lifting her eyes to mine again, she strokes my cock again, slowly, watching my reaction. *Fuck, she is pure perfection*. Again, she pumps my cock beneath the water's surface from the base to the tip, swiping her thumb over its swollen head.

"Kasia," I whisper, nearing the edge. She smirks, clearly enjoying the effect she has on me and my cock, and pumps again. My tongue darts out across my lip, and she adjusts herself so that my cocks tip is at her entrance. She moves it in circular motions around her core while I hold her up in the water, teasing us both. Her body is humming with pleasure, I can feel it through the bond. She needs this as badly as I do. She wants it as badly as I do, and just when the hunger becomes unbearable, she locks eyes with me and lines me up at her opening before slowly sliding down.

We both let out a gasp and freeze in place as she adjusts to my size. She feels euphoric. Unlike anything I've ever felt, and the moment she begins to move her hips, my heart stops. It feels as though our bodies are as one, moving as one. Each grind of her hips has her taking me deeper inside her, as her head falls back. I wrap one arm around her back, holding her closer as she picks up the pace. The waves crash around us as my little dove rides me in the moonlight.

"Oh... My... Gods," she moans. My hands make their way to her round ass, pulling her down harder against me as she cries out into the night air with pleasure. She rides me as my hand guides her down harder and deeper until I'm completely sheathed inside her. Her heat clenches around me as she nears her release. I'd be lying if I said I hadn't dreamt of how good she'd feel, but being inside her, being this connected to her feels even better than I expected.

"Tell me, little dove... have you been drinking the tea Agatha brings you?" I groan as I pull her down on me hard. She smiles, as her head falls back.

"You mean the special blend of Thalla Mint tea she brews for all the ladies of court who wish to avoid a child?" she asks coyly. Lifting her head, she brings her lips mere inches from mine, she runs her tongue along my lips "I drink every... single... drop," she whispers, slamming her lips over mine—a growl crews in my chest at her playful yet incredibly sexy antics.

Every part of her feels completely and utterly perfect. My side of the bond and hers become connected, and my skin pricks with tiny bumps sending a chill rolling through me. She rests her head on my shoulder, as she picks up the pace. I kiss her neck, inhaling her intoxicating scent before lightly sinking my fangs into her flesh. Just enough to break the skin, to taste her on my tongue.

"Don't stop, please... don't stop."

A low moan of pleasure slips from her lips, as she wraps her hand around my neck, pulling my mouth into her neck deeper. Slowly bringing my fangs back to her neck, I bite down. I bite deeper this time, so that when I pull my fangs from her flesh, tiny streams of blood trail down her neck. I run my tongue through them, welcoming the sweet metallic taste of her blood.

"Fuck, you taste fucking divine, little dove," I whisper as my lips brush against her ear.

"Xerxes, I-"

I throb deep inside her, watching her bring herself to the peak of pleasure, as she sinks down on my cock. Her body shakes in my grasp, her tightness clamping around my cock as she finds her orgasm. With the mound of emotions coursing through her body as she rides the wave, she loses hold of her magic, and two snowy white wings sprout out of her shoulder blades to rest against her back. I chuckle, grabbing her hips, as I keep her motions going. I intend to fuck every ounce of her release out of her. The white wings glow in the moonlight, as she brings her face to mine. Her cheeks are flushed with a dusting of red, like a wild rose, and the moment her eyes lock with mine, I catch a flash of something I didn't expect. Acceptance.

She believes me. She believes everything we've told her. Everything I've been feeling for her, she finally feels too, and for the first time, she's not hiding it. I combust. Pulling her down on myself one last time before I come undone. Filling her with my seed, marking her like I was always meant to.

Having both found release, she collapses against my chest as we wade in the waters of the cove. Our hearts beat erratically as we share panted breaths. This moment was worth it all. The years of searching, years of feeling alone because no one believed me when I said she was alive. Shedding the blood of anyone who got in the way of me finding her was all worth it. At this moment, she is exactly where she's meant to be, and I will never let anyone take her from me.

Her breathing slows, as she slowly unwraps her legs from my waist and climbs off me. Tucking her hair behind her ears, she clears her throat, but it's her expression that has my attention. It's that of regret. Despite now feeling everything I have felt over the years, and finally starting to believe she is who we've all been saying she is, she regrets what's happened between us on this night.

"We should get back."

"Don't do that, Kasia. Don't try to pretend this didn't happen." My voice cracks as I plead with her. Internally, my heart is breaking. Part of me knew it would take more than simply being with her, to keep her, but I had hoped it would at least lessen the coldness. Bring us closer even.

"I'm not!" she snaps, as she brushes past me, her white wings parting the water behind her. I watch as she grows annoyed with them treading water behind her.

"Then where are you rushing off exactly?"

"It's late, Xerxes. We should get back to camp and get some rest." Though she won't admit it, I know exactly what she's doing, and I'd normally play along. I'm done playing. My jaw clicks with annoyance as I return to the shore.

When I get there, she pulls her red gown over her still-damp body. My blood boils in my veins as I grab her chin in my hand, forcing her eyes to mine.

"This isn't happening. We will not go back to pretending you don't feel everything I feel, not now that I've had you. *Marked* you."

"I told you it meant nothing!" she seethes, tearing her face away.

"I don't give a fuck what you told me. We both know how much your mouth likes to spit lies. Just look at those wings. Tell me, little dove. You claim you're no Satori. Well last I checked, they were the only bloodline in the realms to have wings like that."

She ignores me and continues to pull the thin dress up the best she can with wings on her back. As she brushes her hair back, the small mark on her neck from my fangs is exposed. It's already beginning to heal itself. Inhaling deeply, I do my best to calm my tone.

"What are you doing?" I ask.

"Getting dressed, *Lord*. After all, I wouldn't want you to kill anyone for seeing me naked when I simply walk back into camp," she hisses before storming off down the trail, back to the camp.

Bringing my hand to my face, I rub my brow and release my breath. Fuck. Even now, her venomous tongue gets me going. There's no controlling it. My cock twitches like it didn't already fill her just moments ago. Standing in the moonlit cove, naked and alone, I accept that my anger only worsened things. Silently cursing myself, I begin to pull on my own discarded clothing when a familiar song carried by the cool wind bellowing across the lake meets my ears. Nymeria.

My head snaps to the dark waters of the cove, where I find the siren. Her piercing eyes fixated on me with a look of hatred and defiance, letting me know she saw everything, and she isn't pleased.

Chapter Thirteen

KASIA

After our encounter in the cove, I've done my best to keep my distance from Xerxes. Though I was forced to share a tent with him, I slept alone. I was wrong. I was wrong about everything.

As we set off in the early morning, the glowing mushrooms light our way through tall ferns as we make the last trek to the oracle's cottage. Once again on Oscar's back, with Xerxes's strong arms wrapped around me, my heart beats frantically in my chest. I keep my eyes forward and my mouth shut as I focus my thoughts on the thick, white, feathered wings that randomly sprouted from my back. I've found release many times, with many men. But never have I sprouted wings, or felt the things I felt with him.

My gut churns. So many thoughts and questions flood my head, but one thing is unshakeable. One thought grows throughout the day while the others slowly fade in the chaos. *Him.* Xerxes, and the moment we shared in the cove, the way being with him felt, has completely overtaken me.

My heart aches to pull his arms around me closer. To feel his warmth as I allow myself to drown in his rainstorm scent all over again. I run my fingers over the now fully healed mark along my neck where his fangs sank into my flesh. The gesture sends a chill down my spine. *Mine.* I can still feel him. Under my skin. Across it. The ghost of his gentle touch haunts me like a craving, and as the day carries on, the harder it is to ignore.

Sex has always been a resource to get what I want or need. To draw attention or distract. A job. But with Xerxes last night, it was completely different. For the first time, I felt truly desired. I felt the passion in his kiss, the love he has for me crawled across my skin and through our bond as he filled me, marked me under the stars.

It was all so perfect. I almost fell for it. Almost believed it was real and that his feelings were real. But I know better than anyone, that love makes you weak, and all men are the same. He will claim he cares, and he'll use me for my body until the next pretty girl comes along who excites him, and then I will be forgotten. Discarded like rubbish, all the while he'll have me completely fooled into thinking I actually mean something to him. I've seen it happen to enough women back home in Lethe. Thankfully, I was never weak enough to fall for the frail attempts of men to win my heart; my body, however, was a different story.

Senna rides up beside us on Raven. Orion is missing from his usual place behind her, probably off dealing with some issues with the men. Her long red hair is flowing down her back today, blowing in the cool wind that bellows through the trees under the forest's canopy.

"Orion needs you at the back of the pack. One of the horses is injured, and he could really use your help," she explains.

Xerxes's arm tightens around my middle, causing me to tense as he pulls on the reins until Oscar stops. Climbing off, he nods to his sister before heading back to Orion without so much as offering me a glance. His coldness doesn't go unnoticed with Senna, and she lifts her eyes to mine in a confused glance. I wish I could blame him. Be angry at him for his coldness, but I can't.

I deserve it.

I've done nothing but push him away since I got here, and the moment we finally come together, instead of allowing us to grow closer from our moment of intimacy, I've shut him down completely. Doing my best to keep away from him, and when he and his questions are unavoidable, I've done nothing but give him excuses that even I know are lies when they slide off my tongue. I don't need Xerxes mind reading powers to know that, and neither does he.

It wasn't nothing.

He was right. It was everything.

Gripping Oscar's reins I urge him forward, with Senna remaining at my side. Her silence reminds me of my guilt. Knowing my attempt to mess with Xerxes caused her pain she didn't deserve.

"Senna, I owe you an apology."

"Ay? What for?"

"The other morning. When I mentioned Orion in my bed, nothing happened." She crinkles her nose with a slight smile. "It's just that- Well... Sometimes, your brother gets to me, and for some reason, I instinctively do things that I know will bother him."

"Now that I understand," she laughs. "But I'm confused about why you think I care if Orion was in your bed."

"You don't have to hide it from me. I saw the pain that was reflected in your eyes when you heard my comment. I may not know you well yet, but I know the look of hurt in one's eyes better than anyone else. Hearing it hurt you and Orion; I think it was clear to everyone there he did not like you hearing it. Which tells me he knew it would hurt you, too."

"I-"

"Stop. You don't have to deny it," I snicker. "It's not my place to tell you who you can or can't be with, and I won't pretend it is. Orion seems like a good man, and if he makes you happy then you deserve it."

"I wasn't going to deny it. Lying isn't exactly my talent. I was only going to ask that you keep this knowledge between you and me. At least until we find a way to let Xerxes know. Keeping him in the dark has been much harder these last few months. He did try to catch us out yesterday when I went to visit him, and I thought maybe I could just keep denying it... but that seems pointless now. Especially if you have picked up on it."

"Well, I can confirm Xerxes does indeed know, and it wasn't from me. He's known the whole time."

She pulls on Raven's reins, stopping. "That sneaky little shit, the whole time?" she spits. Unable to contain my amusement, I laugh, as she looks over her shoulder to where Xerxes and Orion are at the back of the line. "He's lucky I have the restraint not to give him a piece of my mind in front of his own men."

"Indeed, I imagine you have much to say to him," I chuckle. "Though, unfortunately for him, I don't share such restraint."

"Ah, yes. Word has spread around the court of your venomous tongue towards the High Lord. I'd be lying if I said I didn't enjoy watching it. Whether he wants to admit it or not, he needs it, and I think we all know you're the only one who will ever get away with it. He's soft for you."

I let the gravity of her words sink in. I know Xerxes is soft for me and that my treatment of him isn't what he or anyone else is used to him receiving. Maybe that plays a part in what makes it so enjoyable for me. Knowing he never knows what to expect from me and watching his eyes darken and fill with lust. I've never known a man to get so aroused by me giving them a piece of my mind. Or maybe it's knowing that all it takes is a bit of sass from me to have that effect on him.

"Finally," Senna says under her breath.

"Hmm?"

"We're here." Her voice leaks with exhaustion as she points ahead of us toward a small clearing in the thickness of the forest. The closer we get, the thinner the trees become, revealing a small cabin made of large birch logs, and outside it stands a woman.

Her dark skin is the perfect contrast to her cloudy white eyes. She's older but easily one of the most beautiful yet terrifying-looking women I've ever seen, and her attire is unlike anything I've ever seen back in Lethe. Black metal rings coil around her neck like a collar. The rings seem to weave into a large headdress resting on her thickly braided hair. Xerxes appears at my side, halting Oscar's advance and aiding me off the tall horse's back. His firm grip on my sides as he lifts me off and places me softly on the ground next to him sends shockwaves through my body. Turning his attention to the strange woman, he bows at the waist, surprisingly catching me off guard.

"Viserra."

"My Lord," she smirks, greeting him with a soft smile as she approaches him. They exchange a soft embrace. It's clear this woman is important to him. Turning her eyes on me, her expression changes to one of concern. "I wondered how long it would take you to seek me out, though I'll admit I am pleased it was sooner rather than later. Come child, we have much to discuss."

"You knew we were coming?" I question.

"Viserra is the last Oracle of the Seer Tribe. She has the gift of sight, Birdie. Among other great talents," Orion explains as he reaches us. It's clear whatever kept him and Xerxes at the back of the line exhausted him. His breaths were shallow and panted.

"Ah, yes, well, thank goodness for my gifts. However, without them, I would still know that you, Orion, only came with the hopes of drinking all my Berry Brandy," she says, cocking a brow at Orion. Bowing his head, Orion smirks and places a hand over his heart like he's wounded.

"You wound me, Viserra. How could you possibly think I'd travel all this way just for your delectable Berry Brandy? Once I heard of Xerxes' trip to visit, I felt obligated to ensure they arrived here safely." The group chuckles, sensing his sarcasm.

"Mhmm, I am sure. Just take care this time. We don't need you going on another berry brandy bender," she smiles. Turning her attention back on me, her eyes soften. The buzzing under my skin grows. I've come to learn it's my magic reacting to my emotions, and though I've had no training, understanding what it is has already been some help in controlling it. I can manage my emotions better, keeping my magic in check. It's hard work, but it's better than risking hurting someone. Taking my hand in hers, her eyes lock with mine.

"I know you have questions and concerns, and I know that to you, I am a stranger, but I was once a great friend to your mother, and I hope that one day we can be just as close," she explains with a gentle tone as she tucks my hair behind my ear. "You look so much like her."

"I do?"

Her smile grows, "Come, let us help you remember her. Remember who you are." She guides me towards her small cabin, with Xerxes close behind me.

"Do you think you can help her?" Xerxes asks. Viserra chuckles, finding humor in his doubts.

"While the power of the Salome potion may be one of the greatest mysteries of the realms, I assure you, it is no match for me."

"Viserra," Senna asks as she reaches our side. "I read in one of Father's old apothecary books that there's a possibility the Salome could go deep into her mind now; there may be no way of retrieving everything. That the potion will have become a part of her itself, is this true?"

177

Viserra stops at the front of the cabin and sighs, "You are right, Senna. There will be some things I cannot retrieve, but those memories will be a tiny fraction. She will remember enough to know who she is."

"Will I remember them? My parents?" The question shocks even me. I don't know where it came from. It slipped from my lips before I could even think or process the question in my head.

"Ah, well," she smiles, "your parents were the type of leaders that are hard to forget. They cherished and loved you deeply, so I imagine you will have no problem remembering them. Now, you all stay out here. Give Kasia and me a few moments."

"I-"

"Xerxes, I already know what you're going to say. You can join us if you promise to let me do what needs to be done. It may cause her some pain, but you cannot intervene, so if you cannot control yourself, stay outside." With that she guides me inside her cottage, Xerxes following in silent agreement behind us.

Immediately, I'm hit with the scent of foreign herbs and flowers. The small cottage consists of one large candle-lit room with designated spaces. There's a small cot off to the left side of the cottage, pressed firmly into the corner with a small table beside it. Shelves of books cover the walls along with a large hearth with a roaring fire, and hanging from the ceiling are bundles of dried herbs and flowers. In the center of the cottage is a large wooden island with various vials and jars filled with many different things, from the glowing mushrooms that fill the forest to black, inky liquids. It's cluttered but cozy.

Viserra guides me to a small wooden chair next to the large island to sit down as she makes her way to the kitchen area of the room. She grabs a large jar from the top of her shelf before returning to me. Placing it down on the table before me, she stands behind me, pulling my thick white locks from my face, and begins to braid it. Xerxes clears his throat from the other side of the island as he watches.

"You're sure she'll be okay, right? I know you said she could experience pain, but how much?"

Lifting my eyes to his, I find them filled with concern. He's nervous. His body is stiff, and his breathing has all but halted. While his eyes are widened and locked on mine, I notice the ripple in his jaw as he eagerly waits for Viserra's response. Unmoved by the tension Xerxes is putting off, Viserra continues to braid my hair, tying it off when she reaches the bottom.

"I cannot say how much pain she will experience, but yes, she will be fine. I would not risk doing something that would put her life at risk. You know this."

"Forgive me, Viserra. I just-" he pauses mid-sentence as Viserra approaches the jar she left on the table. It's filled with a whitish-grey powder of some kind, like ash.

"Xerxes, you need not explain. I know," and with that, she opens the jar, coating her fingers in the fine substance. I should be nervous and afraid, and maybe somewhere deep inside me I am, but right now, knowing Xerxes is so close, I can't help but feel safe. His concern in itself is a comfort. The pain they speak of cannot be worse than the pain I felt throughout my life. The pain of growing up thinking I had no one, no family, that I was never loved. Some pains heal and fade over time, like the scars on my back, but that pain will haunt me forever, permanently etched into my heart.

Gripping my chin, she forces my eyes to hers. "Are you ready to learn your story, child? Are you ready to learn your truth?"

"Yes," I say with confidence. She smiles, releasing her hold on my chin as she returns to stand behind me. Viserra presses her ash-coated fingers firmly to my temples, and instantly, a searing pain barrels through me. I thought I knew pain, but this is unlike any pain I've ever felt. It's as though the blood pumping through my veins has been replaced with fire. It burns, and I can feel it coursing through every fiber of my body, but the worst is in my head. Visions of people I don't recognize flash in my head. A woman with long white hair and gentle icy blue eyes. Valleys of green and lush meadows of wildflowers, places I've never been. Or have I? I grip the arms of the small wooden chair tightly, and though my eyes are forced closed from the pain, I can feel Xerxes at my side. I can feel his worry. My pain is his pain, and I never understood it as clearly as I do at this moment.

Viserra quietly chants some words I don't understand behind me as the burning sensation grows in intensity, and then it stops. All the pain is gone. Slowly, I open my eyes. Xerxes is on his knees beside me, his hand resting on my leg as he scans my face for answers I don't have.

"I- I don't feel any different."

"You won't. This won't be a sudden change, child. Years of memories are stored in your head, and they have been dormant for decades. It will take time for them to come forward, but they will, and when they do, I will be there to guide you through them."

"You intend to return to Eventide with us?" Xerxes asks as he rises to his feet.

"I do. She will need me for more than just the return of her memories. Her magic is strong and hasn't even fully begun to show itself. She will need training and guidance that only one who fully understands can provide for her."

Bits and pieces of their conversation hit my ears, but my head is like a cloudy haze. Squinting my eyes, I shake my head to clear it, but it isn't until Xerxes senses my distress and pulls me up from the chair and into his arms that things seem to calm. The feeling of being in his arms pressed tightly against his rapidly beating heart, causes time to freeze and all the chaos and fog in my head to clear. Though I may not be sure of anything happening in my head, there is one thing I am sure of now. *Him*.

"You're okay, little dove. I'm here; I have you," he whispers, pulling me closer as he gently presses his lips to my forehead.

"Thank you," I reply, my voice muffled by his chest. With my words, he releases a breath I didn't know he was holding. His body frees itself from the stress and the worry.

"This is normal. It will be like this for some time while your memories slowly work their way to the surface." I turn my face from Xerxes's strong chest to bring my eyes to hers.

"They won't all come back at once?" I ask, suddenly eager to see and learn more about the woman with the white hair.

"No. They will return in fragments; some might not make sense at first. They can be visions of people or places. You could be walking down through the halls, and suddenly, something will smell familiar. There is no way to tell which memories will come forth or when that is up to them, but we will face it together, Kasia."

"Thank you. For everything, Viserra," I reply, suddenly feeling immense gratitude to this strange woman for wanting to help me.

"Child, there is no need to thank me. While I may not have supported the choice your mother made in taking your memories, I understand why she felt she had no other choice. I am blessed to be the one to return them to you, to return *her* to you," she expresses. "Now, we should be going. The camp is a few hours' ride away, and it will storm something fierce tonight."

Xerxes chuckles, releasing me from his hold only to take my hand as he leads me out of the small cottage. Orion, Senna, and some of the men are waiting anxiously outside, but before they can question us, Xerxes waves them off, but to no surprise, Erebus ignores him. He reaches my side with his tail wagging excitedly behind him as I bend to pet him gently.

"Ay, mate, it's bloody bollocks, we're meant just to sit out here all this time, and you're not even going to tell us if that old hag's voodoo did anything?" Orion utters under his breath. "We didn't even get any berry brandy," he sulks.

"This old hag's voodoo worked just as it's meant to. Make no mistake, I may be old, but my ears can still hear just fine, Orion," Viserra counters. A small laugh slips from my lips, and Xerxes doesn't miss it. His eyes lock with mine as he lifts me back onto Oscar's back with a smile of his own. Viserra climbs to share a horse with Gage, one of the older and most trusted guards.

"But what about the berry brandy? Can we at least nab a couple of pints to bring back to Eventide to celebrate your successful voodoo then?" Orion questions with hopeful eyes.

"I gave it to Nefeli and the centaurs when she visited. I knew I wasn't going to be here to drink it and thought it would be more appreciated there," Viserra replies with a smirk.

"Ah, but if you're coming to Eventide, that means it worked then, ya?"

"Orion, we can talk about it when we reach Eventide," Xerxes shouts to the group before climbing behind me. Unlike earlier, I welcome the cage of safety his arms provide me. "You did good, little dove. We have a few days ahead of us until we return home. Rest now." I don't fight him. Instead, I lay myself back, cradling my head against his chest. While he leads the men back down the trail, my head fills with visions of who I can only guess to be my mother.

Chapter Fourteen

KASIA

Since returning to Eventide, the icy blue eyes of my mother have haunted me. After Viserra freed my memories, nothing much else has come through. At least not as clearly as her. Everything, every vision, is nothing but a moment of a life I do not remember. Not yet, anyway. There's a song, a lullaby of some kind, that plays repeatedly in my head even when I'm awake. Yet no one I have asked has heard it, not even Viserra. However, she confirmed it is my mother I continue to see. I look just like her, though I've yet to see her full face. Our hair is the same silvery white shade, and in all of my visions she wears it down freely. What I have seen of her is beautiful, and though she's nothing more than a fragment of my memory, I can feel the love she had for me.

My long, crimson silk dress bellows behind me as I make my way through the halls of Eventide and out to the court where Viserra has been meeting me for training. It's probably my favorite gown yet, with a low-cut corset beautifully embroidered with intricate vines in gold thread that hugs my tits tightly. At the waist, the silk pours down my lower body with two thigh-high slits on each side that reveal my toned legs with each step I take through the halls.

It's only been a few days since we returned with Viserra, and though she's been nothing but kind and supportive, I struggle to open up to her about the full extent of my memories. Though I know that everyone is concerned for me, I need the time to process things myself before I'm ready to share the things coming to light. Free from the heat of the palace, the cool night air of Calathe I've grown so accustomed to assaults my lungs.

Lifting my eyes, I find myself in awe. Though I don't want to admit it, there is beauty in this magical foreign land—the black-to-indigo gradient that becomes the backdrop to an ethereal glowing crescent moon. Millions of twinkling stars move across the night sky, similar to the snowflakes in Lethe, and though I'm the furthest I've ever been, I feel at home.

It rained last night, and the storm was fierce, leaving the grounds covered in thick layers of mud. I secretly hoped that Viserra would cancel training and allow me to spend the day soaking in the hot bath with a book, but I should've known better.

These early mornings have been tough on me, especially without proper sleep. My body and mind are exhausted and drained, but I enjoy the visions that keep me up– the flashbacks to moments from a past that I don't remember. The moon's glow shines over the courtyard as I approach to find Viserra crouched down in the middle of a large circle that's been etched into the mud of the courtyard. She's wearing a long dark wool cloak with an oversized hood as she continues making markings on the earth with her hands.

"Ah, about time you drag yourself out of bed, child."

"Sorry," I apologize. "I'm still adjusting to this whole *always-night thing*," I say.

She chuckles. "Yes, well, that will indeed take some time to get used to, especially when you do not get the sleep that your mind needs," she hints as she lifts her ghostly eyes on me. I still don't understand why, if not blind, her eyes appear so clouded. Her focused gaze locked on mine is simply haunting. Like looking far off into a sky of storming clouds. "Tell me, Kasia, what memories kept you from resting on this night?"

It isn't the first time Viserra has tried to pry answers from me regarding my memories, or lack thereof, and I know I should be able to trust her. She's given me no reason not to, and yet... I don't. But then again, I've always struggled to trust anyone. It took me years to trust Sage, and she raised me.

"None, Viserra," I answer with a tone that does little to hide my annoyance. "Now, can we move on?" An expression of doubt forms on her face, and she crosses her arms across her chest. I roll my eyes. Every morning brings the same questions, the same pushing for answers I'm not ready to share.

"Her mother," his husky voice says from behind me. Chills crawl over my skin. My heartbeats increase with his presence. As he reaches my side, his rainstorm scent washes over me, filling my nose with its calmness. "Her dreams are of nothing more than her mother, her eyes mostly, and a song... nothing I am familiar with, but could be important to Lethe."

"No," she replies, "If it were important to Lethe, someone would know it. My guess is it's a lullaby. Important only to the Satori line." I ignore their conversation, turning my sights on Xerxes.

"Stay out of my head!" I seethe. I'm angry, but part of me is also hurt. His mind games feel like a betrayal. It's one thing for him to know I was lying about my memories, but to take them from my head and explain them to someone I clearly did not want to trust with the information is another.

"Good morning to you, too," he smirks.

"Kasia, you have to stop keeping things from me," Viserra states.

"Why?" I spit, turning my glare towards her. "These are *my* memories. *My* visions. Why must I share them before *I* am ready?"

She exhales. "Well, I was hoping today we'd have some progress, but I can see you still plan to continue being difficult."

"Wanting to keep my visions to myself until I am ready to share them does not make me difficult. Yes, I am having visions of a woman. A woman you have already informed me to be my mother. I've also already told you about the song; you knew nothing about it. Half of what I see does not make sense until I see it a few times. Forgive me if wanting to keep these visions of this woman and her song to myself for a while makes me difficult. I only just got these tiny fragments of myself back, and I did it for all of you! Because you all told me I could save Lethe. The *least* you could do is allow me time to process them myself before taking them from me!" I snap.

"Kasia—" Xerxes begins, but I don't bother to listen.

Enraged, I storm off towards the forest, no longer caring what excuses he has. We both know it won't be the last time he invades my privacy and thoughts. Usually, I can just shrug it off. At the very least, I'd have some smart-ass comment back to him. But this time, it feels different; it feels like he's taking something from me that I'm not ready to give yet. *How could he do this? I just got her back, and already I fear losing her.*

"Kasia, stop. Please," his soft tone shouts from behind me. The bond linking us allows me to feel his pain and his regret, causing me to spin around.

"Why?" I manage to croak.

"I am sorry. I never meant to hurt you," he gently says.

"You didn't," I scoff, trying to hide my emotions. I've gotten quite good at it over the years, but hiding anything from Xerxes is nearly impossible.

He sighs, rolling his eyes. "Oh, will you please stop? Stop the lying, the pushing, the need to fight me on *everything*! I know what you are thinking. I know how you really feel. About me, about being here, about everything. I *know*!" He does know. There's no way for me to keep my thoughts and feelings to myself while I'm here. Not with the bond and his Gods-forsaken ability to read minds.

"Those were *my* memories. *My* memories to share when *I* felt ready to share them," I spit as my face drops, hurt written across my features.

"They were. You're right. I *should never have taken that from you, and for that,* I am sorry. I thought I was helping." he whispers as he approaches me. I spin around, giving him my back. I can't do soft right now. Not with him. Not with how badly my body aches for him. "Viserra means well, I know... I know you do not trust her, but please if you won't trust her, then trust me," he pleads.

He doesn't touch me, but I can feel him. I can feel his body so close behind me that it hurts. Every fiber of my body, soul, and magic wants me to touch him. Craves to bring him closer. To feel him against me again. I've kept my distance since the lagoon. He fought it at first. He tried everything to get me to open up again, which got him nowhere. But after a few days, I saw less and less of him. It hurt, but I knew it was for the best. That didn't stop me from wondering if he, himself, suffered as I did.

His touch on my shoulder pulls me back from my thoughts. It's soft and gentle as his hand moves from my shoulder to my long, wavy hair. I wore it down today; without proper sleep, I barely had the energy to get in this gown, never mind deal with my hair. His hand weaves through my long locks, softly brushing the exposed skin of my shoulders and back. I trust him, even if I haven't admitted it out loud. I know he knows it, and I suppose if he trusts Viserra, then I should at least try to, even if it is only to help me figure out the chaos in my head.

"Little Dove," he begins, but I interrupt before he says anything else.

"Why do you call me that?" I ask. The words slip from my lips before I can even register the question. Spinning myself around, I take a deep breath. His expression is one of pain and regret, and I realize it then. I don't need his powers of the mind to know how he is feeling at this moment. I don't need the bond between us to know how genuine his apology is. "Why do you call me 'Little Dove?'"

"Before Draven, when your family ruled over Lethe, the flags around the kingdom carried their emblem. Your family's emblem and color." I eye him, confused as to what this has to do with the nickname he gave me the first day we met, well, the most recent first day we met. "A dark red flag with a white dove. Kasia, you are the last Satori heir, the last of your bloodline. The last dove."

"Little Dove," I whisper as the pieces fall into place in my head. "My wings..."

"Only those of the Satori bloodline have the wings of a dove. So, you see, you are *my little dove*," he says, pulling me against his hard chest. I smile, though, to some, it may seem like something small, some unimportant fact about a dead kingdom; his nickname has a new meaning to me. My wings, which have remained dormant since our night in the cove, now have a new meaning. Xerxes presses a soft kiss on my head. "*Mine,*" he whispers against my hair.

The possessive comment should've enraged me, but it doesn't. At this moment, everything about him feels *right*. This feels right. The bond connecting us buzzes through me, clearly content with how close he is against me.

"You have to stop doing that," I whisper softly. Pulling back, he looks down at me, confused by my statement.

"Doing what?" he asks.

"Saying things that make me want to kiss you," I admit.

It amazes me how easily he can calm me. Just a few moments ago, I was so angry, so hurt, I didn't even want to look at him, let alone be held in his strong arms. But here I am, melting against him, with everything completely forgiven. It occurs to me then that I have even forgiven him for bringing me here, for holding me captive and refusing to let me return to Lethe, to Sage. I don't know when I did, but the anger I once felt has since been replaced with understanding.

"Ah, well, I make no promises. I rather enjoy the feeling of your lips on mine, among other things," he smirks.

Unable to control the smile that forms on my face, I shove him in the chest playfully. "I should get back to Viserra and apologize," I say.

"You don't need to apologize to her. She understands. We all do. But you *should* get back. From what she has told me, you've been progressing well with the training over the last few days, and I don't recall any wind blowing through with that little tantrum you just threw."

I must admit, at first, training with Viserra was something I loathed. It's so hard to keep my head focused with all the thoughts that constantly spin through it. That was until she showed me meditation and how she uses it to calm her senses and magic. It's helped me and taught me to control my emotions enough to wield my powers.

"She informs you on my progress?" I question, finding it odd he has made the time to check in on me or my training with how I've been treating him since that night in the cove, especially with how busy he is with his duties as High Lord.

He places his hand on the small of my back as he guides me back to the courtyard. "Anything involving you always comes first, little dove."

"You're reading my thoughts..."

"No, I don't need to. I know you think I've kept my distance because I don't care, but that's where you're wrong. I've kept my distance because I know it's what you wanted. What you needed after that night—"

"I don't want you to keep your distance anymore," I admit, quickly cutting him off. "I... I'd like it if you didn't."

Without another word, he scoops me up in his strong arms, carrying me the rest of the way till we reach the high outer stone walls of the courtyard, where he places me down gently. Cupping my face in his hands, his whiskey eyes darken as he watches his thumb brush gently across my bottom lip.

Patience has never been a talent of mine, and unable to handle his lust-filled stare any longer, I grab his collar, yanking him down to my lips. His kiss is full of passion and hunger. So gentle, yet frenzied and full of a need for more. A need that echoes through my body from his soft lips. His fangs scrape against my lips, sending a shudder through me as his hand fists the hair at the nape of my neck. When I begin to melt, to crave more of all he makes me feel, he breaks the kiss and rests his forehead against mine.

"Godsdammit," he whispers through his panted breaths. "Little dove, you are lucky Viserra is waiting on you."

"Oh? Why is that?" I ask with a smile. I run the tip of my nose along his jawline, making him shiver.

"Otherwise, I'd be fucking you. Right here, right now, against the nearest tree," he explains as he releases me, guiding me into the courtyard. "Return to Viserra. I have things to attend to, and I'll return before you're finished to walk you back to your chambers," he adds before turning to head towards the barracks.

"Wait."

"What is it?" he asks, surprised I have called him back.

"Stay with me."

"I wish I could, but I have meetings regarding the veil and—"

"No," I smile, cutting him off mid-sentence as a genuine smile forms on my face. "Tonight. I'd like it if you'd stay with me."

"Alright," he smirks, clearly proud of himself. "Now return to Viserra, little dove. She'll have my head if you keep her waiting longer than you have. I'll be back for you." His words do something to me, and I feel excited and content for the first time in my life. I watch as he walks away before I head back through the stone arch and into the courtyard.

Viserra is still hard at work with the markings etched into the mud. Though Xerxes told me I don't need to apologize to her, part of me can't help but feel like I should. "Viserra, I—I want to apologize."

"Child, it is I who should apologize," she responds. She doesn't look up from her work. She continues digging her fingers into the thick layers of mud, forming symbols and signs I don't recognize. "You have been through much in your life, and I should be more patient. It is just that I fear our time is limited when it comes to preparing you and your magic for what is to come."

"What are these markings?" I ask, completely disregarding our previous conversation as I try to understand the shapes and their meanings.

Slowly, she rises and scans her work. "These are the sacred markings of my tribe. The tribe's seers were well known for their connection with nature. They believed they were one with the earth, as we still believe today. These symbols are used to protect from outside energies." Absorbing her words, I wonder about her people and their history. I pace around the large circular symbol she marked and stands within, studying the markings, searching them. For what I don't know, but something about them feels important.

"What do they have to do with me? With my magic?"

"As a Satori, your power is of nature," she explains.

"But Xerxes said it's linked to my emotions—"

"And he was not wrong. Though your power stems from the very nature around you, it is, in fact, linked to your emotions. It's why when you're angered, a storm will replace the once sunny skies, or why when you feel the nature around you—"

"Feel it?"

"Yes. The connection. The link. When the forest hurts, you hurt. When you heal, the forest will also heal." With her words, the bits and pieces of the story I've been told of my family and their death finally fall into place.

"Lethe... the curse..." My eyes widen at the realization.

"Ah, yes. You see, child. When your parents were killed and their blood split, the land, the magic, it died with them. Though not in the same way."

"But that means I can fix it? Right? I can break the curse, free Lethe—"

"One thing at a time," she chuckles. "First, you need to learn to harness that power. Welcome it instead of fighting it." Once again, returning to her knees, she places her palms flat on the earth's surface. Viserra tips her head toward me, signaling me to do the same. Thanks to the slits of my gown, when I lower myself to the ground, my knees sink into the cool, thick mud. But I ignore it, eager to follow Viserra's directions. I place my palms flat on the muddy surface of the earth like her.

"Let it in," she whispers.

I close my eyes, unsure of what I'm supposed to feel. "I— I don't know what I'm feeling."

"Shhh, Child. Slow your breathing. Relax and do not overthink it. You are one with nature. Open yourself up to the earth, to the forest around us, and let it in," she whispers.

My breaths slow. Inhale. Exhale. My skin buzzes as I try to concentrate on the coolness of the wet earth. The sound of the wind through the trees, the scent of rain that still lingers in the air. My head fills with visions of my mother. Her long white hair moves as she spins around in a valley of red roses, but she isn't alone this time.

This time, she carries a small child with matching hair that flows in the wind. It's my mother, and she is holding me, spinning me around and around in her arms as she sings the song that has played in my head for days. We spin and spin, and just when I'm about to finally see the face of the child in her arms, a loud scream erupts, and the vision changes. My mother's song and laughter were replaced by blood-curdling screams and visions of her long silver hair, stained in blood, as she lay dead on a floor of marble.

Startled, I pull my hands from the earth, breaking our connection. Viserra rushes to my side, clearly sensing something isn't right.

"What is it, Child? What did you see?"

"I saw—I saw my mother, but then I saw blood. So much blood," I stutter, clearly shaken.

My chest rises and falls quickly, and my heart pounds in my chest. I didn't need to see her face to know whose blood-soaked hair lies on the marble floor. Lifting my hands to my head, I close my eyes, trying to remove the visions and thoughts from my head. Only to realize my hands are dry. There's no wet mud coating my fingers. I bring them to my face to inspect them before turning my sights on the ground around me. The entire courtyard, which was filled with thick mud just a few moments ago, is dry. Viserra's markings are now gone as if it had never rained.

"You dried the earth, child, and with it, the protection runes were erased."

"Oh—I'm sorry I didn't—"

"Do not be sorry. You harnessed the energy, Kasia. You allowed the connection to form. It worked."

"But the visions I saw... At first, they were good. I saw my mother. She was dancing in a valley of red roses with me in her arms."

"Magic *always* has a balance, Child. With the good, you must also accept the bad. That's enough for today."

"I have to agree with Viserra on that matter," Xerxes adds as he enters the yard. Erebus is with him, and since I'm still sitting on the ground, he wastes no time rushing to my side, nudging me with this large furry snout, his way of checking if I'm alright.

"I'm okay, buddy," I whisper, scratching him behind his ear. He sits down, kicking his leg against the ground as his tongue hangs out the side of his mouth. "What a good boy."

Reaching my side, Xerxes kneels down and wraps me up in his strong arms to cradle me for a moment before he looks over me. Though my hands are free from the mud, my dress is ruined, and my legs are covered in dried earth. "Well, looks like someone needs a bath," he says, kissing my head.

"She did well, Lord," Viserra explains as she gathers her things.

"I never doubted she would. Thank you, Viserra. Truly."

Viserra turns her sights back on me. "Rest. I'll see you tomorrow, bright and early."

"Thank you," I utter as I let myself melt into Xerxes's arms. He turns away from her to carry me back into the palace with Erebus at our side.

"I don't know what happened, little dove. But I felt your distress. You don't have to tell me, but—"

"No," I whisper, cutting him off mid-sentence.

"No?"

"No. It's okay. I want to tell you," I admit truthfully.

"Well, first, you need a bath."

"You mean, *we* need a bath?"

He freezes as the realization of my words hits him. "Is that an invitation?"

"Nope, it's an order. After all, I *am* a Satori. The rightful High Lady of Lethe, right?"

"Well, my lady. However, could I refuse?" he chuckles as he makes his way through the halls, with me tightly curled up in his arms.

Chapter Fifteen
XERXES

It's been weeks since Kasia asked me to return to my own chambers. I have spent weeks sleeping beside her, bedding her whenever I please, yet I still fear it's just a dream every morning I wake next to her. Laying here next to her in bed, I wonder how in the Gods I got so lucky to be bonded to her eternally. As she lies in my arms, completely vulnerable and exposed, I know for certain I have never seen anything more beautiful and serene. Thick eyelashes lay softly closed as she smiles in her sleep. Gently, I brush her starlite like hair from her face, causing her to stir and my breath to hitch in my throat. I don't want her to wake up, not yet. I want to savor her like this.

I've dreamt of this day—this moment. Waking up with her beside me has been something I've always wished for, though I never thought it would actually happen. Especially with how much she fought our bond in the beginning. I don't blame her for it. Her instincts lead her to protect herself in every situation, and while that is a side of her I will always accept, I'm thankful that she's finally seeing how badly I wish to be able to protect her, too. My entire being lives and breathes to ensure no harm comes to her and keep her happy. *I'll do whatever it takes.*

Waking up in my chambers and my bed is another thing I am thankful for this morning. Laying in the moon's glow as it shines through the large cathedral windows of my balcony doors, I welcome its energy against my exposed skin. Though there are preparations to make for when Draven comes through the veil, I find myself unwilling to leave her side. The only thing that forces me to slide my arm out from under her slowly is the fear of losing her. Because Draven *will* come, and I will take *no* chances regarding her safety. Now that I have her, now that I can hold her, there is *nothing* I will not do, no one I will not destroy in order to keep her.

"Do you plan just to lay there and watch me all day?" she whispers as she nuzzles closer to my chest before pressing soft kisses up my neck.

"Why? Does it bother you? Because I can't think of anything better to wake up to."

"I can," she mumbles in the crook of my neck.

"Oh? Well, please... Do tell me, then. What could I be doing that is better than watching you sleep?" I chuckle. My cock hardens as she presses her heat up against my thigh. Lifting her head, she rests her chin on my chest as her minty green eyes lock with mine. This morning, they're sparkling, full of life and happiness. I'll admit it's something I had accepted I'd never see from her, and yet, every day that passes, her guarded walls crumble more, and those eyes show it.

"I can think of many things that are much better than that," she responds.

"That is but your opinion. Mine, however, is slightly different. There is only one thing better than laying here watching you sleep. Only one thing better than knowing you're safe and sound in my arms." She rolls her hips, grinding herself against me.

"And what is that, High Lord?" she purrs.

"Watching you submit to me."

She pauses for a moment before a laugh erupts through her. Lifting her head, she turns her gorgeous smile to me. "I'll never submit to you," she laughs playfully.

Quickly, I flip her over onto her back as my arms suspend me over the top of her. Calling on my wings, they stretch out from my back above us, blocking out the moon's glowing rays. Reaching over my shoulder, I pluck one of the thick black feathers as a grin forms on my face. Below me, Kasia looks entranced yet confused. Her eyes are taking in the sheer size and beauty of my wings.

Taking the delicate feather between my fingers, I brush it along her skin, tracing the curves of her collarbone down to her perky breasts. Softly. Gently. She shudders under the touch as small goosebumps form across her skin.

"You're submitting to me right now," I whisper, lowering my mouth to her pointed ear. I climb off the end of the bed. Kasia pushes herself up to her elbows, curious as to what I'm doing, but before she can object, I grab her ankles and pull her down the bed so her legs hang off the end of the bed. A shocking scream erupts from her, followed by another playful giggle. Kneeling down between her legs, I continue to trace the curves of her body with the feather, circling her breasts and gliding its softness across her peaked nipple. She doesn't fight me. Her breaths begin to come in short and shallow as I tease her.

It slowly glides down her stomach, reaching her hip, where it traces around the wide curve of her hip before reaching her pelvis. Her back arches off the bed as I drag the feather across her heated core, but I don't stop. Not where I know she craves my touch the most. Not yet. The feather glides across it and down her gorgeously toned legs slowly until it reaches the tip of her toe. Dropping the feather, I grab her foot and bring it to my face, where I gently kiss her feet and legs.

"Every fucking inch of you is exquisite, little dove," I whisper, pressing my lips softly against her inner thigh. I settle myself between her legs and look up at her sprawled out on the bed before me. The sight of her alone, white hair that glimmers in the moon's glow fanned out on the bed beneath her. Her milky skin, glowing in the moonlight as soft moans slip from her full lips, has my blood pumping.

"Stop teasing..." she begs, pushing herself up on her elbows. I cock a brow at her, my face nestled between her thighs. The scent of her arousal has my mouth watering.

"I can taste your desire."

"Then stop talking and do something about it," she spits with a coy smile.

"The thing is, while I will never tire of your venomous tongue or the affliction it may bring me, right now, in this moment, you have submitted to me. So, I get to say when we're done, and I'm just beginning. I have dreamt of this moment and everything I want to do to you." Lifting my hand to her core, I press my finger into her dampness slowly. Letting herself fall back into the bed, she whimpers as I ease a finger inside her. Then another, causing her back to arch off the bed and her hands to fist the silk sheets. Her body shudders as I pump them in and out of her, watching from the floor between her legs. I am mesmerized by how her body melts and reacts to my touch.

"Oh Gods..."

"I will never tire of watching you unravel at my hands, little dove. Knowing my touch, my kisses—" I whisper, pressing kisses up her thigh as my fingers continue to slide in and out of her, "can have you begging," I press another soft kiss, higher this time, "and have those sweet sounds slipping from your lips." Another kiss, "Your pleas for more belong to me." Another kiss. "Every whimper—" another kiss, so close to her heat, her scent is intoxicating, "every fucking inch of you... is mine," I growl before replacing my fingers with my mouth.

A rumble echoes from deep in my chest as I lap my tongue through her folds. She tastes decadent, earthy and sweet. Unlike anything I've ever tasted before, but now, having had her, tasted her, I know I'll never stop craving her. She squirms on the edge of the bed, her hands rushing to my head, where she threads her fingers through my hair, gripping it tightly at the root.

"More... Xerxes, I need more," she cries out, pulling my face deeper into her.

"Say it. I want to hear you say it," I mumble against her core. "Say you're mine." I circle my tongue around her swollen clit, watching as she trembles and squirms.

"Yours," she breathes as she nears her first orgasm. Bringing my mouth down on her clit, I suck it into my mouth and watch her inch closer to that edge. Bringing my fingers back to her core, I slide two inside her and curl them slightly.

"Xerxes..."

"Don't be afraid to go over the edge. Soar on those wings, little dove," I whisper before bringing my mouth to her clit once again while my fingers continue to pump in and out of her. A sharp cry of pleasure forms on her lips as her orgasm courses through her body. I pull my fingers from her, running my tongue along her as she rides it out, tasting her, leaving no drop of her precious juices behind. *Mine.*

When she comes down from the high, I rise to my knees between her legs. Her ass hangs off the edge of the bed, her legs spread open and wide before me. I allow myself a moment to take in the sight of her swollen core and how it glistens in the moonlight for me. Suddenly, her foot is rubbing along my hardened shaft, drawing my attention. I grin, lifting my eyes to hers. She sucks her plump lip into her mouth, biting down on it with her tiny Fae fangs with anticipation.

"Are you just going to stand there, or are you going to fuck me, *High Lord*?" she asks with a frivolous tone before her eyes return to where she's running her foot up and down my cock.

"You know... We could've been doing this for months if you'd been less difficult."

"No."

"No?" I ask, my lips pulling into a smile.

"I didn't even like you until hmm...let me think..." she explains, scanning the ceiling with her eyes. "Ah, yes. Until I saw how big your cock was."

"Oh, is that so?" I reply, gripping my cock tightly in my hand. I stroke it slowly, watching her eyes as they follow my hands' movement. "And just what is it about my *big cock,* that you love so much?" I whisper as I line its tip up at her opening. Her body stills, her eyes glazed over with hunger as she watches eagerly awaiting.

Holding my cock firmly in my hand, I swirl the tip around her opening. Beads of precum leak out, mixing with her arousal as I spread it around her. Slowly, I push the tip inside her, a low hiss slipping from my lips as her tightness squeezes my cock.

"All of it," she whispers as another soft moan escapes her. I come undone. Losing all control as I thrust into her hard and fast.

With each thrust, I'm drawn to be deeper inside her, like our bond is almost punishing me with how good she feels wrapped around me. She quivers, wrapping her legs around my body and pulling me into her.

"Fuck..." I hiss as she clamps down around me. The sounds of our flesh coming together echoes around our chamber, the bed shaking with our movement. I bet every Fae for miles around can hear us, hear her, but I don't care. She is mine, and I am hers, and at this moment, nothing else matters. The bond connecting us hums under my skin as our bodies come together in a fit of passion and longing.

"Harder. Gods yes!"

"There are no Gods here, little dove." I answer as I pound into her, "Just you and me, and it is my name you will cry out for while I'm inside you." Suddenly, her hands are on her breast, squeezing and pinching her peaked nipples.

"Xerxes..." I look down on her as I bring my thumb to my mouth, licking it before I lower it to her swollen clit. Circling it, I grind my hips, thrusting myself deep inside of her. Bending over, I bring my mouth to her ear, running my tongue along its pointed tip.

"Fuck, that's it, Kasia. Look how well you submit for me."

"Oh yes..." With that, she finds her second release, taking me over the edge with her. My cock pulses in the deepest part of her, pumping her full of my warm seed. A guttural growl vibrates through my chest as I empty myself inside her, my body collapsing over the top of hers on the edge of the bed. Our breaths are short and shallow, and our bodies glisten in a layer of sweat. We lay there for a few moments, catching our breaths as our hearts race and our bond hums with content.

Pushing off her, I look down on her glorious body, flushed and ravished in the moonlight. Every inch of her smells like mine, and I can't help but grin.

"Come," I whisper, taking her hand and pulling her off the bed. "Let's get you cleaned up." I guide her through the bedroom, over our discarded clothes from the night before, and into the large bathing chamber. Reaching into my well of magic, I summon a tether of moonlight in my hand and toss it into the air above the bath's steaming waters. The tether breaks apart, shattering into tiny specks of glowing moonlight that float above the bath like tiny stars.

"What are they?" she asks, her eyes sparkling as she looks up at them, mesmerized by their beauty. I chuckle.

"Think of them like tiny specks of dust, but each one holds some of the moon's energy, allowing them to glow."

"They're beautiful," she whispers.

"They are, but their beauty is unmatched when it comes to yours," I reply. She snaps her eyes to mine, releasing my hand as a soft smile forms on her face. She steps into the steaming waters and submerges herself to her shoulders with a sigh. Grabbing the vials of oil and soap from the table, I follow her into the water. Floral-scented steam rises into the air of the room, instantly relaxing me.

Finding a seat along the ledge, I sit down and place the vials on the side of the tub before pulling a giggling Kasia to sit on my lap, where we soak for a few minutes, welcoming the relief on our sore muscles that the heat provides us. I grab the bottle of lavender soap from the side of the tub and pour some of the liquid into my hands before massaging it into her thick, white hair. She melts into my touch as I wash her. As the suds slide down her hair and onto her back, I work my way down, massaging the soap into her scared back and shoulders.

She moans and sighs as I work her tense muscles with the suds of lavender soap, her cute little ass grinding against my lap. Slowly, she spins around to face me, her eyes glazed with lust as she straddles my lap and wraps her arms around my neck. Her eyes scan my face as she brushes loose strands of damp hair from my forehead. She rocks her hips against me. Her core rubbing against my hardening shaft below the water's surface.

"Kasia..." I hiss, gripping her thighs. "This is a dangerous game you're playing, little dove."

She leans forward, bringing her lips to my ear. "I've never been one to run from danger," she whispers with a heated breath against the shell of my ear.

My cock pulses. *This woman is going to be the death of me.* I smirk, ready to give in to her temptations, when suddenly a knock on the door of our room meets my ears. *Fuck.*

"Mate... Mate, I know you're in there, and normally I wouldn't be one too well... interrupt..., but I'm afraid I have to this time. Nefeli is here, and she has word about the camp at the veil." Orion explains from the other side of the thick door.

I growl, which only causes Kasia to grind her hips against me harder. Her pussy glides over my shaft beneath the water as she looks at me coyly. What have I gotten myself into? The feel of her against me is driving me mad, and it takes everything in me not to slide myself inside her and let her ride me over the edge all over again.

"Xerxes...this can't wait," he adds. I can tell by his tone he's serious. There is no humor in his voice.

"I have to go. If Orion thinks it can't wait until we're finished, it must be important."

Her playful smile is quickly replaced with a stern and serious expression."Who is Nefeli?"

"Nefeli is Queen of Culzean. She rules over the Centaurs that live in the Somnia Forest. When word spread of your arrival here, she met with me, and together, we set up the camp at the veil."

"Do you think something is wrong? At the veil, I mean..." she asks, slowly climbing from my lap.

"I'm not sure, but I need to find out," I reply.

She tenses, and her head fills with thoughts of Draven. Concern paints her face as she worries about whether or not it's possible he's here. Gripping her chin in my hand, I force her face to mine. "Do not worry, little dove. You are safe here. I will die before Draven *ever* gets his hands on you." I bring my lips to hers, parting her lips with a fierce stroke of my tongue. The kiss is hard and demanding, causing a shudder to rock through her. I smile, breaking the kiss and pressing a soft kiss to her forehead. "Finish your bath and rest. I'm not done with you today." I smirk as I make my way out of the bath.

"I'm not worried," she spits with that tongue I love so much. But she is, even if she won't admit it. "When— when will you be back?"

"As quickly as I can. I promise," I answer, allowing myself one last quick glance over my shoulder.

Every fiber of me wants to stay, wants to tell Orion to fuck off and to leave me with my bonded. But I know I can't. If he's risking interrupting us, then something big has happened, and I need to meet with Nefeli to find out what it is without causing Kasia to worry. Erebus, who has spent all morning lying on his bed, lifts his head as I enter the bedroom. "Stay with her today." He quickly sits up, his tail wagging as he barks loudly before heading towards the bathing chamber.

Quickly, I pull on my fighting leathers and tie my wet hair up behind my head. My heart races with anticipation of what Nefeli could be here to tell me. A mix of fear and anger coils in my stomach as I exit my room, finding Orion waiting outside.

"Sorry mate, I didn't want to bother you, but it isn't good."

"It's fine, where is she?"

"In the courtyard," he explains as we walk through the halls. "He's here," Orion says with a hushed tone. I don't even need to ask who he means. His words hit me like an arrow through the heart.

"He will not have her, Orion. I will die before he even lays eyes on her," I seethe.

My tone does little to hide my aggression. I turn my eyes to him, and without him muttering a word, I know he has my back.

"No, he won't. I'll meet you in the courtyard. I need to find Senna," he adds, clicking his jaw. Offering him a nod, I watch as he heads back into the palace, searching for my sister. He's clearly as affected by the news as I am, and I know without a doubt that he will happily die by my side if it means protecting Calanthe and those we love, and I *love* Kasia.

Chapter Sixteen

KASIA

Instantly, I feel his absence. The warmth of him that I have come to treasure the last few weeks. Erebus lies beside the large granite bath next to me. The glowing shards of moonlight still linger in the air above my head. They're beautiful; I've come to view each kind of magic, including mine, to be beautiful in its own way. I've also grown used to the night, and although it may remain dark, there is light everywhere you look in Calanthe: the stars, the plants, even my bonded. Thoughts of him bring a smile to my face. We've grown closer as the days have passed in more ways than one.

He's told me of our childhood, and in return, I have told him of my visions, the fragments of memories as they come, with hopes that he can explain them to me. Fill in the blanks and help me understand what I'm seeing. It took a while, but finally, I was able to remember him as a child—Orion, as well, who was just as comical as a child as he is now. I remember the way they picked on me and the way his whiskey-brown eyes would twinkle when he'd pretend he didn't like me chasing after him. I've learned to trust him and with more than just my memories. I trust him with my heart. My life.

It's like I just know he'd never hurt me. Xerxes says he would do anything to keep me safe, and I know he means it. I can feel it. Erebus nudges me with this snout—his way of forcing me to get out of my head. I finish washing, ringing the oils from my hair, and the soap from my skin before I leave the bath. Leaving wet footprints across the marble floor, I grab the thick fur robe from the hook by the door, wrapping it around myself as I enter the bedroom.

The room feels empty without him here, though his rainstorm scent still lingers in the air. Erebus is close behind me, unwilling to let me out of his sight as I reach the wardrobe. Scouring the gowns Glinda had made for me after I finally had the chance to meet her, I pull out a wine-red one with pops of pine green. It's a mix of fine silk and tulle that makes up the skirt. Sliding into it, I make my way over to the full-length mirror. It's beautiful, but what shocks me is my own reflection. I've put on weight since being in Calanthe. My face has filled out and grown a rosy-pink shade across my cheeks. I look healthy and happy. I turn around, pulling my hair over my shoulder to check my back in the mirror. The dress hangs low on my back, revealing my scars to anyone who looks, but I'm okay with that. I wear them proudly, not caring who may see them.

Erebus heads out to the large balcony off the side of our chambers excitedly like he sees something. I follow, curious as to what's drawn his attention. Once outside, the cool breeze hits my skin, carrying the loud crashing sound of the Arachai waves hitting the rocks below. The dense Somnia Forest surrounds the palace, and from up here, not a speck of the light I know to be within it can be seen. The crescent moon shines high in the sky, casting its energy-filling glow over Calanthe.

Though I miss Lethe, I must admit the beauty of Calanthe is unlike anything I'd ever dreamed of. It gives me hope. I hope that Xerxes and Viserra are right, and I could be the key to breaking the curse over Lethe, freeing it from the never-ending winter. I can't help but wonder what beauty it holds underneath the decades of ice and snow.

The cool night air blows past me again, bringing with it the familiar floral scent of Somnia. But that isn't the only thing it carries this time. A moth makes its way over. With one injured wing, it relies on the wind to push it through the air. Cupping my hands, I quickly reach out, placing them under the small creature, giving it a safe place to land. It's weightless, almost like I'm holding a feather, as its tiny legs grip my palm. One of its large, dusted wings hangs off his back to the side. With an injury like this one, he won't last long.

"Look at you," I whisper softly as he walks along my hand. "Broken and scarred, just like me." Though I have a lot more training and much to learn about my magic, something inside me pulls. There's this need to help the moth. It's like he came to me because he knew I could. "Let's see what I can do, okay?"

Cupping my hands around him, I'm careful not to squish him as I reach into my magic the way Viserra taught me. It was ready and waiting as though it knew the moth needed my help. It vibrates through me, and a familiar sensation shoots down my back as my wings make their second appearance. The wind rips around me, grazing my feathered wings as I turn my focus back on the moth. I close my eyes, willing his wing to heal. Willing his pain to be gone as I picture him soaring high in the night sky. The vibrations stop, the wind calms, and I swallow, afraid yet excited to open my hands.

Parting them slowly, I peek inside, only to have the moth flutter out, with both his wings healed as they carry him through the night air. I did it. I'm shocked and cannot do anything but stand there for a moment, silent, as I realize that not only did I heal the moth, but I controlled my magic.

I watch the moth fly about in the air above the balcony, and slowly, he's joined by more moths until there are so many that I cannot count them. They surround me, fluttering about in the air above where I stand. Some of them land around me, on me. Erebus jumps up, resting his paws on the balcony railing as he barks at them excitedly.

My stomach growls—a reminder that, thanks to Xerxes, I have yet to have breakfast. Not that I'm complaining. It was well worth it. I watch as the group of moths fly away, back down to the safety of the Somnia Forest, before I head back inside. Reaching the table, I realize Agatha hasn't brought any food today. I chuckle. I don't blame her. She probably made it as far as the door before she heard us and figured it would be better if she returned later. Erebus reaches my side, where he sits down, cocking his head to the side as he looks at me.

"Hungry boy?"

He answers with a loud bark, and I smile.

"Alright, let's go find some food then. Lead the way to the kitchen." Excitedly, he rushes to the door, and I chase after him. The halls are packed with servants and court members going about their days. Some are cleaning; others are moving things around, no doubt in preparation for the very thing I dread—Draven's arrival. I don't know what's worse. Not knowing when he will come, or knowing that his arrival means danger for this place and its people whom I've come to adore. It means danger for the man I've grown to trust. I know that Xerxes wants to protect me, but how can I sit in this palace, hiding while innocent people die to keep me hidden?

I follow Erebus through the halls and down a narrow stairwell, continuing until a delightful smell hits my nose. Turning the corner, we end up in a large, open room full of ovens and roaring fires with large pots of broth suspended above them to simmer. The air is hot and filled with a sweet, fruity scent that has my mouth watering. Senna and Orion stand on either side of a large table in the center of the room while the cooks continue to work around them. They're clearly having a disagreement about what I don't know, but the tension in the room is smothering. Orion had his wings out today, which is odd. Rarely do Calanthians walk around with their wings out. I can't imagine why. They're beautiful. Rows of thick black feathers that glint in the moonlight. Xerxes' are of the darkest shade of black, Orion's are a bit lighter, almost like charcoal with a mix of ash.

Agatha offers me a quaint nod as I enter the room with Erebus at my side, but when Senna and Orion notice me, they go silent. Their bodies relax as though they're trying to act like nothing's wrong. Assuming it was just some lovers' quarrel, I push it to the back of my mind, eager to get my hands on whatever smells so delicious.

"Well, I didn't expect to see you out and about today, little birdie," Orion chimes, crossing his arms across his chest as he leans against the large wooden table. Though his tone is humorous, it's clear he is distressed. His expression does little to hide it. Lifting a brow, I smirk at him.

"Am I expected to starve then?"

"Oh! Lady, I did come to—"

"Agatha, it's fine." I chuckle, "I'm capable of getting my own food. After all, you have enough to do. What is it that smells *so* divine?"

"Ah," Senna answers as she grabs a plate from the counter behind her. "That would be Mr. Tam's muffins. They're a favorite here: oats, apples, and honey!" She holds the plate out for me to grab one. Picking it up, I bring it to my nose, inhaling its sweet scent before taking a bite. It's fluffy and still warm inside as it melts in my mouth. "Good, right?" she says, placing the plate back. "There's a reason he's famous for them."

Her eyes move from me to Orion in a tense look that exchanges silent words, and I find myself unable to ignore it any longer. "What's going on?"

"Nothing for you to worry about," Orion quickly replies. Senna rolls her eyes, clearly unimpressed with his response.

"Orion, I know you seem to think you have this charm about you, but you really suck at lying. I have met children who can hide the truth better than you, so tell me... What is going on?"

"Xerxes will explain when he gets back, okay?" Senna whispers. Her tone is laced with concern, but I can tell she's doing her best to reassure me. My thoughts trail back to my morning with him and how he was pulled away for something important.

"Does it have to do with the meeting with Nefeli? With Draven?" I ask. Fear builds in the pit of my stomach as they exchange another look, but my question goes unanswered. My magic vibrates under my skin. I remember Viserra's training and do my best to push it back down. *Breathe. Just Breathe.* But it proves to be useless. Knowing Xerxes could be in danger right now and those I've come to trust are keeping me from the truth, I grow angry. Annoyed. "Fine. I'll find out myself since you all want to keep me in the dark."

I storm off, heading right and left down halls I don't recognize, not caring where I'm headed so long as it's away from them. I keep walking until the halls grow colder and darker, and the sounds of the everyday chaos seem to disappear completely. Only then do I stop. Only then do I allow myself to release the breath I didn't know I was holding in. My chest rises and falls as I lean against the cold stone wall. My eyes flutter closed as thoughts of Xerxes fill my head. His eyes and the way they shine in the moonlight. His rainstorm scent as he wraps me in his strong, warm arms. I focus on my breathing, willing myself to calm down, to get a grip on the vibrations of my magic that begs to be released.

Erebus lays at my feet with a small whimper, clearly sensing my distress. When the vibrations of my magic finally calm, along with my quickened breaths, I hear something. Furrowing my brow, I turn my head towards the passages the sound is coming from, unsure if my ears are playing tricks on me. The echo of someone grunting fills the air again, igniting my curiosity. Silently, I head down the passageway carrying the sound, careful not to make a noise. It grows louder and more frequent by the minute, letting me know I'm getting closer. But it's when I turn that final corner that my heart stops. My breath catches in my throat as I lay eyes on Xerxes with a woman I don't recognize, her body pinned against the wall while he thrusts into her.

Luminescent patches of scales glimmer in the light radiating off the small sconces on the wall next to them. Long, thick. black braids cascade down her shoulder and around her face. She moans, her head smacking against the stone wall behind her as he fucks her roughly. Unable to move, to speak, I stand there watching. Watching the man, I thought I could trust betray me. Each pleasure-filled cry. Each echoing smack of flesh on flesh as he buries himself inside her are blades through my tender heart. I stand there, unable to force myself to move or tear my eyes off the scene before me.

Suddenly her eyes open and lock with mine. Her lips pull into a malicious grin as she takes him. All the while knowing I'm there watching. My magic vibrates, its intensity growing quicker than before, but finally giving me the push I need to get out of there. I run back through the maze of dark and unfamiliar passages, with Erebus following close behind me. I trip on the gown, falling to the cold hard ground. Sobs threaten to escape me, and the dress tears up my thigh as I push myself to my feet, but I don't care. My scraped knees burn, but I ignore it. I don't stop. Not until I reach our chambers and the door is locked tightly behind me.

Only then do I allow myself to feel. To fall apart. With my back pressed tightly against the door, I collapse to the floor. My body trembles uncontrollably, and tears begin to spill from my eyes. But instead of wondering how he could do this to me, I wonder how I could be so stupid. So stupid to believe he would be any different from the men I've known in my life. To think he could genuinely care for me. I'm nothing more than a bargaining chip. A means to end the curse in Lethe. An easy fuck.

My mind spins as everything that's been said or done the last few weeks since my arrival replays repeatedly. Every moment shared with Xerxes, the way being with him felt. Every gentle touch, kiss, and moment where he had me believing the poisonous words he fed me like some foolish girl. He played me with my own trick. Though I may still be alive, here I sit, alone in my room, wishing for death to come and find me.

Chapter Seventeen

XERXES

The tension in the courtyard is thick as I head outside. I find the moon nearly full against the starlit sky and Nefeli pacing back and forth, clearly distraught with the news she bares. The air is cold and heavy on the lungs tonight. Though the moon's energy soaks into my skin as it refills my well of magic, I can't shake the gut-wrenching feeling of unease that builds inside me. My guards line the walls of the courtyard, ensuring no one enters or leaves without being seen. A precaution was set up for many reasons, mainly to ensure Kasia is safe.

I nod as I pass Gage and Ron, crossing the open space as I approach the Centaur. When she hears me approach, she rushes to my side. Her long red hair is disheveled, and tears streak her cheeks, but it's the blood painting her strong, fur-covered legs that draws my attention.

"Xerxes," she shouts frantically. "We need to go. Now. The men—they have called for aid."

I quickly search her for a wound, thinking the blood is hers. "What has happened, Nefeli?"

"Drake," she mutters. "He entered through the veil in the night, backed with double the men that our camp held. There are more that enter through the veil hourly. Xerxes, it is a massacre. The men do not have the numbers to hold Drake back. One of my guards was injured but escaped and was able to warn me."

"Where is he? I'd like to speak with him, perhaps get some insight on what we're heading into."

"He passed shortly after he arrived in Culzean. His injuries were extensive, and he got to us too late. However, before he passed, he mentioned in grave detail the bloodshed," she sobs. "Xerxes, I fear we may be too late as it is. We must make haste."

"I am sorry for your loss. He was a brave man indeed to give his life in order to warn us. He shall not be forgotten, Nefeli," I whisper, placing a hand on her shoulder for comfort.

So, this is it. I knew this day would come. I knew Draven would come looking for her; we all did. However, I didn't expect him to send his son in his stead. I thought he would have the balls to come for her. Today, Drake brought war to my realm at his father's command.

Regardless, today, *he* began shedding Calanthian blood, which will not go unpunished.

"Gage." I shout, cracking my neck.

"Yes, Lord," he responds, rushing from his post to my side.

"Gather our best man. The encampment at the veil calls for aid, and we shall answer."

"Right away," he whispers something to the other guards stationed around the courtyard before taking two of them and heading toward the barracks.

"What if we're too late?"

"I pray we are not. Though Drake will suffer for his crimes regardless," I seethe through tightly clenched teeth.

"Something has changed," she whispers, eyeing me. I release a breath. From her thoughts, I know that she means between Kasia and me. Though I always would've given my life to keep her safe, it's different now. Our bond is sealed. She is mine, and I am hers. Nothing and no one will come between that. "You love her."

"I always have."

"Yes, but not like this. This is different than when we last met."

"She is unlike anyone I have ever met," I reply with a hushed tone.

"Hold her close, Xerxes. Especially now. She is the only hope for Lethe—for all of us."

"Don't worry, Nefeli. Kasia has been through enough in her life. I will never let another touch her."

She smiles, a brief relief from the pain she feels so intensely from the loss of her people. "I do not doubt that, friend," she replies.

Gage returns with a group of men; some ride on horseback next to Nefeli while others have their wings out, ready to soar the skies. They will arrive faster than those on foot and be able to provide help faster. With any luck, there will still be some left alive. I turn, giving Nefeli my back in an effort to hide my anger as I focus my attention on the men before me. Men with families, with wives and children. Men I could be sending to their deaths.

"When you leave these grounds, you report to Nefeli. Whatever she says, goes. She is your commander until I arrive," I explain to the lineup of men that Gage had gathered to take. They all reply with a nod, knowing better than to question my command.

"Let us go. Time is of the essence," Nefeli says from behind me.

Turning, I bid her farewell and watch as my men head off to battle behind her. My fists clench at my sides as I storm off towards the barracks. But as I make my way through the courtyard and past the stables, someone's thoughts grow with intensity, making it impossible for me not to read them. *Nymeria.*

I freeze in place as visions of her pinned against a wall fill my head. Not those visions or the fact that I'm fucking her that have me enraged. It's the look in Kasia's eyes when she sees me. When she sees who she believes me to be. Her heartbreak and disbelief shine through her minty green eyes just before she runs off. Nymeria giggles as she slowly approaches me from her hiding place in the shadows, clearly proud of herself and the pain her little game has caused Kasia. A wicked grin forms on her face as she reaches my side; it takes everything in me not to strike her down.

"My, my. It appears *someone* is angry this evening," she hisses, circling me as she begins trailing her elongated nails gently across my chest. My blood boils beneath my skin. I knew Nymeria wouldn't just let it go. "Pathetic. Look at you. All mighty Xerxes worked up over some *nobody.* Some Lethian whore," she spits.

Quickly, I catch her off guard, gripping her by the throat as I slam her against the smooth stone wall of the courtyard. My chest rises and falls with panted breaths of fury as I glare at her. A vindictive laugh erupts through her. "What's wrong, Lord? Did my thoughts have you wanting to recreate the little show I put on for your precious *Kasia*?" she whispers with a seductive tone as her tongue darts out to run across her lips.

With my hand clasped tightly around her frail throat, I lift her off the wall before slamming her head back into it. She cries out in pain before more laughter erupts through her. She knows she's getting to me. I'm falling right into her trap. Kasia's heartbreak finally makes its way through the bond. The betrayal she feels for something this scum has her believing I committed.

"You will pay for your crimes, Nymeria. I warned you to stay away from her."

"Oh, but Lord. I was just having a bit of fun with your new toy. She is so fragile. Poor thing. You should've seen the pain reflected in her eyes. It was just that look that sent me over the edge. She did it to herself, really," she chokes out as my grip tightens around her throat. "I did not make her stay and watch, but she did. She watched you take me in those passages, in all the ways she probably won't let you take her." A growl rips through me as I slam her head against the wall harder. Blood trickles down her neck from the back of her head, but she doesn't stop laughing.

"I will end you for what you have done."

"Not tonight, though," she replies, eyeing me coyly. "How quickly you forget you have dying men waiting for your arrival. If anything, I did the realm a favor tonight." Her words sink in. In my rage, I've completely forgotten Nefeli and the men waiting on me. But how can I rush to their aid when Kasia's pain radiates through me? Igniting every fiber of my being to rush to her side to explain what she thinks she saw. Nymeria cants her head to the side as a wide grin forms on her face with the realization of my internal battle. "So, whose side will you rush to on this night? Your men and the safety of Calanthe, or your heartbroken woman?" she questions as she laughs.

A roar rips through me as I release her, retreating to the middle of the courtyard where I pace, contemplating my options. I want to kill her, to shed every drop of her siren blood so that it floods the courtyard ground. But she's right. Nefeli and the men are counting on my arrival, and yet I'm torn. Kasia's pain is so strong. The level to which she feels betrayed is gut-wrenching, and my bond begs me to rush to her side to mend the heartache she feels. Gripping the pommel of the blade at my hip tightly, I unsheathe it, pointing its tip towards Nymeria. She smirks, a look of disbelief forming on her face as she steps closer to me.

"Take another step, siren, and I will end you here and now," my voice echoes off the walls of the courtyard. Her smile grows, and her body sways as she takes another step towards me.

"No, Lord. You won't. We both know you won't. You're angry, but we both know you won't kill an unarmed woman. Not here, not in the middle of your courtyard for everyone to see," she purrs, taking another step forward. I turn away from her, willing myself to calm down. "You, Xerxes, are too much of a coward. Your subjects would not approve of such an act, and they're opinion means far too—" her voice stops mid-sentence. Then, there is silence before the thudding sound of something falling hits me. Spinning around, I find Nymeria dead, with an arrow straight through her eye.

"She said you wouldn't end her, but she didn't say anything about me." Senna shrugs from the balcony above. "Besides, if she messed with Kasia, she got what she deserved, and your people will understand and respect that. Now go, Nefeli needs you." I pause for a moment. I find myself in complete awe of the ruthlessness of my little sister, but I am also thankful.

"I need to see Kasia first. She needs to know it wasn't me she saw, Senna. The pain, *her* pain. It's eating me alive, I can't... I can't go into battle like this."

"I will take care of Kasia, Brother. Orion is already on his way over there, and if you let him die, I swear to the Gods, your eye will be my next target. You know better than anyone that I never miss." Fuck. I contemplate leaving her, and though every part of me tells me to stay and run to my bonded, I know I have to go. I cannot let Drake take control of the veil. Kasia would be furious with me if I put her before them. At least, that's what I tell myself.

"Fine, but Senna... Make sure she knows, please. I would never betray her that way. I..." I choke out, not wanting to say the words for the first time to someone other than Kasia. Senna looks down at me from the balcony. Her long auburn hair blows in the wind as she nods her head at me.

"I know, Xerxes. I know. Now go. I swear to you, I will look after her."

I turn my focus back to the lifeless siren on the ground before summoning my wings and taking off into the night sky. Pain radiates in my chest as I force myself to leave my bonded when I know she is hurting, but I bury it down. I can explain to her later. Senna will make sure she knows. Her pain will end, but the same cannot be said for the men under attack at the veil.

LOOMING HIGH ABOVE THE VEIL, the scent of blood is heavy in the air, which isn't a good sign. It's silent. My ears are met with no screaming or shouting, and though I have a clear view of the veil, I can see no movement. Corpses litter the forest floor. Death is everywhere you look. Limbs torn from bodies; the natural beauty of the glowing forest foliage hidden behind a coating of freshly spilled blood. Everywhere you look, there are bodies: Lethian, Centaurs, and even my own men. I'm too late. My anger grows as I reach the ground, careful not to tread on any of the fallen. I can see the piles of bodies with my eyes, and my magic hums beneath my skin, but when I lay eyes on a familiar Centaur with long red hair, I pause, and my rage begins to mix with guilt.

I said we would face them together, and we didn't. She died thinking I abandoned her—a failed promise from my lips because of my rage. My fists clench at my sides as I reach her side. Her throat is slit, her once radiant glow dimmed to a ghostly shade of grey as she lays in a pool of her own crimson blood. My body grows cold, and my heart stops at the sight of my friend lying lifeless on the forest floor. Lifting my trembling hand, I run it along the soft hide of her leg. My jaw ticks as a roar rips through my chest, echoing around the forest.

"They didn't stand a chance," Orion says with a tender tone as he approaches from behind me. The guilt he feels is overwhelming. His thoughts are full of frustration and rage for the lives lost in senseless bloodshed. "Drake's men had already taken out the rest of the encampment before Nefeli arrived. They were expecting them and took them out in minutes. I—" he chokes out as he kneels down beside Nefeli's corpse. "I couldn't save them, Xerxes. I couldn't save her..."

"She wouldn't have wanted you to anyways. Nefeli was brave, and she wouldn't have wanted your life to be taken to save hers," I explain with a sorrow-filled tone as I lay my hand on his shoulder in understanding. Tearing his eyes from her, he stands as we approach the veil. I find myself forced to face my own words. However, they don't replace the anger I feel for Drake or the pain I feel for knowing I could have saved them. Nefeli would not have wanted me to be here, not if it was a trap.

"Well, that we can agree on. Though I'm not surprised. Centaurs may be savages, but they're stubborn as hell and so fucking sacrificial," a deep voice echoes from the shadows of the forest. "She wouldn't tell me a damn thing about that bonded of yours or where I might find her," Drake spits as he steps from the shadows and into the open.

The moonlight shines off the blood-free patches of his silver chest plate as he runs his hand through his golden hair. A coy smile forms on his lips as he reaches Nefeli's body and kneels beside it. Pulling a small blade from his belt, using the tip to brush the blood-matted hair from Nefeli's face. "Pity, though. Nothing beats taming a good-looking mare; this one was a beauty."

"You won't get near her," I spit aggressively. Orion steps closer to me as a show of support. He has my back. But behind Drake, at least fifty men mimic Orion's gesture, bringing themself to stand behind the false prince of Lethe.

"No? So, you like seeing your friends cut down, then? Because that is what will happen if you don't bring her to me," Drake replies. "I will slaughter every person in this realm, one by one if that is what it takes to get her. So, the choice is yours."

I don't reply, allowing myself a moment to take in the area around us as I watch Drake's men circle around behind us. "The realm won't go down without a fight, mate. I think you underestimate the support the realm will offer to keep the Satori Heir alive and out of your or your father's reach," Orion counters, never breaking eye contact with Drake. Drake laughs, holding his arms up to his men.

"Funny, is he not?" he expresses, encouraging his men to laugh along with him. "Tell me, Xerxes. What means more to you? Your realm and its people? Or your pretty little lost heir? Because you will not keep them both. However, I will allow you till tomorrow to decide. If Kasia is not handed over to me by tomorrow night, I will bring war to Calanthe and take her. Even if that means prying her from your cold, dead arms as she scratches and screams, *Lord*."

"Bring your army. I will not let you take her," I growl.

"No one will let you take her. You will have to go through every soul in Calanthe to get her," Orion adds.

"Well then. This was a fun conversation," he says with a sardonic laugh as he signals for his men to back away from us. He turns to return to the veil but stops, spinning to face us once more. "One last question, Lord. Since then, I have found myself curious about the matter. Your bonded—is she a scratcher or a biter?" he questions. The fury within me grows as his thoughts move to Kasia in an attempt to envision what she may look like, *feel like*. How good it would feel to take her from me, to ruin her. "No matter. I rather like a good surprise, anyway. Tomorrow, Xerxes. Or I will burn Calanthe to the ground and slaughter everyone in my path," he adds as he turns to make his way back to the veil.

"Mate..." Orion whispers, clearly sensing how ready I am to implode.

"Let's go. I will send some men to retrieve the bodies of the fallen," I reply. My wings beat rapidly through the tension-filled air, before I push off the ground, taking off into the air. The cool breeze against my skin does little to calm my nerves. I wanted to strike him down. I should've, but deep down, I know it would solve nothing. Drake's death won't keep Draven from coming for her. From coming for what belongs to me.

"You have to tell her, Xerxes."

"There is much I need to tell her tonight," I reply. As we soar through the starlit sky, I'm more eager than ever to return to Eventide. To her. I need to explain what happened with both Nymeria and Drake. Most importantly, though, I need to know she is safe that the pain caused by Nymeria is gone. I can only hope that Senna has at least been able to explain some of it to her. Once I know she's okay, I can prepare for tomorrow's battle.

"Go away, Xerxes" she shouts through sobbing cries. Her tone is laced with the heart felt pain that radiates through our bond.

"Little dove, please. You have to know I would never—"

"Leave me alone!"

It's been well over an hour since my return, and still nothing. Though Senna spoke to her, she refuses believe it wasn't me she witnessed tonight with Nymeria. I can't blame her. Siren illusions are powerful, and can be very realistic if the siren casting them is talented enough. Nymeria, well, she's an expert at them. For the first time in my life I feel completely helpless. How can I get her to believe me if she won't even let me in?

"Kasia, *please,*" I sigh, bringing my fists down on the thick wooden door one last time. No response. Just silence from the other side. "Let me in. Let me explain." With my fists on the door, I sink to my knees, resting my forehead on the smooth oak in defeat. I've known plenty of pain in my life, but nothing compares to being shut out by my bonded. Feeling her pain through the bond has me in a chokehold. *I need to get to her. I need her to understand.*

Chapter Eighteen

KASIA

The continuous sound of pounding fists against the thick wooden door wakes me. I push myself up, forcing my dried eyes open. They sting and burn as they adjust to the light of the room. They're irritated and sore from the hours I spent sobbing. The banging continues, louder with each fist that slams down, shaking the door in its hinges. The night replays in my head. Remembering my conversation with Senna and how she explained everything about Nymeria and her tricks. How Xerxes would never betray me.

"Kasia, I know we haven't had much time to get to know one another, but you have to know I would never lie to you. Not about this," she explains, her sincerity laced in her words. "You are everything to my brother, and Nymeria knows that. It's why she did what she did." Senna stands behind me. With my head resting on my crossed arms on

the flat surface of my vanity, I can see her reflection in my mirror from the corner of my eye, but I don't lift my head. The last thing I want is for her to witness me in a moment of weakness.

"I hear what you're saying, Senna, but I saw them. I saw him. With her."

"What you saw wasn't real! It was nothing more than a siren trick. It's how they lure fishermen to the depths, and Nymeria is one of the best when it comes to illusions. Xerxes would never do that to you."

I know shes right. In my heart I know Xerxes would never betray me. He'd never hurt me, not like this. Through the bond I can feel his fear. His pain, and yet, it does not ease the pain I feel. It does not erase the images of him and her from my thoughts. My heart and my head are at war with each other, untrusting and unsure of what to believe.

"At least let him explain when he returns. Please..." she pleads, gently placing a hand on my shoulder.

"I—I don't know if I can," I admit. Trusting is hard for me as is, and though I hear her words and appreciate her effort, this is something I need to figure out on my own.

The knocking pulls me from the internal war taking place within me. I know there is truth to her words, yet my eyes saw it. Clearly.

I saw the look in Nymeria's eyes as he had her pinned against the wall, thrusting into her with the fury and hunger I've experienced from him when we're together—heard the familiar sounds of a man I trusted. A man whom I had allowed myself to open up to about things I'd never told anyone. How could it all have been a lie? Letting myself fall back to the soft mattress, I pull my hands over my ears to block out the sound. Tears I didn't know that I possessed had begun to leak from my eyes and down my flushed cheeks. My head throbs and the pounding fist on the door only grows louder. I know he's out there. I know my pain is causing him pain. I can *feel* it. He's distraught, angry– but it's more than that. For the first time, I can sense his fear. Though, I can't imagine what it is that he has to be fearful of.

"Kasia, *please*," he shouts, with a pleading tone. "Let me in. Let me explain."

I don't respond, struggling to find the willpower to bring myself to speak so much as a whisper as the pain of his betrayal radiates through my heart. How could I be so stupid? I knew this would happen. You could even say I expected it. Years spent guarding my heart to avoid this very moment, this pain I've watched countless other women suffer. Yet, I still allowed myself to fall for him. For the first time, I allowed myself to be vulnerable. Simply because once, a *very* long time ago, we knew each other. *Foolish*. Another sob escapes me, and this time, the sound of my own whimper meets my ears. The banging has stopped.

Did he leave?

Did he give up?

My breath catches in my throat as I fly off the bed with the fear that he has left. I don't know why I care if he did. He hurt me. He betrayed me in the worst way a man could. Regardless, I find that I am still drawn to him. Regardless of what happened or *didn't* happen, according to Senna, I still have these feelings—this pull to him. I stand there for a moment. The stone tiles of the floor are cold under my bare feet as I contemplate the abundance of the new and confusing feelings now coursing through me. I know he didn't do it. I know he *wouldn't*. But I saw it, I saw him. I heard him.

Placing my hands on my head, I shake it slightly and silently beg it all to stop. Beg to go back to where we were this morning, where he held me in the safety of his arms. Where he kneeled in front of me, devouring every last drop of me with that Godsdamn mouth of his.

Footsteps pull me from my thoughts. As I turn my head towards them, I find Xerxes making his way towards me. His eyes are sad and lackluster, their usual glow missing. He moves slowly towards me as though he's afraid of startling me. As though he's afraid I will run, and I do. The small trickle of tears turns into rivers as I run to him. Wrapping my arms around his neck, he takes me in his arms and lifts me off the ground, holding me tightly against him.

"Little Dove—" he mutters.

"Shh... Just hold me. Please," I whisper hoarsely.

For once, he listens. He holds me tightly against him, his warm breath in the crook of my neck as his rainstorm scent fills my nose. For the first time in my life, I feel at home. I feel safe, and I feel loved. Lifting my eyes to his, we lock eyes before my lips slam down on his. His lips part over mine as he pulls me closer, deepening the kiss. It's needy, hungry, and so full of passion that I can feel myself melting in his arms. His fangs nip at my bottom lip, sending a chill down my spine. More. I want more of him. He is the breath my lungs crave, but he breaks the kiss before I can fill them. He sets me down gently on the stone floor and tucks my hair behind the pointed tip of my Fae ear.

"I need to explain before this goes any further."

"No, you don't. Senna already did, and I know it wasn't you. I know—"

"Do you?" he replies coldly. "Then why did you lock me out? Why have I spent the past hour banging on the door to my own room only to have you ignore me."

"You're angry," I reply—a statement, not a question.

"Well," turning his back to me as he runs a hand through his thick hair, "I am angry, but I'm also hurt."

"I know I shouldn't have ignored you. Even without Senna explaining, I know it wasn't you. Though I don't understand it or know who this Nymeria is, I know you wouldn't—" I pause.

"Fuck another woman?" he answers while pacing around the room. "No, I wouldn't. I will not pretend you were my first, the same as I know you have been with others before me. But that was before you, Kasia. There is no one else for me now. Every fiber of my being belongs to you and only you."

I let his confession soak in, suddenly feeling ridiculous for even thinking it possible he would hurt me like that. As the days have passed and my magic has grown, so has the strength of our bond. I feel it just as vividly as he does now. Had Xerxes's feelings for me been untrue, I'd have felt it. But instead, all I ever feel through the bond is genuine concern and *love*. However, neither of us has ever uttered the word that holds so much meaning.

He turns to face me, his eyes still full of fear and anger I don't understand.

"So then, was Nymeria one of the women... from before me?"

"Yes, the siren and I had an arrangement. But the moment I found you and brought you here, I ended it with her. She wasn't as willing to give it up and made it clear she did not like you. I knew that you wouldn't be safe around her." Though I already know he's been with others, as I have, it doesn't make hearing about it hurt any less.

"The cove..." I whisper, suddenly fitting the pieces together.

"The cove is where Nymeria lived."

"Lived?" I ask with confusion.

"Senna killed her this evening in the courtyard. She is dead," he states before changing his tone. "But that isn't what we need to discuss right now. I met with Nefeli—"

"He's here...isn't he?" I don't even need to ask. The look on Xerxes's face, the tension coming off him as he saunters to me. I already know. Draven is in Calanthe, and he is looking for me.

"Drake is here. Nefeli informed me of his arrival and that our men were calling for aid. I was meant to return to the camp with them when Nymeria found me in the courtyard. Her thoughts were filled with her little trick and the pain she caused you. I was enraged. I could feel your pain, and I wanted to rush to you, but I—I couldn't let my men die," he explains. His tone is full of pain and sorrow as he takes my hand tightly in his and pulls me towards the bed, guiding me to sit next to him.

"You made the right choice. I can understand why you went to them and not to me," I reply, hoping it will ease some of the guilt he feels, even if I do not understand it.

His body tenses and his voice lowers to a mere whisper. "Because of Nymeria's distraction. I was too late. When Orion and I arrived, it was a bloodbath, Kasia. With only

Drake and his men left standing among the corpses of my men, my friends." His tone is laced with pain and guilt. "They died for nothing!" he shouts, rising to his feet as he begins to pace around the room again. His fists clenched tight at his sides with aggression.

"They did not die for nothing, Xerxes. Nefeli knew the risks. They all did. They gave their lives to defend their homes and their people. They died with honor."

"Maybe so," he whispers, releasing a breath. "But Drake is still here and now has control over both sides of the veil."

"Does he know I'm here?"

"Oh, he knows. He even demanded I hand you over to him as if I would ever even consider letting him or his father get close to you." I tense with his words, causing him to rush to where I sit on the bed. Standing before me, he cups my chin in his calloused palms. Tilting my face up, he forces my eyes to his. "I will *never* let him have you, little dove. My body will lie with those of the fallen before he will ever come close to you," he whispers.

"I know," I reply. "I know."

Within seconds, his lips are on mine again as he pushes me up further onto the bed before laying me down. He climbs over top of me, parting my legs with his knee, causing me to moan against his mouth. His intoxicating kisses work their way down my body as he gets into position between my parted thighs. Soft, hunger-filled lips make their way down my jaw and neck, trailing slowly across my collarbone to the cleavage of my breast. He runs his tongue across the thin fabric covering my peaked nipple before a growl rumbles through him.

"I will never let anyone touch you again," he whispers as he pulls at the fabric, freeing my breast. Before I can process the moment, his mouth is over my breast. My back arches off the mattress and the need between my legs grows in intensity. I need him. More of him. "No one, Kasia."

"I know," I mutter. He fumbles with his belt; the glint of his small dagger in the moonlight catches my eye just as he sucks my nipple into his mouth, pinching it between his fangs. The sharp pain causes me to cry out. I lift my head, looking down at him. A trickle of blood flows down the curve of my breast. His eyes rise to mine as a coy smirk forms on his luscious lips before he lowers his head and runs his tongue through it. He holds my gaze as he savors the taste of my blood on his tongue before bringing his lips to my ear.

"So fucking delicious. I can't wait to spend eternity with the taste of you on my tongue," he whispers against my ear. Suddenly, strong hands are bunching the skirt of my dress to my waist and lifting me. His hands sink into the flesh of my ass as I wrap my legs around his waist while he moves me back against the stacks of pillows at the head of the bed. Laying me down, his muscular body covers mine as he slides his pants down, freeing his thick cock. With panted breaths, he lines himself up at my opening. He slowly moves the tip in slow, teasing circular motions through my arousal before pushing it through my folds. I gasp and cry out, causing him to bring his lips to mine. I moan against his mouth as he pushes in deeper until he's fully sheathed inside me.

Slowly, he rocks his hips as the sounds of him thrusting into my wetness fill the night air. I grip him closer, my moans mingling with the sounds of our bodies coming together. Once again, I find myself submitting to my bonded. To this man I somehow have complete trust in. The sweat-coated muscles of his toned chest flex with each roll of his hips.

"Stay with me, little dove."

"I'm here," I breathe.

His thrusts grow faster, ensuring that he hits all the spots he knows my body craves.

"I'm... so close," I stammer breathlessly. The way he reads my body and mind, always knowing what I need and where I need it, proves how quickly he can bring me to release. I cry out. I beg him not to stop. I want all of him.

"That's it. Come for me, Kasia." I come undone. My pussy clamps down on his cock as my orgasm pulsates its rhythm. Xerxes doesn't relent, his thrusts growing harder and more frantic. I grip the sheets tightly in my sweaty palms. Our bodies are in unison, moving together with perfection. I urge him deeper as heat pools between my legs.

"Yes... more, Xerxes."

"Fuck. My name on your tongue will be my undoing. Say you're mine, Kasia. Only mine," he commands with a deep and carnal tone.

"Always, my love." With my reply, we find release together. A loud roar rips through him as his cock pulsates in the deepest parts of my as he fills me with his seed. Collapsing on my chest, we share panted breaths for a brief moment, allowing ourselves to come down from the high. Slowly, he lifts his head from my sweat-coated chest, turning his eyes to mine.

"I love you, little dove," he whispers. "I always have, and I always will."

A smile forms on my lips with his confession. Though I knew how he felt, hearing it from his lips is different. It feels different than I expected it would. "I love you too, Xerxes," I reply softly.

His lips pull into that handsome smile I have grown to love as he pushes himself up to bring his lips to mine. Once their softness is pressed against mine, I take a moment to take in what we're sharing. To feel him. Before I lift the small silver dagger from his belt and push it into his back, right above his beating heart.

He cries out. Gasping with the shock of what I've done. The tears I was holding in make their appearance, streaking down my face as I watch his face fill with confusion and panic. Blood leaks from the wound, painting the silk sheets with his crimson blood. It's hot and sticky against my exposed flesh.

"Kasia..." he chokes out as blood begins to leak from his lips.

My heart breaks. I watch the hurt flicker in his eyes at what I've done before he collapses to the bed. It had to be done. He said so himself. He would never let Draven get his hands on me. Xerxes would risk the lives of everyone in Calanthe and the realm itself to keep me safe. But I won't. I slide out from under him and quickly make my way across the large room to the wardrobe. Grabbing my favorite fur-lined cloak, I wrap it tightly around myself and allow myself one last look. One final look at the first man I've ever given my whole heart to. I can feel myself going numb as I head out into the halls. *I didn't kill him. Only wounded him. I had to. He never would've let me leave.*

It's so late at night that the halls are empty and quiet. No servants or court members are wandering about. There is no one to witness me in my escape. No one to stop me. Sobbing, half naked and coated in the blood of the man I love, I take off through the halls, leaving a blood trail of footprints behind me. I make my way through the courtyard where Viserra has spent months training me, and I don't stop running until I find myself under the thick canopy of the Somnia Forest. Though brought here against my will, I've come to appreciate Calanthe and its people. If my life is the cost to keep the realm safe from Draven, then it's a price I will happily pay.

After all, one life lost is better than thousands, and I am hardly innocent.

The glow of the forest I witnessed on our travels to see Viserra is absent tonight. Replaced by a cold darkness that sends chills up my spine as I make my way through the thick foliage on my way to the camp, Drake took over at the veil. It's as though the forest is lifeless. Not a bird can be heard. There is no wind, no floral-scented glowing flowers—just dull darkness with no more than the occasional trickle of moonlight through the thick roof of leaves.

As I get closer to the camp, the glowing torches guide me to a small gatehouse with two dwarf guards standing outside. Long broad axes in hand, they stand with their backs to the gate, staring off into the darkness. With my hands raised in surrender, I slowly move forward from the shadows.

"My name is Kasia Satori, and I'm here to see Drake," I shout.

Rushing to my side, one of them quickly binds my hands behind my back. I don't fight him. Not when they rip the cloak from my back or when the other hits me in the back of the leg with the blunt end of his axe, knocking me to the ground. I don't fight. I don't fight any of them. Not even when they drag my naked body across the forest floor and into the camp do I fight them because the only person I have to fight for is gone.

The dwarves drag me through the camp, past shouting and cheering men until we reach a large red tent at the back of the camp. They release me, letting my body drop to the forest floor before one of them brings himself in front of me.

"Satori scum," he grunts before kicking me in the gut. Once, twice before taking my thick white locks in his fist and dragging me inside. Once inside, soft rugs replace the forest floor, and a savory aroma fills the air. They toss me to the ground roughly before storming off.

"Well. What do we have here?" a deep, male voice chuckles. Bruised and sore, I try to push myself to my feet but find my body is too weak. My arms give out, causing me to crash back down on the rug covered. Footsteps rush to my side before hands brush my hair from my face. My vision begins to fade, and focusing on my surroundings becomes nearly impossible. "What did they do to you?" he whispers alluringly. I lift my eyes to the figure above me, only to find a stunning Fae male with long golden hair that hangs around his pointed ears. Sharp features make up his face, but deep blue eyes are my last thought before everything goes black.

Chapter Nineteen

KASIA

The sound of male voices arguing wakes me. I stir, the small movement sending shooting pains across my torso, causing me to hiss. I open my eyes, pushing myself through the pain to sit up. I don't recognize my surroundings or the voices I hear. I'm sitting on a small wooden bed of thick furs and soft linens. A long, black shirt hangs off my body that I don't remember wearing. Someone must've put it on me while I was asleep. My hair is pulled back into a thick braid on the back of my head, and it smells of mint and roses, like it has been freshly washed.

Scanning my eyes around the tent, I find my fur-lined cloak hanging over the back of a chair at a small table. It is then that everything starts to come back to me. Xerxes, the dagger, his blood on my skin. The look in his eyes when I left him. But I also remember *why* I did it. Not that it helps with the pain or guilt that floods me.

Tears threaten to make another appearance, but I force them down, not wanting to be caught here crying. I turn my attention back to the small table and the small silver tray on it. It contains fruits and wine, with a few pieces of bread and cheese on the side. My stomach growls. The air carries the familiar scent of burning wood, a hint of damp earth mixed in. The tent door flap opens, and the golden-haired Fae male enters. Noticing I'm awake, he pauses briefly. His jaw clicks as he strides toward the small table and fills a small cup with wine. His silver and gold armor glints in the glow of the candles placed around the tent, with not a single dent or scratch on it. The same deep blue eyes I remember lift to mine as he makes to hand me the cup of wine. His hand trembles, but not with fear. With anger. Turning my head away from him, I push myself back up further onto the bed. He sighs.

"Drink, Kasia. Please," he says with a soft yet stern tone.

"No. If you're going to kill me, just be done with it," I scoff.

"Who said anything about killing you?" he replies as he approaches me, putting himself back into my line of sight. "No one is going to kill you. Their treatment of you has already earned them a severe punishment and quite the earful. I assure you." He chuckles, once again holding the small glass of wine out for me to take. Parched and finding myself curious, I take it, sniffing it for any poisons or tonics before tossing it back.

"So, how did you manage to get away from your bonded? Because when I last saw him, it was clear he had no intentions of letting you anywhere near me," Drake questions with a curious tone.

"I go where I want," I snap.

"He doesn't know you're here, does he, Princess?" I ignore his question. Pushing the thoughts of what I had to do to get here from my thoughts.

"What is it you want with me, Drake? If not to shed my blood like your father did my family's?" I choke out as I swallow down the bitter liquid. He laughs again, this time louder and more genuinely than before. I find myself curious about this golden-haired male. He's handsome, even I can't deny that. "I will not let you kill anyone else. Calanthe and its people are innocent. I would rather die a thousand deaths than hide while you destroy it all."

"Well, that is very selfless of you, Princess. However, it's unnecessary. I have no plans to kill you, nor does my father. In fact, I wish to make you my wife."

My eyes widen, my body tensing with his confession. His wife?

"Your wife?" I laugh. "Are you mad? What on earth makes you think I would want to marry you."

"I don't *think*, Kaisa. I *know*. You will be my wife for the very same reason you came here with the intent of dying. Marrying me is how you spare Calanthe and its people."

"I'd rather die than marry you," I retort. "Even I would never stoop so low as to tie myself to a murdering rapist!" I retort before spitting in his face.

He smiles with amusement, wiping the spit from his cheek with a swipe of his finger before sucking it clean. "Murder, yes. I've killed many, but so have you. Though, I'm confused about the rapist part of your little fit."

"You raped Senna! Left her in the halls of Eventide to be found by whoever passed."

He laughs, "Senna? Younger sister to your precious Lord? I won't deny she is a beauty, but I can assure you I never touched her. I do, however, remember the night you speak of. She was raped, but not by me. In fact, I was the one who so happened to pass by during the act. Her attacker fled, and I chased after him. When I lost him, I rushed back to check on her when the servants found me leaning over her. Of course, the guards were alerted, and when I tried to explain the truth, no one believed me. So, I was blamed for it."

His story churns in my head as I scan his face for any sign of dishonesty, but to my shock, there is none. He is genuinely speaking the truth.

"It doesn't matter. I can't marry you," I reply sharply.

His expression hardens as he begins to pace the small space. "Why? Is it because of him?"

"No," I mutter. The confession hurts more than any pain I've ever felt. "He has nothing to do with it." *But he does. He has everything to do with it.*

"I don't think you understand. My father will kill you, and the people of Lethe will continue to suffer if we do not marry. I—" he pauses, "I understand you have a bond with the High Lord, but what if I told you there was a ceremony we could perform to break it."

"I will never—"

"No? Do you no longer care for the people of Lethe, then? Because without you by my side, as my wife, my father will continue to rule over the realm. I think we both know how well that is going for its people."

I sit silently on the bed, pulling the blankets against my chest. I can save them. I can save both realms and all the people living within them without it costing my life. For a moment, I catch myself thinking about the pain Xerxes would feel if I were to break our bond, but then I remember he can't feel anything right now.

"So, if I agree to marry you, will your father spare Calanthe as well?" After all, that was why I came here, ready to surrender my life to keep Drake and his men from laying waste to the beautiful realm I have called home for months.

"No one in Calanthe will be touched. There is no reason for it now that you are here. I never enjoy the killing of innocents, but I had to find you."

 For some reason, I find myself believing he doesn't enjoy the kill. Something about him is different from most men. He's softer. "And what exactly does breaking the bond entail? Do we need to break it in order to be wed?" I ask.

"A simple vow, followed by a blood ceremony. Where we will be creating a bond between myself and you."

"Bonded to you?" I say, tilting my head in surprise.

Widening his arms in a questionable stance, he smiles coyly. "Am I really that ugly that spending eternity bonded to me would be so horrible?"

I turn my gaze away from him, even considering this plan feels like a betrayal to Xerxes and our bond. But what harm can it do? I've already betrayed him once, and though breaking our bond will cause us both more pain than the blade I embedded in his back, I don't see any other way. A single tear leaks from my eye, and I wipe it with the back of my hand. "Fine, I'll do it."

He sighs, bringing himself to sit on the bed next to me. The bed dips with his weight. He brushes his knuckles over my arm, sending a chill through me. "I promise no harm will come to you, Kasia. If you choose to trust anything, let it be that," he whispers.

"Don't touch me," I snap, pulling my arm away from him.

My magic vibrates under my skin, sensing my annoyance with this new male. Wind ripples around the tent outside, reacting to my magic. He chuckles, running his hand through his long golden hair as he rises and heads towards the tent door.

"They said you were powerful... but I didn't see that coming," he confesses proudly. "No wonder you thought my father wanted to kill you. I can only imagine one with magic such as yours would think everyone wants to take them out."

"You know *nothing* of my magic."

"I know you struggle to control it," he replies. "Sure, you do have some hold over it, but not entirely. How much would it take you to lose that little bit of control, though, Kasia? Tell me. How long can you keep it on its leash?"

"Keep pushing me, and I will show you just how well I can let it off its leash, *Drake*," I spit. I meet his eyes with a hateful glare that he seems to find amusing.

"I'll get you some dinner. I imagine you're hungry. You've been out for a while. There is hot water there for you to wash with if you'd like," he explains, as he points to a large ceramic bowl next to the bed before he heads out of the tent.

Finding myself alone again. I sit up, pulling my knees to my chest and wrapping my arms around them. I tuck my head into them and slow my breathing in an effort to calm the magic that brews within me. Drake was right. With all the emotions flowing through me, my magic is gaining its hold and becoming harder to control. My heart is broken, and yet I can't allow myself to feel the pain. I need to push forward. For Lethe. For Calanthe. I need to marry Drake. I need to forget about Xerxes, how he made me feel, and the moments we shared. *I need to forget about all of it.*

I sit like that for a while, allowing myself time to grasp the storm brewing within me. Once I have it under control, I crawl to the edge of the bed where I find the wash bowl that Drake spoke of. Dipping my hands in, I splash some on my face. It's cool, letting me know it's been there a while. I take the small towel next to it and pat my face dry before placing it back and climbing off the bed. I slowly make my way around the tent, taking everything in. For a royal tent, there isn't much luxury. I see a large wooden chest of clothing, extra armor, and a few stacks of books on the floor beside it. The small table is covered with maps of the land, and the silver tray of wine and food is placed carefully over them.

I step lightly on the soft rugs, the night's chill kissing against my bare legs. The shirt I find myself wearing barely covers me, reaching just below my ass. Pinching it, I sniff it before inspecting it. It's soft, unlike any fabric I've ever worn before, and it smells like freshly fallen snow with a hint of oak moss. Musky and earthy, reminding me of the forests back home in Lethe.

"Well... you certainly look better in it than I do."

I jump, startled by the deep sound of his voice from behind me. Drake enters the tent with a plate of food in his hand. He pauses, taking in every inch of my body with his stormy blue eyes. Quickly, I grab my fur-lined cloak from the back of the chair and wrap it around me as my cheeks flush.

Drake chuckles, placing the plate down on the table. "It was a compliment, Kasia," he explains as he pulls the chair out for me to sit. I roll my eyes, taking a seat in the chair.

"Your compliments are wasted on me," I say. His hand snaps to his chest like I've pained him with my rejection. Picking the fork up, I stab it into a piece of roasted meat on the plate before bringing it to my mouth. The meat is smokey and charred to perfection. Melting in my mouth before I swallow it down.

"Your words hurt me so. Do you truly hate me so much that you can't accept my simple compliment?"

"Your father *killed* my family."

"Exactly. My *father*. I had nothing to do with it. I wouldn't have killed them."

"No? So, you didn't want my throne?"

"Now, that I did not say, but there are other ways of claiming a throne without having to shed innocent blood."

"Did you help him? Tell me. You fought by his side that night, did you not?" I question, pushing the food around the plate with my fork.

"I did, but I was young... Naive. I didn't know any better back then," he sighs. "I was blind to my father's cruelty, to his lies."

"And now? Are you still blind to it? If what you say is true, how have you allowed things in Lethe to get so bad? How do you sleep when you know the people suffer?"

"Why do you think I am here, proposing a marriage to you?" he shouts. Releasing a breath of frustration, he brings himself to stand before me. "I am *not* my father, Kasia. I will not lie to you. I am not here claiming to be perfect. I have shed blood, as you well know, but I do not wish to watch the people of Lethe suffer anymore."

"What do you know of their suffering? I lived it, Drake! I survived it alongside them. I spent nights searching for children who *vanished*. Did you know that too? Those children have been going missing from the orphanage for months! Never to be seen again."

"I do not claim to know what it was like for you, or what it is like for them. All I know is what I see for myself. However, when it comes to the missing children you speak of, I did know."

A wrathful laugh erupts through me. "You knew? And did *nothing*?" I snap.

He shrugs, unbothered by my tone. "I knew they were better off," he admits.

"Better off? How is a missing child better off?"

"Honestly, I'm surprised your *precious* High Lord didn't tell you," he says, words laced with sarcasm.

Furrowing my brows, I find myself confused by his statement. What could he know about Xerxes that I do not? "Tell me what?"

"That he was the one responsible for the missing children," he explains, grabbing a piece of smoked meat from my plate and popping it in his mouth. "He and the Lord of the Naga from Amazath, that is. They had been taking kids off the streets in Lethe for *years* and bringing them to their own realms. I knew it was happening, and I allowed it. I even went out of my way to ensure my father never found out."

"I don't believe you."

"Right, because admitting that you also know nothing about me would be too hard, right?" he spits. "You don't know enough about me to hate me. My father may have earned that reaction from you, but I have not." He's right, even though I hate to admit it. I know nothing of Drake, other than rumors. Since being here, he has only shown me kindness, and patience even. Perhaps he isn't as cruel as people make him out to be. Not that it matters. He'll never be Xerxes. Breaking our gaze, I fiddle with the hem of the black shirt.

"He was saving them?"

"Yes. My guess is that he was coming into Lethe looking for you...and couldn't turn a blind eye to the suffering."

"Sounds like him," I mutter. Rubbing his face with his hands, he brings himself to kneel before me.

"Kasia, I'm not trying to be him, nor do I want to take his place in your heart. I don't expect you ever to have the same feelings for me that you do for him. However, it would make our lives easier if you could at least *try* not to hate me. I promise you, I am not this monster you seem to think me to be. I will be kind to you and to the people of Lethe." His eyes darken, and the weight of his gaze grows heavy, causing me to break it before pushing him aside and returning to the bed.

"I'm tired," I whisper, no longer wanting to continue this conversation. I no longer want to think about how it felt to drive the blade through the back of the man I love. The man who was secretly helping Lethe's people. *My* people.

"Right. Well, I suppose it is late. I can never tell in this fucking realm," he replies, rising to his feet. I climb into the comfort of the bed, covering my body with thick fur blankets as I watch him clean up the dishes and leftover food. "I'll be back later. You should try to rest. We head back to Lethe tomorrow," he explains as he makes his way out.

"Drake!" I shout, causing him to stop.

"Hmm?" His head snaps in my direction, locking eyes with mine.

"Thank you for allowing them to take the children. For keeping it from your father," I whisper. A smile forms on his face before he heads out of the tent. The moment he's out of my Fae hearing range, I swallow the lump in my throat and attempt to get ahold of my magic before I let go of everything I have been holding in. The dam holding back my tears collapses as rivers of salty liquid streak down my heated cheeks, staining the pillows. Pain radiates across my chest, and my body trembles. Sobs slip from my lips, and I find myself reaching through my bond, needing to feel something, anything from him for comfort. But I get nothing. I Feel nothing from him. Nothing through his side of the bond. My stomach churns with fear. *Did I miss my mark? What if I pierced his heart?*

Suddenly, a small piece of him trickles through the bond in response. Weak, but there. I sigh with relief through sobs as I pull the blanket up closer to my face. He's alive. That's all that matters.

Chapter Twenty

XERXES

Long silvery hair shining in the moonlight. Piercing minty green eyes. Soft moans and ethereal-sounding laughter. Visions of Kaisa, my bonded, flood my dreams. Her soft skin pressed against mine. The way she crinkles her nose when she giggles, her warmth. Then suddenly, it's all gone. Replaced with pain. Searing through my weakened body. I can still feel the blade's mark on my back as the memory of our last moments together replays in my head until I wake. My eyes snap open, taking in the room—a thick layer of sweat coats my chest, and the air smells of burning sage and incense smoke. Senna sits at the end of my bed, her nose stuck in a book as she reads with red, puffy eyes like she's spent hours crying. But it's her blood-stained gown that draws my attention. Confused, I raise my hand to my head, the pain growing worse by the minute. *What happened?*

"Kasia... Where is Kasia?" I stammer with a cracked voice. Tossing the book, Senna rushes to my side with widened eyes.

"Shh... rest, brother. We almost lost you," she pleas, gently pressing a damp cloth along my brow. My throat is parched and scratchy, causing me to cough and clear my throat.

"What happened? Where is Kasia?" The sounds of the door opening and closing echoes around the room. Senna ignores my question, doing her best to keep her thoughts from me. But it's no use. She's struggling to tell me the truth of what's happened. She's afraid for me.

"She's gone, mate," Orion explains as he reaches us. "She stabbed you and took off into the night."

"Erebus was locked out of your room, barking for hours like he knew something was wrong when Agatha heard him. She opened the door to let him in and found you," Senna explains as she rinses the cloth in a bowl of water next to the bed before wiping her hands on her gown. Erebus whimpers from the foot of the bed, letting me know he's here and concerned for me. "I could kill her," Senna spits angrily.

"You will watch your tone, Sister."

"Are you serious? She almost killed you, Xerxes!"

"Senna, he's right. You heard what Niko said. She missed his heart intentionally. She didn't want to kill him, or she would've. Kasia is ruthless, especially with a blade in her hands. She knew he would survive," Orion explains defensively. It's clear he doesn't like arguing with my sister, but like me, he sees why Kasia did what she did.

I don't even have to ask where she's gone. I already know, and though I should be angry and feel betrayed, I am flooded with worry. I try to push myself up, but the pain intensifies. I ignore it, knowing I must get to her before it's too late. Reaching down my bond, I can feel her. Sensing my pain, Senna grabs a small amber vile from the table, popping the cork off before bringing it to my lips.

"For the pain. Niko's made it," she whispers as I swallow it down. It's sour and tastes like rotten fruit, but its relief is almost instantaneous. Within moments, the pain subsides, and I can sit up.

"We need to go. Now. Orion, ready the men. We're returning to Drake's camp," I command.

"Mate, she isn't there," he sighs. "Drake took her back to Lethe. He plans to marry her. It's all over the realm. They're to be wed tomorrow night."

An uncontrollable laugh erupts through me. Senna and Orion look at me questionably, clearly confused in my amusement. "You don't truly believe that, do you? Kasia can't be that stupid!"

They exchange a look before turning their gaze back to me. I rise from the bed, quickly going to my wardrobe to pull on my fighting leathers. My body is tense, and I'm careful not to injure myself more.

"Xerxes, stop. You're in no condition to travel. You need to rest," Senna shouts as she approaches me. She grabs my chest plate to stop me from putting it on. A low growl rumbles through me.

"Senna," I say sternly. "You will not stop me from going back for her."

"She's in Lethe! For God's sake, have you heard *nothing* of what Orion has told you?" she shouts. Her thoughts fill with anger at me for not listening or letting it go like she wants me to. But how can I? Kasia is a part of me.

"I heard *everything*! And I do not care! I don't care where or what realm she is in. I will never stop until she is back here with me, where she belongs," I explain, trying to keep hold of my temper.

"They will kill you, Xerxes, and the people of Calanthe with you. She knew this. Don't you think she knew what she was doing by going there?"

"He will kill her, Senna! Draven cannot allow her to live when she's as powerful as she is!" I seethe with annoyance. "Think about it! She is the one person in all the realms who can take him down, and not only that, but it is *her* throne he sits upon. Her birthright. He will not let her live; you can be sure of that."

She freezes, taking in my words as she tries to make sense of them before turning her eyes back to mine. She knows I'm right.

"I'll ready the men and inform Niko that—" Orion begins but is cut off mid-sentence.

"No need. I heard, and I am with you, friend," Niko explains as he enters the room. His long, black-scaled tail glints in the moonlight that radiates through the open balcony doors as he slithers towards us. "I will travel back to Amazath and gather my men. I failed da girl's parents twenty-three years ago. I will not make that mistake again," he explains, nodding.

Fastening the straps of my armor, I return his nod. "Your support means more than I can express, Niko."

"Aye, just make sure you rest until then. Your body can't yet handle wielding a blade." Reaching into the well of magic provided by my moonstone ring, I summon a small tether of moonlight. It takes great focus and mental strength with how weak I am from blood loss, but I don't let it show. I smirk, twirling it between my fingers.

"Who says I need to wield a blade?" I reply cockily.

Niko exhales loudly. "Rest. I do not feel like having to restitch you simply because you were too stubborn to listen to instructions long enough for your Fae magic to heal you. We will meet at the veil—in a day's time," he adds before leaving the room. I begin to pace around the room, planning our attack in my head. They'll be expecting us; we need to be smart about things. Who knows what could be waiting for us on the other side of the veil?

"She... She went there knowing he'd kill her. Didn't she?" Senna stammers, coming to the realization of why Kasia did what she did. Why she left. I sigh, sensing my sister's pain and guilt for the way she spoke of Kasia before she fully understood.

"She knew what would happen, and I never would've allowed it."

"That's why she... I am such an idiot! I'm coming with you," Senna says with a commanding tone. "We have to try. We owe her that much."

"We're going to do more than try. We're going to get her back, and anyone who even thinks to try and stop me will meet their death," I growl.

My blood boils beneath my skin. Drake's life will be mine for taking her from me. Even if she willingly turned herself in, he knows who she belongs to. He knows of our bond and what it means. My blade will meet his heart before I ever allow him to sever it. I turn my gaze on Senna and Orion. Their hands clasped tightly within each other's for comfort, but their faces carry expressions of determination.

"Go. We'll meet tomorrow." Orion says firmly.

"Brother..." Senna whispers, but I raise my hand, signaling her to stop.

"I will be easy on myself tonight, Sister. I only want to bathe in peace. Orion, take her back to her chambers. Stay with her and Kenji for the night," I command. He nods in reply. "Make sure she sleeps. There will be plenty of time to read when we return and this is all over." I smirk. A small smile forms on Senna's face, and I spot a small sparkle in her eyes before Orion guides her out of the room, closing the heavy oak door behind him.

Alone, with no one but Erebus, the room grows silent. Slowly making my way to the bathing chambers, a shudder rips through me. Everything in here smells of her. Through the bond, I can feel her, feel her pain. But it isn't physical pain. Her heart hurts. Stripping off the linden trousers I woke up in. I toss them to the side before stepping into the bath. Its heated waters wrap around my tense and sore muscles like a blanket, easing the pain and stiffness. Ducking myself under the steaming waters quickly, I surface, wiping the water from my face as thoughts of Kasia fill my head. Could she really believe marrying Drake will save her from death? I smile, wondering how well Drake is coping with that sharp tongue of hers I love so much. Knowing her, she's not making anything easy for him, which offers me some peace of mind—*one more night.* I tell myself. *One more night before she's back, here in my arms, abusing me with that Godsdamn mouth of hers.*

WHEN WE REACH THE COURTYARD, I find my best soldiers lined up along the wall. They are all wearing the same signature Calanthian obsidian chest amour that I wear. Thick black chest plates that curve along the body with a small moon etched into the center and two openings on the back, allowing them to have their wings out. The helmets cover from the nose up and have small black feathers above each ear. A suit that was designed by my father to be strong and durable but also, lightweight, and easy to fly with.

"The men are ready when you are, mate. Gage has picked his best men. We'll get her back," Orion explains as he mounts onto Raven's back.

Offering no response, I finish strapping the saddle on Oscar. Today, I feel nearly completely healed. Thanks to the tonics from Niko and the moon's energy that shined on me all night as I slept on the balcony. My well is full, and my wound is no more than a pink discoloration on my skin.

The courtyard is full of tension this morning. Anticipation of the battle to come weighs heavy on the men. They're afraid, and they should be. Lethe's army is no joke. Their soldiers are well-trained in all forms of combat. If rumors of Drake's brutality are true, many will die on both sides, especially now that we no longer have the element of surprise on our side.

"Good," I reply, climbing onto Oscar's back before patting his head between the ears. He huffs, clearly eager to get going. Senna approaches, wearing fighting leathers that match Orion's and mine, with her bow and quiver strapped tightly on her back. Her thick auburn hair is pulled into a thick braid that hangs over her shoulder. Reaching Raven, Orion offers her a hand to help her up, and she accepts, taking the seat behind him and wrapping her arms around his waist.

"Senna, where do you think you're going?" I question with authority.

"You didn't really think you'd be going without me, did you? I'm the best shot in your ranks, and you know it. You need me."

Sighing, I whisper, "What I need is to know you're safe."

"If you think I'm going to stay back and twiddle my thumbs while you're all out there risking your lives, you're sadly mistaken, Brother. Kasia is as much my family as yours, and I will be helping bring her home," she replies sharply. Orion and I exchange looks of defeat, knowing when my sister has her mind set on something, there is no changing it.

"Keep her close to you, Orion."

"Ay, mate. That, you don't have to worry about. You just worry about getting your girl, I got mine, and no one is getting close to her."

"You two act like I need protecting, but how many times have I saved your asses?" she snickers cockily. My lips pull into a smile, as do Orion's, as we sit silently for a moment with Senna's question going unanswered. She grabs the reins tightly in her hands.

"That's right. Now, if you ladies are done with your bickering, we should get going."

Erebus sits beside Oscar. His snout tipped up towards me as he whines. He misses her and shares the same concerns for her that I do. A moth flutters by the corner of my eye, pulling my gaze as another joins it. And then another, until the sky around us is filled with hundreds of moths as they soar high into the night sky. Their luminescent dusted wings glow in the moonlight like moving stars.

"A good omen," Senna whispers. I snap my gaze to hers in time to see a small smile form on her lips. "To be seen off by the sacred moths of Somnia is a good omen."

"Did one of your dusty old books tell you this?" Orion asks, looking over his shoulder at her.

"You'd be surprised what you can learn from my *dusty old books*," she retorts. "I know one in particular you could learn a lot from, actually," she adds.

"Oh, bloody hell, not this again," Orion sighs sarcastically as he rolls his eyes. Senna smacks his shoulder playfully before pressing a soft kiss to his cheek.

My hand grips the pommel of the dagger on my side— the same dagger Kasia plunged into me right after confessing her feelings to me. Even with a blade buried in my flesh, my heart had never been so whole. That same heart aches for her and the sacrifices she felt she had to make to protect as many lives as possible. She's shown the selflessness of a great High Lady.

"Gage, where is Viserra?" I ask, wondering why she hasn't joined us. The oracle wouldn't allow us to leave for Kasia without her. Not after everything they've been through together.

"No one has seen her, Lord. She wasn't in her chambers," Gage replies.

"Ron, check again." Something doesn't feel right. Where could she be? "Check everywhere. We can't leave without her. Kasia will need her." I order.

"Brother, we can't wait—" Senna explains, but I cut her off mid-sentence.

"No, we can't, but we also can't show up without her," I reply. My patience thins by the second, and the hair on the back of my neck prickles. *Something isn't right. Viserra would be here.*

The wind rips past us as we wait in the moonlit courtyard. Titling my head up to the night sky, I exhale deeply, welcoming its glow as it slowly refills my well of power. I find my thoughts trailing back to Kasia and the look of surprise on her face that night in the forest when she healed the tiny sapling. Reaching for our bond, I wait, feeling for her warmth to shine through. She's okay. She's alive. I swell with relief as I send my own magic through the bond. *I'm coming for you, little dove.*

Chapter Twenty-One

KASIA

The cold winter air of Lethe once again fills my lungs as I stand on the high balcony of my new room in the Fairewny Palace. My home. Or, at least, the place that was meant to be my home. Being back in Lethe has brought a mix of feelings. Knowing my parents walked these halls and slept on the same beds brings new light to how I view the realm. My heart has always ached for the suffering of the Lethe people, but knowing who I am–who I am meant to be–I know now I have to do everything in my power to help them, even if that means bonding myself to the son and heir of the usurper who stole my throne and killed my family.

The thought alone feels like a betrayal. It shouldn't, not after what I've already done to him. I never thought I would miss feeling him as much as I do. The trickling of his magic through the bond is something I long for, though I know in Lethe, it will never come. I know it's only a matter of time before he comes here looking for me. Even still, I spend every day praying that he won't, at least not until the bonding ceremony with Drake has taken place. After that, he won't have any reason to come looking for me.

Footsteps through the echoing halls meet my ears, followed by the sound of the key in the lock before it clicks open, and Drake enters. I hear as he closes and locks the door behind him before striding across the large open room to the balcony. He sighs with his approach, causing me to spin around. Leaning against the door frame, he crosses his arms around his chest as a small grin forms on his face. His long golden hair is pulled up on the top of his head in a messy knot, showing me a clear view of his haunting blue eyes. Tonight, he's under-dressed, with no armor or weapon at his side. Just simple black trousers and a thin cotton shirt unbuttoned at the top, hanging open enough to reveal a part of his toned chest.

He cocks a brow in my direction, "So I hear you not only threw your meal at the guard this time, but you also disarmed him and stabbed him in his thigh with his own blade."

"The soup was as cold as the snow that plagues this realm. If you ask me, you should be ashamed that your guards are too lazy to bother heating food before serving it to royalty. He had it coming."

"You know, you could at least try to be nice to them. Your quarrel is with my father, not the—"

"He is still breathing, is he not? I was nice," I reply. "And do not speak of my quarrels like you know me. My hatred for your father extends to every man who obeys his orders. That includes the guards who stood by his side while he slaughtered my family's blood. *Your* guard is lucky. All he will have is a nice scar. We both know I could've done much worse."

"I don't doubt that. In fact, I rather enjoy this violent side of you," he chuckles as he makes his way towards me. "I can see why Xerxes liked you."

"Do not speak of him!" I snap. His expression changes with my response. The once playful and flirtatious sparkle in his eyes dimmed with my tone. Spinning around, I turn my attention back on the kingdom below me, watching as the people of Lethe go about their day. From here, I can see the tall chimney of the orphanage I once called home. Smoke billows in thick puffs that float up to mingle with the clouds. The sky is grey and dreary, as it always is, and I find myself wishing for the starry sky of Calanthe.

I have grown to miss much of Calanthe in my time here. The people, of course, but as I stand here looking over the land, it's the magic I find myself lost without. It's odd to find myself lost and missing something I never knew I had. The silent vibrations of my family's magic coursing through my veins, the scents, and the creatures. The way the moon's glow seemed to bring everything to light.

Drake clears his throat as he brings himself to stand next to me. "Let's get out of the cold. I will have the maids bring new hot soup for both of us. We can play a game or read. Whatever you'd like," he whispers with an apologetic tone.

He knows he's upset me, and though he may be my captor, part of me feels that he genuinely cares for me. Drake always makes sure I am safe. He has been true to his word on that. He often checks in and finds his way to my room at night to spend time with me reading, playing cards, or even painting. Looking down, I fidget with the hem of the thick cloak draped over my shoulders, feeling guilty. I want to hate Drake, but I don't. How can you hate someone who has been nothing but kind to you? Someone who's done nothing but try to make me feel welcome and kept his word to me about every promise he's made me thus far? Inhaling deeply, I fill my lungs with the frigid air before turning without a word and returning to my room.

Back inside, I'm instantly welcomed by the warmth that chases away the cold that has seeped into my body. My hands and face begin to thaw, thanks to the roaring fire constantly tended to by the servants Drake sends in. Hanging my cloak on the post by the bed, I adjust the floor-length cream-colored silk dress I chose to wear. It's low cut around my chest, with an intricately stitched bodice of the most beautiful lace I've ever seen. The seamstress must've spent a great amount of time on it, as tiny crystals that glint in the fire's glow are sewn into the pockets of lace. Rows of beautiful white feathers drape down my shoulders and the length of my arms–the closest thing to wings I have here.

I head to the small table and chairs set up by the fireplace. The room they've locked me away in is lavish, and though most would be grateful to find themselves having the opportunity to stay in such luxury, I don't. Everything I see or touch takes my thoughts back to my parents and childhood. Was this my room? Theirs? Did the trinkets and books Drake reads me at night belong to my family? Have I heard these stories before? I have had no memories return since being back in Lethe. No flashbacks and no sign of my wings. However, that doesn't surprise me since I have yet to learn how to summon them when I *actually* want them.

The palace here is much different from Calanthe and different from what I expected from looking at it from the outside. It is mostly constructed of large, elegant, and beautifully carved arches and pillars, so it blends perfectly with the winter landscape. Viserra once told me Lethe was covered in vines of the most beautiful red roses, but walking the halls and finding nothing but dull white walls with the odd gold fixtures, I find it hard to believe. Lowering myself to one of the small chairs, I grab the crystal decanter off the table in front of me and pour myself a glass of the amber liquid the Lethians call bourbon. After I bring the glass to my lips, I take a sip and swirl the liquid–equal parts smoke and spice–around my tongue, savoring its flavor before swallowing it down.

"What should we play today, then, Princess?" Drake asks as he sits in the other chair across from me. Lifting my eyes, I find his are full of curiosity as he rakes them across my body, focusing on the places my skin is exposed.

"I think I'd prefer skipping a game tonight. I'm rather tired."

"Okay," Drake nods. "If that's what you want. We can just sit here in silence."

"Perfect," I reply, returning to the flickering flames of the fire, doing my best to tune out the world around me. I am desperate to feel anything besides the pain I feel without him. *Xerxes*. I know by now he must've woken up. He said once before that he could feel me, even though I couldn't feel him. Is it the same now? Can he feel how broken and lost I am without him? How I wish it had been my own heart I plunged the blade into instead of his.

"May I ask something?" Drake questions, pulling me from my thoughts.

Keeping my eyes fixated on the flames, I reply. "When have you ever asked?"

A humorous laugh vibrates through him. "You always have some sassy thing to say back, don't you? I can't help but wonder why you seemed so shocked by my mentioning of Xerxes helping the orphan children or even seemed to care so deeply about what happened to them."

I sigh. Knowing as much as I don't want to answer his questions, he won't stop until I do. Truthfully, I have nothing better to do. "I care because I was one of them."

"Well, I know your parents were killed, obviously, but that doesn't—"

"No," I whisper, keeping my eyes on the fire. "The night before my family was killed, my mother had my memories wiped before she dropped me off with Miss Sage. I grew up in that orphanage for twenty-three years, never knowing who I really was or was meant to be. Those children, Miss Sage... they became my family... my home... And before I was taken to Calanthe, I did everything I could to keep them from freezing and starving to death in this Gods-forsaken realm."

A loud laugh erupts through him. My eyes snap from the fire to him. I glare at him with confusion. "You were *right* under his nose. The entire time!" he laughs, bringing his hand to his chest. "Well, if that isn't the best thing I've heard in a while, I don't know what is," he explains.

"I'm glad you find the life I was forced to live because of your father funny."

Sensing my annoyance, he pauses. Quickly clearing his throat as though to seem more serious. "I apologize, truly. It wasn't your misfortune I found funny, but I can understand why my reaction would make it seem that way," he apologizes.

Though his tone seems sincere, I pull my eyes from his, returning them to the flames. Moments of silence pass between us as I watch the flames dance. My thoughts trail back to one of the days I spent training with Viserra, where she taught me that, though more fire is man-made, it stems from nature. She spent all day trying to have me focus on controlling the tiny flame of a candle she lit, surrounded by unlit candles. She wanted me to light them all from one flame. I tried for hours and hours with no luck. It wasn't until annoyance with myself for not being able to do such a simple thing, mixed with the fury I felt for Viserra and the way she talked down to me during the training, that I unwillingly controlled the flames and the once tiny flame spread from one candle to the next and the next until the table was covered in glittering flames. What I'd give now to have the same control of the flames in the hearth next to me. But where I had grown used to the vibrations of my magic within me, there is now no more than an empty echo.

"Do you know how absolutely stunning you are, Princess?" Drake whispers. Pulling my eyes from the fire, I turn my attention back on him. Removing the small black ribbon from his hair, his golden curls tumble down his face before he runs his hand through them. "Especially in that dress. The white feathers suit you. I think I shall be lucky to call you wife and have you at my side to rule over Lethe. I hope in time you can grow to care for me as deeply as you do him—"

"Stop."

"Why does the mere mention of him bring such hostility from you? You're the one who willingly came to *me*, Kasia. You came here expecting to die. Yet when I tell you it will not be death you receive but the chance to live, so long as you marry me, you act as though you'd rather the alternative."

"Because I would," I retort.

"You will come to love me, Kasia. The bond will force us to develop feelings for each other; there's no denying it. Once the bond with *him* is broken, we—"

"Enough!" I shout, rising from the chair. "Do not speak of him as though he doesn't exist! You know nothing of the bond he and I share. Whatever bond I find myself cursed to share with you will never amount to what I have with him. *Ever.*"

"Fuck," he sighs, rising from the chair. "When you say things like that, I want it even more. Your love and loyalty for him is beyond anything I've ever seen, even from other bonded couples. What you and Xerxes share is—"

"I swear to the Gods, Drake... If you mention him again, I will break your jaw!" I shout angrily.

His eyes widen with shock for only a moment before his smile turns smug. "Do it," he challenges.

Typical. Men in Lethe have *always* been predictable, thinking they know everything and underestimating women. My fists clench tightly at my side, trembling with anger at how easy it is for him to speak of the bond to someone else when he knows nothing of either of us or our bond. I want to hit him, but I don't. I close my eyes and remember the training that Viserra taught me to control my emotions—slowing my breathing, inhaling through my nose, exhaling out my mouth in slow, deep breaths.

"I think you need to leave," I mutter before opening my eyes.

"What? No, Kasia. Listen, I... Fuck," Drake whispers. Running his hand through his hair, he pulls on it at the root as he moves to bring himself closer to me, but I back away. "I didn't mean to dismiss what you shared. I'm not doing any of this right. I've never genuinely cared for someone. This is new for me." He gestures between the two of us with his hands.

"You? Care for me?" I scoff with a harsh laugh, crossing my arms across my chest. "I am nothing but a power move for you and your father. You want the support of the Lethian people, and the curse lifted. Both of which you can't get without me. That's all this is. You know it, and so do I."

"No. That may have been how it started out, but the time we have shared together has changed that," he admits. "I may not know what you two share, but I assure you I don't enjoy breaking it. Not when I know the pain it will cause you."

"Then why are you doing it?"

"Because despite how evil you think me to be, I have true feelings for you. Completing the bonding ceremony with you is the only way I can save you, the only way I can save Lethe and make the realm better for its people."

"If this ceremony ever actually takes place. We've been here for days and have not heard a word about when it will occur. Nor have I seen your father yet, which is surprising considering the man spent how many years looking for me."

"Count your blessings." Drake laughs. "My father can be intense. Besides, I'm the charming one." I catch myself smiling at his cockiness and quickly avert my eyes to the ground, not wanting to see it. "Well, I suppose I should see what happened to our soup. It should've been here by now, and Gods, I don't want to see what you'll do if it arrives cold for the second time," he explains. "I'll be back."

I nod, watching as he strides across the room to the door.

"Drake!" I shout, catching his attention. He stops, spinning around to face me.

"Hmmm?"

"I don't think you're evil," I admit.

He smiles at me and winks before he lets himself out of the room, locking the door behind him to ensure I cannot leave. Alone again. I slump back down in the small chair with a huff. Ironically, the two men who hate each other both seem to want to lock me away in a room with fine things, thinking that makes it any less of a prison. The difference in Calanthe was that I at least had my magic flowing through me, my memories, and Erebus. Here in Lethe? I have no one. No one except Drake. Who, I've come to realize, isn't anything like people portray him to be. He isn't evil like Draven. He's kind and honest. At least so far. While most women would be happy to be able to one day call him their husband, regardless of how kind he is... he isn't who I want.

He isn't Xerxes. My heart aches for my bonded, for the man I left behind—the man I need to forget.

Chapter Twenty-Two

XERXES

The hum of the full moon's magic does little to silence Kasia's pain and heartache that trickles through our bond. Regardless, I welcome it as it refills the well of power carried by my family ring, knowing I will need it in the battle to come. Rolling my shoulders, I stretch the healing muscles along my back. Mentally, I'm ready; with any hope, my Fae healing will also have my body ready. The pain radiating down my back is a constant reminder–not of the betrayal she hates herself for, but of how much I let her down. Had I done my job as her bonded, she never would have left. She would have trusted me to find another way to save Calanthe without her having to give up anything, let alone her life. Every fiber in me misses everything about her: her smile, sweet scent, and sharp tongue. Though I'm sure she's giving her captor a piece of her mind, I find myself wishing it was me who was being inflicted by its venom. Soon enough, I will be.

"There's no sign of Viserra, Lord," Ron explains as he approaches me from behind.

Turning my eyes to his, I nod. "Fuck. Where the hell could she have gone?" I reply.

"Who knows where that ole bat ran off to. She could be in the forest doing more of her voodoo tricks, or looking for more of those horrible-smelling herbs she likes to collect from around the palace for all we know." That's the last thing we needed. I wanted Viserra with us. Kasia is going to need her, and truthfully, I'd feel better having her at my side in this.

"We can't wait for her any longer, Xerxes. We have to go, now," Senna explains with a soft tone. I know she's right. I nod in return, taking Oscar's reins in my hand.

Though it means we'll be traveling without the oracle, I must admit that I'm eager to get going. "Alright, well so be it. We don't have time to waste waiting for her to be found." Orion's eyes find mine, and his thoughts fill with the question even though he isn't brave enough to ask me. "She's alive, Orion. I can feel her."

"Aye, this is one of those rare moments where I'm thankful for your annoying little mind-reading habit. Well, I guess that's good, then. I never doubted the little birdie. She's probably giving them a piece of her mind, that's for sure. I wonder how many she's killed," he jokes —doing his best to lighten the mood. Tension has been high since my injury. Many of my people have gone to the furthest part of the realm to avoid being mixed up in the chaos between our realm and Lethe. They blame Kasia for Drake's murderous rampage when, really, it's me they should blame. I am, after all, the one who brought her here in the first place, knowing he would come looking for her.

"I'm sure they learned very quickly how resourceful she can be after growing up in the poverty they created," I reply, the two of us making our way through the halls and towards the courtyard where the men Orion and Gage gathered await. "I suspect Drake left men guarding the veil we must take out before we can actually get through. Any word from Niko yet?"

"Nothing from Niko. Not since he left, anyway. But he's probably on his way to the veil as we speak. You know how much he hates missing out on the action." Orion laughs as we head out of the courtyard and into the Somnia forest.

PERCHED HIGH in the dense treetops of the Somnia Forest surrounding the veil, my men and I scope out the encampment left behind by Drake. At least fifteen Lethian guards move about, pacing the perimeter and guarding the entrances to the veil. They're expecting us, but not from the sky. The thick black feathers of our wings and the obsidian armor will keep us blended into the night sky until the last second–until it's too late for them to defend themselves. Orion blows out a whistling sound, mimicking one of the local Calanthian birds, drawing my attention. A trick we use when we want to communicate but remain hidden, it can be quite useful.

Looking over, he does not speak. Instead, his head fills with visions of the plan he and the men have decided upon, knowing I will read his thoughts. He's found a weak spot in their defense and wants permission to take two men down with him while we take out the rest. But I have a plan of my own. Signaling him to hold off, I dig into my well of power, lifting one of the burning logs from the small brazier lit outside the largest tent. With a flick of my wrist, the log lands in the middle of the fabric roof of the tent. We watch as it rolls down, setting fire to the tent along the way until it hits the roof's edge and lands on the forest floor. I repeat the same action. Diving deeper into my fully charged well of power to set all their tents ablaze. The Lethian men run around frantically in the chaos, and that's when I signal Orion to move in.

Like a swarm of ravens from the treetops, we fly down, landing on the unexpecting groups of Lethian guards. Senna and some of my men are armed with bows, sending waves of arrows ahead of us on our descent, while others are armed with blades. They waste no time slashing throats and limbs once they're in range. Though my men are able to pull on their power in Calanthe, they're all well-trained in all forms of combat. I made sure of it. This way, they were always ready for war, regardless of the realm we were in–a choice Draven should've made as well. Though his men may have the durable weapons crafted by the dwarves of Lethe, they lack knowledge on how to use them.

Now, on the ground, I return my focus to my well of power. Thankful for the full moon's energy tonight, I summon two small daggers, each one fused to one of my hands. Orion and I work together, taking out a small group that was caught trying to flee. Their tents continue to burn down around us, sending thick trails of billowing smoke through the air and into the night sky. The once silent night has been interrupted by the sound of battle, blood-curdling screams, and metal clashing with metal. I strike down every enemy I come across. My ears are deaf to their pleading cries as tunnel vision kicks in. Nothing else matters.

The only thing I see or feel is my bonded. Her soft skin, the way she always seems to smell perfect, and how her minty green eyes give away her lust when her mouth is spewing venom. But I will not stop until I get Kasia back. If I have to shed the blood of one hundred men and water the forest floor with the blood of Draven's men to get to her, I will.

"Woooo!" Orion cheers, holding his sword up to the sky. "That's the last of them. Lethian scum." He spits on the corpse of the closest fallen man. "That's for Nefeli, you bastard!" He stomps his foot on the corpse of a dwarf man, a deep gash across his torso and empty eyes. Senna looks at him with disgust.

"Was that truly needed? He was already dead, you idiot. I hope you know I'm not going to be the one washing brain matter off your boots," Senna shouts at Orion, crossing her arms over her chest with annoyance. He smirks, before running over to her. I watch as he wraps his arms around her, lifting her in the air as her expression quickly changes and a giggle escapes her. Though my heart aches, I'm happy for my sister and best friend. It's nice to see them finally accepting their feelings and allowing the world to see it rather than hiding it.

Releasing my power, the daggers dissipate back into my well. I wipe my blood-coated hands across my trousers before lifting my helmet off my head.

"Gage!" I call out.

Stepping over bodies on his way toward me, Gage replies. "Yes, Lord?"

"Any sign of Niko?"

"No, I'm afraid not." Fuck. Without Niko and his men, the battle in Lethe will be tough. My men will be without their magic or Fae healing and will be highly outnumbered. Worst of all, they will be expecting us, and we have no idea what we're walking into. Even still, I know we can't wait. The bonding ceremony could occur at any minute, and I refuse to let anyone break what we have. No one will take what belongs to me.

"We can't wait for him," I express. Gage and Orion exchanged a look before nodding. Around us, the men check over the fallen, ensuring no Lethian guards are left alive. I sigh, turning my back to them as I approach the veil. Standing before it, its bluish glow reflects against my blood-splattered skin. I can feel its ancient magic humming with mine. Senna approaches behind me, placing a gentle hand on my shoulder.

"We will get her back, Xerxes." she whispers.

"We will do more than that, Sister," I reply, turning my eyes to hers. "Tonight, I will ensure no one is ever a threat to Kasia again. Tonight, Draven will meet his death, and I will return to Kasia what was stolen from her so long ago." Senna nods in agreement.

Slowly pulling back from the veil, I turn around to find my men in line and awaiting orders. Their eyes are full of loyalty, and their heads are filled with visions of the families and friends they wish to protect–even if it costs them their lives.

"Gage will take three men and wait here for Niko. The rest of us will travel through the veil. It won't be easy. We have no idea what awaits us on the other side." I shout as I make my way toward the men. "Drake took something that belongs to me and wishes to make it his; I cannot allow that to happen. The battle will be tough. Many of you may die, but none without honor. This is for Calanthe, your families, and your children. We will succeed, no matter what it costs. It's an honor to be your High Lord and fight at your side through this," I explain. My fists clench tightly at my sides as the determination to get

Kasia back sets in. "Tonight, I will polish my sword with the blood of the usurper, Draven, and his heir!" I shout. The men cheer and throw their fists up in the air with excitement.

A smile forms on my lips as I turn my sights back on the veil. Orion approaches behind me, and his thoughts are full of all the things that could go wrong, especially with Senna with us.

"Since when do you ever worry about losing a fight?" I ask, moving my eyes from the veil to his.

"Well, since I had something to lose, I suppose," he replies.

"What would my dear sister think to hear the man she's swooning over turned to mush on the battlefield?" I smirk.

"Aye, let's keep this sentimental moment just between us, mate. Your sister can be quite intimidating when she wants to be, and she'd never let me forget it," he replies with a chuckle as he pulls his helmet back over his head. "You ready? Like truly ready? There's a chance we're already too late, and we could be rushing right into a trap."

"We're not too late. I can feel her still, but I have no way of knowing for how much longer. As for the trap, I'm hoping for it."

"Huh. It seems my cockiness has rubbed off on you tonight then." He pats his hand on my back. "Let's get your little birdie then, mate," he adds. Looking over my shoulder, I see Gage had chosen his men, and the rest have lined up behind me, ready to head through.

"Let's go. See you on the other side," I reply before quickly heading through the veil.

Everything goes dark.

THE STREETS of Lethe are deserted. Not a soul can be found as we make our way through them. The cold winter wind bellows across the valley, ripping its way through the alleyways, blowing abandoned pails and the shingles off the roofs. I had expected to have been greeted by more of Draven's men on the other side of the veil, but instead, we found the encampment abandoned. At first, I assumed it was a trap of some kind, but when we managed to make it all the way to the village without seeing anyone, I knew something else was happening, and I don't want to admit it. I can guess just what that is.

The ceremony.

"Where is everyone?" Senna asks as she trudges through snow as deep as her knee.

"Probably hiding inside. Can you really blame them? Look at this place. It's a miserable, frigid wasteland of a dead realm," one of the men scoffs.

Orion lifts his eyes to mine. He clearly shares the same fear as me–that the ceremony has already started.

"We need to hurry," I command. Flying would be faster, but with the wind as strong as it is, flying would be dangerous. I take off running through the streets, my exposed skin welcoming the stinging pain from the cold as we approach Fairway Palace. The closer we get, the more I can feel her through the bond, reassuring me there is still time. Not much, but I have a chance.

Senna reaches me. "This is where she grew up?" she questions, her tone doing little to hide the disgust and pity she feels towards my bonded after seeing the conditions she was raised in. Looking around, I scan the familiar streets of broken wooden and stone homes. Roofs caved in, and torn tapestries cover the broken windows in an effort to stop the cold winter draft from entering the small homes. It smells of soot and death. No one should ever have to live in a place like this, let alone an entire village.

"This is nothing compared to what most of Lethe suffers, trust me," I reply.

As we near the town center, we find the street packed with crowds of people, both Fae and dwarf alike, all huddled together as they slowly make their way through the streets towards the palace. Towards where the ceremony is no doubt about to take place. Fury builds in my chest, and without thinking, I shove the shivering people aside as I storm my way through the crowd. My men and Orion follow behind me, encouraging people to return to their homes and escape the bitter cold. Knowing by our wings that we are not of Lethe, most listen, afraid for their safety. But not all.

The closer we get, the stage in the center of the village just outside the palace becomes clearer through the blowing snow. I pause, my heart catching in my throat as I lay eyes on Kasia. She's making her way out onto the stage with Drake at her side. Her eyes remain at her feet as she stands next to him, her long white hair blowing freely in the wintry wind. I find myself in complete awe of how beautiful she looks—wearing a dress so pure white that it blends in with the snow around us—a diamond-jeweled bodice around her middle, pushing her tits tightly against her. White feathers hang from sheer lace sleeves down her arms. But it's when my eyes catch the glint from the tiny, winged tiara on top of her head I realize how much she looks like a true Satori in this moment—my *little dove*.

Orion brings himself to stand next to me, clearly noticing I've stopped. "What do you wanna do, mate?" he questions. His tone does little to hide his concern. Especially when his thoughts speak so loudly of his fear that my love for her will get us all killed.

"I can take Drake down right here and now. One arrow, Brother, just say the word," Senna adds, reaching my other side.

I watch, unable to tear my eyes from my bonded on the stage. But when Drake places his hand on the small of her back, guiding her to the middle of the stage, any composure I had left melts away. A roar rips through me, echoing around the buildings around us as I push through the crowd with my fists clenched tightly at my sides until I'm at the front of the stage.

Drake and Kasia's heads snap in my direction. A smug grin forms on his face. He knew I'd come for her, and his thoughts tell me he's thankful I did. My chest rises and falls quickly with anger.

"Ah. Just when I was beginning to think you wouldn't show up," Drake says with a cheerful tone. "Now that everyone is indeed here, let's get this moving along. I'd rather like to get out of this cold, as I'm sure they all would, too."

"No!" I shout. Lifting my eyes to Kasia, she holds my gaze as her thoughts fill with silent pleas to stop. To go back to Calanthe. I shake my head in response before turning my eyes back to Drake. "You took what belongs to me, Drake, and I will not leave here without her. She is *mine*, and I will have her if that means taking whatever is left of Lethe down in the process, Drake. I will do it."

"I think you're mistaken. I didn't take anyone from you. Kasia came willingly and agreed to be my wife in exchange for the promise that the people of Lethe and your realm will be spared. You should be thankful, really. This is an important moment for Kasia and I. After what she has sacrificed for you and your people, it's a shame you're here to try and ruin it for us."

"You're a fool if you truly believe that," I retort with a growl. "You're far from stupid Drake. Think about it. Kasia is the one person who can steal your father's throne. The one true threat he faces. Do you think he will just allow her to live? Simply because you were naive enough to bond yourself to her? He won't!"

"He will not harm her! Once we are bonded, he will allow her to live, and the peace between realms will return. He gave me his word!" Drake replies. Kasia pulls away from him, keeping her eyes on the ground as she contemplates the new information. Even she knows what I say is true.

"And what weight does the word of a murdering usurper hold?" I question. "If you do not allow her to leave with me, he will kill her the moment the ceremony is completed.

"You're wrong!" he shouts.

"For once, the Calanthian High Lord speaks the truth, son." Draven's voice explains as he treads up the stairs and onto the stage. He is sporting the same unkempt shoulder-length golden hair as the last time we met, only this time, a deep pink scar marks his face. Crossing from his hairline down his left eye to his cheek, clearly, someone almost got close enough to take him out. It's a shame they failed. You'd think he'd be dressed in finer attire for a celebration, but instead, it is steel armor decorated with his crest that he seems to have chosen for this occasion. His outfit is completed with thick shoulder pads, heavy boots, and wrist guards strapped tightly on the end of each hand. To anyone paying attention, it's clear he knew we'd be coming, and the menacing smirk on his face upon seeing me and my men in the crowd only confirms it.

Seeing him so close to Kasia has my heart racing. Her eyes snap to his, and her thoughts fill with rage and sorrow for her family, who died at his hand. She wants revenge. She wants to shed his blood in the same way he did to her family. Draven brings himself to stand in front of Kasia, inspecting her. With a gloved hand, he takes a piece of her straying white hair, bringing it to his nose before he chuckles, releasing it. "Pretty little thing, aren't you? To think you managed to evade me for so many years. Your stupid mother should've let me kill you the day I took her life. Then you would've been spared the life you were forced to live."

"Do not speak of my mother. She had no part in the way I was brought up! That was your doing. Lethe may be cursed in a never-ending winter and forced to live without magic, but you are the true curse to the realm!"

Kasia spits. Draven chuckles, finding humor in her tongue. Fire burns within me as I find myself proud of her bravery.

"The bonding ceremony was more of a tactic—a way to break the curse over Lethe. The girl is *nothing*. I may have stolen the throne, but I am Lethe's rightful ruler now. Her power will *always* be a threat, along with her name. The only way I can assure she never becomes a problem is to bury her next to her mother." Draven explains.

"You gave me your word, Father!" Drake shouts, placing himself between Kasia and Draven. The protective stance confuses me, though I find myself thankful. I can tell from his thoughts that he cares for her, that his father's confession angers him.

"Yes, well. As the High Lord stated, my word isn't worth much these days. It's tough times," he explains mockingly. He signals his guards with his hands, and they surround us in the crowd. Diving into the small well of power my ring provides, I summon a tether of moonlight, twirling it between my fingers as the corner of my lips pulls into a smile.

"Well," Draven adds. "Now that the children are looked after and everyone understands, let us begin."

And with that, chaos breaks out.

Still no sign of Niko.

Chapter Twenty-Three

KASIA

The air fills with the iron-rich scent of blood. I find myself unable to move. Frozen in place as though time itself had come to a standstill. The frigid winter wind bellows through the village, causing my hair to whip about as I take in the scene surrounding me. Through the veil of falling snowflakes, I find Xerxes's and Draven's men in a heated battle. Senna is perched on a tall pillar in the center of town, her large black wings blocking the wind at her back as she takes aim with her bow. Men fall one by one, each arrow meeting its mark. Seeing her here, fighting for me, sends a chill through me, especially after what we have been through together.

All around me are men shouting as their blades clash. Somehow, amidst the chaos, my eyes find him in the swarm–Xerxes. I squint, watching as his large, winged frame makes its way toward the stage, leaving a trail of

Draven's men behind him. His expression is one of pure rage. Moonlit sparks flicker around him as his blade meets the flesh of any man in his path to me. My heart beats rapidly in my chest. I never expected to lay eyes on him again, not after everything.

"I won't let you kill her!" Drakes shout loudly, drawing my attention. Standing between his father and me, he draws his sword and takes a protective stance.

"So protective of your future bonded. How noble of you, Son." Draven chuckles. "Though it will not stop me from doing what needs to be done, even if that means burying you next to her," he adds with an aggressive tone.

Drake charges at his father, but Draven is ready for him and draws his sword in time to block his son's attack. I gasp, my eyes widening with shock as I watch Drake take on his father in an attempt to save my life. I knew he wasn't as cruel as his father. You could even say I'd grown to care for him—as a friend—in the days we spent together. Though, I never expected him to take on his father or risk his life for mine.

I stand there, frozen, as I watch the battle unfold. Drake is faster than his father, causing Draven's blade to slice through the air and miss its mark. Draven, however, is larger, stronger, and has centuries more war experience than his son. Blow for blow, they battle on the stage while the war continues between Xerxes's winged men and the Lethian guards around the town's center. My body trembles uncontrollably. Fury builds inside me as I watch more innocent blood being spilled on Lethe soil for one man's greed—*Draven's* greed. An older dwarf soldier wearing Draven's crest and colors quickly approaches the large stage. His eyes fill with hatred as they fixate on me from behind his steel helmet. I ready myself, knowing he either means to subdue me or kill me himself, but neither will happen without a fight. It won't be easy without a weapon, and my hands being so cold from the winter wind that they hurt, but that's half the fun. After all, I have a lot of pent-up emotion inside me, and it's been months since I got to shed the blood of one of Draven's more than deserving men. The men I spent my life hunting, killing just to survive and provide for those in need.

That's when the reality of everything I'm fighting for becomes so much clearer. Marrying Drake might have kept me alive, and it may have spared Calanthe. But what of those who suffer in Lethe? Even if the curse was broken, would things have changed for the low-born? Drake said he'd help me protect them, but how could he do that with Draven still sitting on the throne?

The guard nears. His snow-covered boots stomp on the wooden stage as he approaches me. Bringing my arm back, I ready myself for the self-inflicted pain I'm surely about to feel. I swing my arm, aiming for the rugged dwarf's jaw. But just before my fist finds its mark, his eyes widen, and a gurgling gasp slips from his lips. Blood leaks down his frostbitten lips, and his axe drops to the snow-covered stage with a thud that rings through my ears despite the chaos around us. He grasps frantically at his chest with both hands until they wrap around the shaft of a large arrow protruding from his middle. He collapses face first at my feet, and that's when I notice the black feathers on the back of the arrow—Orion. Feeling annoyed, I lift my eyes in search of the bastard who stole my kill.

"Ay, Birdie," he calls out from the rooftop of one of the homes. His large black wings flap behind him as he takes off, fighting against the wind. He lands next to me with a coy smirk on his face.

"I had him, just so you know!" I snap, crossing my arms over my chest.

"Did ya now? With no weapon *or* magic?" he questions sarcastically with a light tone. It amazes me how, in the heat of battle, he's able to laugh–like men around him aren't dying by the minute. Though I suppose after so many, you become numb to it. Numbness, I can understand.

"He was half my height, for Gods' sake, Orion. Besides, I've taken them out with plenty less than I have on me now."

"Well," he says, bending down to pick up the fallen dwarf's axe. "Now you can take them out safely," he adds, handing me the small iron axe.

As I take it, Xerxes reaches us, his broad chest rising and falling with panted breaths beneath his obsidian armor. Bringing himself to stand in front of me, I'm faced with the blood of his victims splattered across his armor. Slowly, I lift my eyes to find his whiskey-brown eyes full of vexation. Fear isn't an emotion I'm used to, but right now, fear and guilt have my heart beating rapidly in my chest.

Quickly his hand wraps around my middle, pulling me into him. I release a breath I didn't know I was holding as a single tear glides down my cheek. I expected him to hate me; part of me hoped he would so we wouldn't be in this situation. But at this moment, I find myself thankful he came. I was wrong to do what I did. I see that now. Nothing I could've done would've saved Lethe.

"I've got you, little dove," he whispers, kissing softly against my hair. I can feel his hot breath against me. My eyes flutter shut, and for a brief moment, I allow myself to tune out the battle around us. "Did you really think all it would take to be rid of me was a dagger to the heart?" A soft laugh builds in my chest as he holds me tightly against him. "Come, let's get you out of here."

"No," I say firmly, snapping my eyes open. Pushing myself away from him, I lift my eyes to his. "I'm not leaving. Not until all of this is over." Clenching the axe tightly in my hand, I keep my eyes locked with his. A loud growl vibrates through him, his expression changing from relief to annoyance, just as a blood-curdling scream rips through the air. Snapping my head toward the source, I find Drake on the ground. His back is pressed against the snow-covered stage as Draven stands above him. A dark and twisted expression forms on Draven's face as he pulls a blood-coated blade from Drake's stomach. Shock and fury take hold of me as I watch Drake struggle. Pressing an arm across the wound in his abdomen, he struggles to back away.

"You had to fall for her, didn't you? Useless bastard. I ask *one thing* from you in your entire life, and you can't even do that properly. You are weak, just like your mother," Draven proclaims as he steps closer to Drake. He drags the tip of his blade across Drake's chest. Blood leaks from his stomach wound, leaving a crimson trail in the pristine white snow below him as he crawls away. Nearing the edge of the stage, Drake has nowhere to run as his father closes in.

I watch as the tip of Draven's blade slices through the fabric over Drake's heart just as Drake lifts his kind blue eyes to mine. In them, I see a silent goodbye as he accepts his fate in the winter wind of Lethe–a farewell from yet another person willing to die at Draven's hand in order to protect me. Before I know it, my feet are moving, running across the stage as quickly as possible. Ignoring the shouts from Orion and Xerxes behind me, I rush to Drake's side. But I'm too late. Draven pushes his blade through his son's chest, piercing his heart.

MELISSA MCSHERRY

My feet stop abruptly as I fall to my knees. The axe slips from my hand to the snow as familiar vibrations begin to build inside me, humming through my body—so much blood and death. Draven will stop at nothing to keep what does not belong to him. I watch as Drake's body goes limp, his freshly spilt crimson blood melting the snow around him. The vibrations grow in intensity. My lip trembles as my rage grows. Anger for my parents, whom Draven stole from me. For the people of Lethe, who suffer daily because of his greed. Now, for Drake, my friend who cared for me when he could've been cruel and gave his life to protect mine. Anguish and sorrow consume me until the humming inside me becomes uncontrollable.

A loud scream rips through me, and with it, a surge of power–my power. A large gust of powerful wind rips around me, knocking men off their feet. My scream echoes off the buildings around us. Tears I'd been fighting trail down my cheeks, freezing in the cold air. Every emotion I've held in over the months of discovering who I am and where I came from is coming to the surface. Odd sensations trickle along my back just as my large dove-like wings sprout from my back. The powerful wind I summoned causes the snow to whip and circle around me like a protective barrier, and thanks to Viserra, I'm able to control it.

Pushing myself to my feet, I set my eyes on Draven. His head is cocked to the side with curiosity, and his eyes are full of hatred as a smug grin forms on his face.

"Kasia!" I hear Xerxes shout from behind me. I ignore him, unwilling to break eyes with Draven. His jaw clicks as he inspects me from afar, sizing me up for the challenge. "Kasia, please," Xerxes continues to beg with panted breaths. He's fighting–the sounds of metal on metal behind me only growing louder. The battle around us seems unphased by my show of power or my wings. Good.

"Well, there's the last little dove I've been looking for now. Don't weep, love. I'll have you reunited with your parents and my son soon enough. Perhaps I'll even mount your wings on the wall above my throne. A keepsake to remember the decades I spent searching for you." Draven yells through the arctic wind. Gripping my hold on the wind, I will it away, no longer wanting any barrier between myself and my target. "You know, I thought of your parents as friends. I didn't want to take their lives. They could've avoided it if they'd just given me what I wanted instead of making me take it," he adds as he continues to circle with a predatory gaze. "But you'll be a good dove, won't you? Just kneel before me, in front of everyone here. Face your death bravely, and I promise to spare the lives of your precious friends."

An uncontrollable laugh erupts through me. "I am a Satori. The last living dove. I will *never* bow to you, a usurper who wears a stolen crown decorated with the blood he shed of the people he slaughtered."

"Oh, you will. Or I will take everything from you."

"You're mistaken, Draven. You have taken enough from me. Today, I take something from you." My voice is clear and laced with determination. "This night, I will rest my head on a silk pillow in my parent's palace while your corpse rots in the ground next to the son you never deserved."

"Feisty, I see. Your mother was, too, until the very end. She was stronger than your father when it came down to it. She took her death bravely. Your father, however, begged in the end. Pissed his pants right where you're standing." He laughs. "I'll never forget the terror that haunted his face when I took his head. The way, even in death, it was forever etched into his voidless—"

I charge at him with the small axe gripped firmly in my hand. Swinging at him, Draven pauses. His expression changes to excitement as he meets my axe with his blade. He is much larger than me but surprisingly fast.

"Kasia! Stop!" Xerxes yells. "Where the fuck is Niko!" Having witnessed my attack on Draven, Xerxes tries to approach me. He wants to stop me. I can feel his fear, his determination to keep me from risking my life. But I have to.

Draven and I continue to exchange blows as I will my magic to the surface again. The wind around us begins to pick up speed again, creating a wall of snow and wind between us and everyone else. Out of Xerxes's sight, his fear grows so strong it's painful, catching me off guard. I slip up, and Draven's blade finds the flesh along my right bicep. A hiss slips from my lips as he laughs when I retreat a few steps to examine the wound.

"Did you think this show of power would scare me?" he asks, gesturing to the tornado of snow around us. "I know what power you have, but even with your Satori blood, you're no match for me. The Gods have always given me everything I have wanted," he explains as he walks towards me. I ready myself for his attack. At the last moment, I spin, using my wings to knock him back a few steps. He growls, clearly angered by the move. "You're just making this harder on yourself."

Warm blood drips down my arm, painting the icy white snow around us with specks of crimson. It practically freezes on impact, making the ground beneath us slippery. I study his movements, remembering what I learned over the years of fighting, looking for weak spots and patterns. Draven lifts his sword above his head, revealing a hole in his armored chest plate under his arm–a difficult spot to hit and not usually fatal for a Fae. However, without access to his healing powers, it's just the spot I need.

I swing my axe hard, but he lifts his blade and pushes against me. Even with the wind blowing around us, I can hear Xerxes pleading, begging me to let him in–but I won't. I won't risk his life. Draven will take no one else that I love. I spin before swinging and bringing the axe down hard again. This time, I catch him off guard and graze his face. He growls loudly and charges me.

Readying myself, I know this is my only shot. With his rage, his movements are less organized and more erratic as he comes at me, his blade held high above his head with both hands firmly wrapped around its pommel. His battle cry echoes around the wind enclosure as he nears. Lowering my axe, I point its blade up and swing upwards into him as he approaches.

Silence. The wind stops. Draven's eyes widen. Everything goes numb. The humming disappears, and my lungs release a gasping breath I didn't know they were holding. I know I hit my mark when I feel the warm liquid leaking down my hand. With my arm trapped tightly under his, I can't move it. My hand is still firmly wrapped around the handle of the axe; I'm pinned. Gurgling, bloody sobs leak from Draven's mouth as he slowly starts to collapse. Quickly, I use the last of my strength to lift his arm, freeing my hand in an effort to remain on my feet. But something is wrong; even with my hand freed, I fall with him. When our knees hit the frozen stage, a sharp pain radiates through my torso. It's then that I realize Draven's blade also found its mark and is now embedded in my stomach.

Xerxes reaches my side, sliding across the snow-covered stage as Orion grabs Draven, pulling him off me. Unable to speak, I mutter words that don't make sense, but I know Xerxes understands me. The bond relayed to him what my words cannot.

"He's dead," Orion whispers, as he and Xerxes exchange a look.

Blood pools around me, and though I never thought it possible, each second seems to get colder. My body grows weaker, and my bond with Xerxes seems to dwindle. I'm dying. I should be afraid, but I'm not. Because with my death, I know that Lethe and its people will be free.

The town center, which just a few moments ago was filled with the sounds of battle, is silent. Xerxes lifts me into his lap, gently tucking my feathered wings so my back is pressed tightly against his chest before softly brushing the stray hairs from my face. Gazing up at him I find his face pale and his brows furrowed with worry, and although his grip around me is firm, I can feel his body trembling.

"Stay with me, little dove. You can't leave me, not now. I just got you back." he whispers as his breath tightens.

Chapter Twenty-Four

KAISA

"Where the fuck is Niko!? This never would've happened had he shown up like he said he would!" Xerxes yells aggressively, his voice laced with hurt, as he pulls me tighter against him. Orion paces about the stage. His blood-coated hands are pulling at his hair. Behind me, Xerxes's chest rises and falls rapidly in short, panted breaths. "You'll be okay. I've got you. You'll heal, and we'll go back to Calanthe." He's wrong. But even he knows that.

"No," I mutter, my voice barely a whisper. "I won't."

"Gods, Birdie! Why did you come here? Why didn't you let us help you... of all the times to be your stubborn self..."

"It wasn't your fight to fight..." I choke out. "Not this one. Draven... was mine. It was my fate to bring him to his death. My choice."

"And what of mine? My fate was to protect you, to spend my life with you. I chose that fate, and you took it from me the moment you kept me from helping you," Xerxes snaps coldly. He is hurt, just when I thought I could never hurt him more than I already have.

"You're angry. Good... It will make letting me go easier."

"None of us are willing to let you go, Kasia. You are part of our family now, and we need you here," Senna admits as she comes into view.

"Don't you see, little dove?" he whispers sorrowfully. "Letting you go is not possible for me. Not now. If you go, you will take me with you. My mind, my heart, and my spirit. I will be nothing more than a hollow husk of a High Lord without—"

"Mate, look," Orion says as he directs our attention to the area in front of the stage. Bodies litter the ground, but it's not them that has silenced the crowd. It's the melting snow, the rays of sun that have crept out from behind the grey clouds for the first time in decades, melting the thick, blood-tainted layers of snow that make up the town center.

With my magic fleeting and the spilling of the last dove's blood, the curse has been broken. Lethe is finally free.

Chapter Twenty-Five

"**K**asia!" I shout, shaking her frail, cold body. No. She can't be gone. I won't allow it. "Kasia!" I beg, pleading silently to the Gods not to take her from me. Not now. Orion rushes to my side. He lifts Kasia's hand from her wound as he inspects it.

"She's not gone yet, mate. But she doesn't have much time left. We have to get her back to Calanthe," Orion explains. Around the stage, my men have taken control. Draven's men, having witnessed his death, have surrendered, and fallen to their knees.

"No. You cannot move her. You'll only do more damage," Viserra's voice emanates over the crowds as she approaches the stage with Niko slithering behind her, leading a team of armed Amazathian guards.

"Where the fuck have you been? We needed you, and you were nowhere to be found!" I seethe, my eyes locking with Niko's. I thought he was my friend. I trusted him. A mistake. One that my bonded now pays for with her life.

"That does not matter now. We can discuss it after," Viserra explains. Reaching our side, she quickly kneels beside us, inspecting the wounds for herself. "We need to remove the blade. Hold her still." I do as she asks, gripping Kasia tightly against me. Placing my lips against her floral-scented white hair, I watch Viserra unravel her scarf from around her neck. Lifting her eyes to mine, she quickly pulls Draven's blade from Kasia's stomach, replacing it with her scarf.

Kasia doesn't move. Doesn't make a single sound of discomfort.

"I meant every word, Lord. Dat, I can promise. Twas my intention to meet you at the veil as planned."

"Then why didn't you?" Senna asks, stepping towards Niko with aggression. Her fury is equal to mine. I don't need to read her thoughts to know that—her stance before Niko is firm. Senna seeks the same answers. For Kasia, yes, but also for the men we lost in the battle. Niko not showing up cost us many lives–many men who will not return home to their families.

"Iker," Niko snaps. "Da bastard had been communicating with Draven behind ma back. He made a deal. Draven had told him he'd come for Amazath if Iker didn't cooperate," he sighs. "When I returned to gather ma men, Iker slipped a tonic in my drink, had me incapacitated, and threw me in the dungeon wit any of ma men who refused to follow him."

"So, to protect Amazath, he took it from you? To rule himself?" I ask with confusion. Viserra slowly lifts the scarf from Kasia's wound before checking her pulse.

"No," Niko continues. "To protect Amazath, he kept me from aiding your fight against Draven."

"And you, Oracle. Where were you?" I ask, turning my fury on the Viserra as she continues to tend to Kasia.

"I saw a vision of Iker's plan. I went to stop it," she admits. Her eyes never meet mine. Her focus is solely on my bonded.

"Why didn't you tell us?" Orion shouts. "We could've handled it together."

"Because you were needed here," she retorts. "I understand your anger and fear, but you must understand that this was *her* fate. *Her* choice. There was nothing you, I, or even Niko could've done to change what the Gods meant to happen," she sighs.

"Sneaky bastard. I never trusted him. I knew there was something snakey about him!" Orion spits as he begins to pace around the stage. Niko raises a brow at him, not finding Orion's snake pun regarding the Naga funny.

"She's fading fast," Viserra interrupts.

"What do you mean she's fading?" Senna questions with concern. "The curse over Lethe has been broken. Magic is already beginning to return to Lethe. She just needs a few moments of rest, and she will heal."

"No. She won't. Not in time to save her anyways," Viserra admits. Numbness takes over as I hold her fragile body closer to me. This can't be it. It cannot end like this; we haven't had enough time together.

Hearing the truth, Orion cries out with frustration. Kasia's body begins to slide down my chest, a sign of her weakness growing. "There is something I—"

"No." Niko cuts her off.

"Don't!" I seethe, snapping my eyes to his. "You do not get to silence her. Not now and not about this."

"He has a right to make this choice for himself, Niko. I will not take that from him. Not today," she replies with a soft tone.

"What choice?" I ask with a concerned tone. Why I asked, I don't know. I know in my heart there is no choice. I want Kasia. I *need* her, regardless of the price.

Clearing her throat, Viserra lifts her ghostly white eyes to mine. "There may be a way I can save her. But the cost is great. For both of you."

"Do it. I don't care about the cost as long as it keeps her with me."

"Xerxes—" Senna begins, but seeing the look in my eyes, she stops herself. She knows I will do anything, whatever it takes to keep Kasia. Her words against it are wasted, as are those of anyone who tries to convince me not to do it.

"You may not, but what of Kasia? Will she feel the same?"

"Kasia did not ask my feelings regarding her turning herself in to save us all, as you know. So, I do not need to know hers for this. If she will live, do it, Viserra."

"There may be a way I can move some of your life force into her," she explains. "But to do so, I will need your ring." Sliding my finger in my mouth, I pull the heirloom ring free from my blood-coated fingers with my teeth before dropping it in my palm and handing it to Viserra. "There's one more thing. You will both be mortal. You will remain Fae and have access to your powers. However, you will be giving up your immortality, causing you to age like mortals and eventually die."

I allow her words to sink in as my eyes roam to the woman in my arms. Her white hair matted and soaked with blood, like the day I found her in that cell. The sun's rays shine down on her beautiful face. She looks peaceful, and though there was once a time when I would have given anything to see her resting this peacefully, I find myself wishing to witness the crinkles in her nose once again when she laughs. The way her luscious lips pull into a smile when she's assaulting me with her venomous tongue or the rosy flushness of her cheeks when she finds release. Gently, I brush her hair from her face and tuck it behind her pointed Fae ear, knowing there was never a choice to make. I will die a mortal death so long as she is by my side.

My little dove.

"I'll do it."

Chapter Twenty-Six

KASIA

The sound of muffling voices I recognize meet my ears. Sweet floral scents fill my nose, and a comforting warmth radiates through my body. Cracking my eyes open, I allow them a moment to adjust to the bright light of the room I find myself in. Light? My eyes snap to the window, where I expect to find the grey skies of Lethe or the Starry night skies of Lethe, but instead, I am greeted with clear blue skies. Golden rays of sunshine pour through the floor-to-ceiling windowpanes of the large room. At my feet, Erebus barks, startling me.

"Erebus!" I choke out on shaky lips. Pushing myself up on my elbows, I reach for him as tears begin to streak down my face. Running my hands through his thick black fur, I rest my head on his, as he pants and whines excitedly. "I missed you so much."

"He hasn't left your side since I brought him here," Xerxes explains in a deep voice. I pause, exhaling deeply before turning my eyes to him. He's sitting beside the bed in a chair that's clearly too small for a man of his stature and looks terribly uncomfortable. His hair is down, hanging loosely around his face. His whiskey eyes lock with mine as a gentle smile forms on his face. "Hi, little dove."

"What happened?" I ask as fragments of the event unfold in my head. Drake's death at his father's hand. The return of my magic, my wings. The snow and Xerxes's pleading shouts—his pain through the bond, the sounds of battle, and the scent of death. My eyes widen, and my hand rushes to my stomach, where I remember the wound from Draven's blade. I should be dead. Viserra. Niko. I remember them arriving, but then everything is blank.

"How am I alive?" I question, turning my eyes back to the whining dire wolf before me. Erebus lays across my lap, resting his head on my leg as I scratch behind his ear.

Leaning forward, Xerxes rests his elbows on his knees, "What is the last thing you remember?"

"Viserra. She and Niko arrived. You were arguing."

Xerxes growls. "About Niko's lover, Iker. He had Niko imprisoned. Iker made a deal with Draven to protect Amazath. All he had to do was stop Niko from coming to my aid, and Draven would spare Amazath."

"So that's why you were so outnumbered..."

"Yes, but there is more. It's been revealed that Iker was also the one who aided your parents in removing your memories. It was he who gave them the scales needed to create the potion. When Niko refused them, he went behind Niko's back."

"But why? What would he gain from that?"

"We aren't sure yet," he admits. "Viserra has been looking through his things for any clue as to what his plan is."

"Is?" I ask with confusion.

"Iker escaped with a group of Niko's men that were loyal to him. No one has seen him since. Viserra hasn't been able to see anything since having seen Niko imprisoned. Do you remember anything else?" His tone does little to hide the rage he feels for Iker.

"No... I remember you all arguing, and then... I don't know what happened after that. Where are we? How is there sunlight?" I ask curiously. Looking around the room, the decor seems familiar, but this isn't a room I've ever stayed in. Tall ivory walls with ornate gold fixings make up the large room. Thick layers of ivy vines climb around the corners. The wall to my left is entirely made of floor-to-ceiling windows open to a clear view of the crystal-clear blue sky. I drag my eyes lower and see white and gold granite floors. In the center of the room is a large crystal chandelier in the shape of a dove. "We're in Lethe... but how?"

Gently, I slide out from under Erebus, placing my shaky legs on the cool floor before slowly standing and making my way toward the large windows; my jaw drops as I look out below lays cascading valleys of lush green grass sprinkled with beautiful red roses like the ones in the vision of my mother. Tall mountains make up the backdrop of the view, with a river of fresh water going down the mountains and through the valley all the way to the village–to Lethe.

"You broke the curse, little dove. You freed Lethe," Xerxes whispers as he approaches me from behind. Softly, he presses his lips to my shoulder, sending a chill down my spine.

"But... how? How am I alive?" I ask.

"Viserra instilled some of my life force within you. To keep you here. Your Fae healing, though slow, did the rest," he explains.

"Your life force? But that means—" I halt as the realization of his words hits me.

"I am mortal, as are you."

"Why? Why would you do that?" I sob, the guilt becoming too heavy for me to bear.

He laughs. "Must I really tell you again? There is no life for me here, not without you. I'd rather live and die as a mortal so long as my time here is spent with you next to me."

Turning to face him, I place my palms flat against his chest. My cheeks streaked with tears as I sob. "I could feel myself dying, Xerxes. I felt so cold, so broken by what I did to you. I would've done it again if it meant keeping you all... Senna? Orion?"

"Everyone is fine," he chuckles, wiping the tears from my cheeks. "Orion and Niko have been overseeing the repairs needed in the village. There is no longer a divide among the people. Everyone has contributed to the rebuild, whether high-born or low-born. Senna is fine as well. She fought bravely and is back in Calanthe, ensuring things run smoothly while I am here. Everyone is safe, Kasia. You don't need to worry."

"And Draven?..." I choke out.

"Dead. We burned his body and buried his ashes in an unmarked grave."

"Drake?" Guilt forms in the pit of my stomach for asking of my captor.

Xerxes tucks my white hair behind my pointed Fae ear as his mouth pulls into a small smile. "We buried him in the royal cemetery, next to your parents and the other members of your family. He died protecting you, and though I might not have liked him, my quarrels with him were forgotten when I witnessed his loyalty to you. He cared for you and gave his life for you; I am thankful for that."

"Oh? So, you're not jealous, then?" I ask coyly.

"Oh, I'm plenty jealous of the time he got to spend with you, but I also know there are so many ways in which I have you that he, nor anyone else, ever will."

"Is that so?"

"I have something for you," he whispers with a laugh. Turning his back to me, he walks to the large table against the wall by the door. I watch as he pulls open one of the top drawers and pulls out a satin sack before pushing it closed and making his way towards me. "Close your eyes." I do as he asks. A nervous feeling begins to form in the pit of my stomach. Like thousands of fluttering butterflies have taken flight inside me, his rainstorm scent hits my nose as he lifts something, placing it on the top of my head. Withdrawing his hands, I can feel the loss of him as he retreats a few steps. The sounds of his boots on the granite floor echo around the silent room. "Open them."

Opening them, I find Xerxes kneeling on the floor a few feet away. "What are you doing?" I ask with a laugh. His eyes light up with my question and a smug grin forms on his handsome face.

"Kneeling before my High Lady, of course," he admits. *High Lady?* Slowly, my hand rises to the item placed on my head. I remove it, bringing it before my eyes. My voice catches in my throat as I take in its beauty and meaning.

"It was your mother's, and now it is yours," he adds. Silver and gold vines and dove-like wings make up the base of it, with small diamonds woven throughout. They sparkle in the sun that shines through the window behind me, creating specks of light on the walls around the room.

"But how? I thought it was lost in the chaos..."

"Orion found it in the melted snow," he explains.

"It's so beautiful," I mutter before carefully placing it back on my head.

"It is. But not as beautiful as you, though, little dove," he adds seductively, pulling my attention. Turning my eyes back to where he's kneeled, I watch as he slowly begins to crawl towards me with eyes full of hunger.

Amused, I fold my arms across my chest. "I'm sorry, but is the *great* High Lord Xerxes on his knees before me, or did that blast of power exhaust me more than we thought? Am I hallucinating?" I question playfully.

Reaching my feet, he slowly slides his calloused hands under the silk robe and up my legs. "Little dove, I will spend the rest of my mortal life on my knees before you if that is what it takes to make you happy," he replies with a guttural tone. His hands push the silk fabric of my robe up my body as they continue their assent up my body.

A familiar heat builds between my legs from his touch. Locking his eyes with mine, he slowly rises, bringing his head between my thighs. Xerxes glides his hot tongue through my folds tantalizingly slow, teasing me before sucking my clit into his mouth. My head falls back against the thick windowpanes behind me knocking the crown to the floor, and my hands find his thick hair. Soft moans slip from my lips, and my eyes flutter closed as he devours me.

A knock on the door causes my eyes to snap open. Against my center, Xerxes growls with frustration.

"Sorry, mate, but uh... well, you're needed in the village. Both of you," Orion chimes from the hall. An uncontrolled laugh builds in my chest at how familiar this situation seems.

"Glad you find it so amusing," Xerxes whispers before swiping his tongue through my folds again. I whimper a laugh, my body twitching in his grasp as he teases me.

"Fae ears, mate. Can't you guys just pause? Briefly, of course. You have your entire now mortal lives to do... well... that," Orion stutters.

Xerxes sighs, releasing his hold on me as he rises to his feet. His chest rises and falls with annoyance, but a smile forms once his eyes lock with mine. Orion knocks on the door again.

"Orion, I swear to the Gods. We'll be out in a moment," Xerxes snaps, doing his best to sound serious. Bending down, he presses a gentle kiss to my forehead, "Let's go before I'm forced to remind my best friend that, though I may be mortal, I can still kick his ass."

"I heard that!" Orion shouts. "And I don't need reminding. I'm fully aware of how big and bad you are. Just hurry up, mate. They're waiting on you. Both of you. Birdie, don't let him distract you again with his so-called charm," he laughs. "I'll meet you guys down there."

Xerxes and I both laugh. "Before we go, I was hoping to ask you something," he adds.

"Of course. What is it?" I ask, finding myself curious.

"Well..." he admits as he grabs a thin cotton sweater from the wardrobe and wraps it around me. "I'd like to remain here, in Lethe. If you'll have me."

Stunned by his confession, I turn to face him. "But what about Calanthe?"

"I'd step down as High Lord and pass the title to Senna, who would rule over it with Orion at her side. It's not something I have taken lightly, but my life is with you now, for whatever life we have left. I want to spend it with you—and this," he gestures to the realm on the other side of the thick windowpanes. "Lethe is your home. Senna will make an honorable High Lady. She's agreed, but the choice ultimately is yours." My heart swells in my chest. I can feel his fear of rejection through the bond.

Cupping his jaw with my palm, I lift myself on my toes and rub the tip of my nose with his. "There is nothing I would love more than you have you here, ruling over Lethe at my side," I whisper before bringing my lips to his. The kiss is soft, weak, and full of passion. His arms wrap tightly around me, pulling me closer as he deepens the kiss. A growl rumbles through his chest. His fang nips at my bottom lip, breaking the skin. The sting causes a pleasurable moan to slip from my lips.

I laugh, breaking the kiss. "We really should go, or he'll just come back."

Xerxes sighs loudly with annoyance. "Fine, but you're mine tonight."

"I'm yours *forever*," I reply softly. He smiles, taking my hand in his as we make our way out of the room.

The halls of Faireway have changed since Draven's rule. All signs of his color and crest have been removed and replaced with those of the Satori Family. *My* family. For the first time in my life, I find myself feeling truly at peace.

Though Iker is still out there, and we know nothing of his plans, I know together we will overcome it. It won't be easy, and we have much to do. But I have hope for the future of Lethe and its people. With the crown of my fallen family resting on my head and the hand of the man I love intertwined with mine, I realize just how far I've come. At this moment, I realize that my virtues, which I once thought to be weaknesses, will make me the High Lady that Lethe deserves.

Acknowledgments

Truthfully, I don't know where to begin when it comes to thanking people. This book was incredibly hard for me to write. Life just kept throwing me curve balls, and at one point, I was very doubtful I'd have it finished in time. Thankfully, I have an army of supportive friends and family who never let me doubt myself and were more than willing to help me with anything I needed to meet my deadline. Words cannot express how thankful I am because this book would not be here without them.

Dana, thanks for listening to all my late-night and early-morning rants and always knowing what to say to pick me up. Thank you for putting up with all my dark and depraved ideas, regardless of how ridiculous they are. P.S. Thanks for the pick-me-up Gingerbread latte, even though it smelt like bandaids.

Renee, you are a machine. Thank you for putting in the long hours editing and picking through everything with such a fine tooth comb. I know it was as stressful for you as it was for me, but I truly appreciate everything you have done for me.

Taylor. Girl, your comments always hype me up. Thank you for your regular check-ins to ensure I was staying on task and focused and for reminding me that every word counts as progress.

To my BETAs (Janie, Bridget, Victoria, Tierney, Heather), I appreciate all of you for the feedback, comments, sharing, and promoting, but most importantly, your patience. You never once made me feel pressure to get it done, and watching your reaction videos along the way meant everything to me.

To my ARC team, thank you for sharing, supporting, and reading my story. I hope you enjoyed following along with Kasia and Xerxes.

Lastly...

Mom. Through this, you have been my biggest supporter. You have never once stopped believing in me, even on the days when I doubted myself. Not once did my late-night calls go unanswered. You were always there when I needed you. Thank you for being the best coffee supplier, cheerleader, and open ear a daughter could ask for. I love you.

Printed in Great Britain
by Amazon